SHE DIDN'T EVEN WANT TO THINK ABOUT HOW SHE HAD GOTTEN UNDRESSED.

Her navy sundress was only a few feet away, draped over the arm of a wingback chair. Candace bent to grab it. But she didn't move fast enough.

"Nice view," said a voice from behind her.

She spun around, at the same time wrapping the sheet tighter.

He held nearly a foot's height advantage over her. His hair, still wet from the shower, was slicked back in a dark wave. Deep blue eyes that appeared almost black in the half-light of the room studied her with clear amusement.

Her gaze traveled down, past his bare muscular chest, following the vee of dark hairs to the waistband of a pair of checkered silk boxer shorts. The satiny material stopped mid-thigh along his lean, defined and—okay, she had to admit it—inordinately interesting legs. She jerked her attention back to his face.

He's gorgeous.

He grinned.

And he knows it.

<u>BOOK YOUR PLACE ON OUR WEBSITE</u>
<u>AND MAKE THE</u>
<u>READING CONNECTION!</u>

We've created a customized website just for our very special readers, where you can get the inside scoop on everything that's going on with Zebra, Pinnacle and Kensington books.

When you come online, you'll have the exciting opportunity to:

- View covers of upcoming books
- Read sample chapters
- Learn about our future publishing schedule (listed by publication month *and author*)
- Find out when your favorite authors will be visiting a city near you
- Search for and order backlist books from our online catalog
- Check out author bios and background information
- Send e-mail to your favorite authors
- Meet the Kensington staff online
- Join us in weekly chats with authors, readers and other guests
- Get writing guidelines
- AND MUCH MORE!

Visit our website at
http://www.kensingtonbooks.com

THE BRIDE WORE CHOCOLATE

SHIRLEY JUMP

ZEBRA BOOKS
KENSINGTON PUBLISHING CORP.
http://www.kensingtonbooks.com

To my Nana
who taught me to be fearless and to pursue my dreams.
To my mother
who gave me my sweet tooth, but not her metabolism.
And finally to my husband and children
who know that the way to my heart is always through
a hug and a Reese's Peanut Butter Cup.
Preferably in that order.

Candace's Fit-for-a-Groom Chocolate Mousse Cake

1 cup granulated sugar
2 cups butter
1 cup water
1 teaspoon instant coffee
1 pound high-quality, amazing-tasting semisweet
    chocolate
8 eggs, beaten slightly

Put the oven on 350 degrees. Grease up a 9-inch spring-form pan (and if it helps any, pretend the pan is a good-looking man). In a saucepan, heat sugar, butter, water, coffee and chocolate, stirring like your life depended on it (and actually it does—this is *chocolate*). Remove from heat when chocolate is melted and smooth. Take one taste to ensure you've used good-quality ingredients.

Okay, take another, just to be positive.

Stir in those eggs and ignore that nasty phase before they're properly mixed.

Now it's time to let it go. I know, I know. It looks good already but truly, you have to cook it. Salmonella and all that. Wouldn't want your groom to be indisposed on the big day. Pour the gorgeous chocolate batter into the pan. Bake 45-50 minutes. Try desperately not to think about the cake until after the timer goes off. Remove from oven and while it's cooling, put on "Chapel of Love." When you're finally in that wedding mood, indulge. Liberally.

CHAPTER 1

Candace Woodrow stared at the gooey, sunken mess inverting onto itself like there was a Hoover under the table. "This was supposed to be a groom's cake, not a pancake."

Rebecca poked at the chocolate failure. "Did you cook it long enough?"

"I thought I did," Candace said. "I lost track of time because Trifecta needed to go out."

"I've seen you with that dog." Maria wagged a finger at her. "Taking a three-legged dog for a walk is a comedy of errors." She gave an indulgent smile to Candace's shelter-rescued mutt, dozing in the front part of the shop, separated from the kitchen by a glass door. "We still love ya, Trifecta, even if you are a living tripod."

Candace laughed. The best thing about working with her friends every day was the laughter. Without them, she swore she'd have gone crazy planning her wedding.

Two years ago, the three of them had started Gift Baskets to Die For in the basement of Candace's Dorchester duplex. Within a year, their food-themed baskets had hit it big with the corporations in Boston, allowing them to open a storefront in a quaint building not far from Faneuil Hall

Marketplace. Business had been brisk enough to pay both the rent and decent salaries for all of them.

Candace's life was settled, secure. On an even, planned keel. She was twenty-seven, three weeks from being married, and her life was chugging along on the path she'd laid out.

Everything was perfect—except the cake.

"Maybe the eggs were spoiled," Candace said. "I mean, look at this thing. It's an overgrown hockey puck."

"It's a sign." Maria nodded and her shoulder-length chestnut curls shook in emphasis. "Yep. Definitely a sign."

Rebecca shushed her. "Will you stop with that? This is Candace's wedding we're talking about. Don't make her more nervous than she already is." She took another look at the cake. "I think you just underbaked it. Besides, this was a trial run. We'll make another one before the wedding."

"What if it *is* a sign?" Candace threw up her hands. "Look at all that's gone wrong with my wedding. The DJ I booked had a heart attack—"

"He said the wheelchair won't stop him from spinning CDs," Rebecca pointed out.

"If he doesn't electrocute himself with the IV drip," Maria added.

"And then last week Father Kenny ran off with the church secretary."

"Who turned out to be a Daniel, not a Danielle like we all thought." Maria grabbed a raspberry thumbprint cookie from the Tupperware container on the counter and took a bite. Maria Pagliano's method of dieting involved buying the latest issues of *Cosmo*, *Glamour* and *Woman's World*, picking and choosing the parts she liked from their diets of the month, then chucking the whole thing on weekends.

"Don't forget the fire at the dress shop. I still can't believe the store burned to the ground, and with your dress inside." Rebecca twisted a scrunchie around her straight brown hair, creating a jaunty ponytail. On Rebecca Hamilton, almost any hairstyle looked good. She had one of those long, delicate faces made for Cover Girl. "It was kind of heroic, though, how that cute fireman kept you from going in after it. He saved your life."

"I would have rather he saved my dress," Candace muttered. "At least I have insurance. But I still need to find another dress. I can't get that particular one anymore and even if I could, there's not enough time to order it."

"You haven't bought one yet?" Maria's jaw dropped. "But Candace, the wedding's only three weeks away."

Since Candace had said "I will" to Barry, it had been one disaster after another. If she put stock in things like signs, she'd have called off the wedding months ago. But she didn't believe in any of that. It was a string of bad luck, that's all. Marrying Barry was the right choice, she was sure of it. Candace had never made a move in her life that she hadn't thoroughly researched, planned and analyzed.

Well, except one. But that had been a long time ago. Ever since then, Candace had subscribed to the "more control is better" life mantra. That's why Barry was so perfect for her. They matched like plaid and stripes.

On her marrying Barry list, the pros had far outweighed any cons. Now if Murphy's Law would just see that, too.

Candace sighed. "Between the business and all those last-minute glitches, I haven't had time to find another dress."

Rebecca looped her arm through Candace's. "Tonight, we're going dress shopping, and then we'll get good and drunk because tomorrow is Sunday, our day off, and we don't have a single delivery due on Monday."

Of the three of them, Rebecca was the oldest by four months and thus had become the unofficial decision maker. She was also the thinnest and the only one who came equipped with both an iron will and a Blackwell-worthy fashion sense.

And, as the sole married one, the wisest when it came to matters of weddings and bridal gowns.

"Wow. An instant vacation." Maria grabbed a second cookie and finished it off in two bites. "I hope the bar is well stocked."

Rebecca gave her a wry look. "You mean you hope the bartender is well built."

"Yeah, that, too." Maria smiled. "But if he doesn't know how to make a killer margarita, what good are looks?"

Candace laughed. She picked up the cake disaster and threw it into the trash, then dropped the springform pan in the sink to soak. The bell over the shop door jangled and a second later, an enormous backpack wrangled through the door into the kitchen.

"Grandma?"

Candace's petite grandmother twirled around, spinning the king-size bag in the kitchen with an ease that belied her age—and nearly took out the Cuisinart on the side counter. "I'm making a pit stop," Grandma Woodrow said, swiping at her brow. The bag dwarfed her, and made her seem even smaller and thinner than she was. "Lord, it's hot out there for June."

"What are you doing with that thing?"

"Hiking. What else would you need a backpack for? George is taking me hiking next month along the Appalachian Trail. I'm following the Paul Revere Trail today so I can break it in." Grandma lowered the dark green bag to the floor, slipping her arms out of the metal frame. She tugged off her Red Sox ball cap and fluffed up her short gray hair, using the toaster for a mirror.

Grandma was seventy-six but told everyone she was fifty-eight. Even Candace fell for the age lie once in a while and forgot her grandmother had been collecting social security for more than a decade. She'd inherited Grandma's hazel eyes and the long blond hair she'd had in her youth, but not Grandma's wild, adventurous personality. "When are you going to get old like other self-respecting retirees?"

Her grandmother waved her hand in dismissal. "Never. Old equals dead. Besides, I'd have to buy a rocking chair and I don't even like to rock." She grinned and gave Candace a wink. "Unless I'm rocking with George, of course."

"Stop! Too much information." Candace poured a tall glass of lemonade from the refrigerator and handed it to her grandmother, then pushed the container of cookies across the counter. Grandma scooped up three of them immediately. Candace smiled. Grandma never could resist any of the shop's baked goodies. Every evening after work, Candace brought home a few cookies and dropped them off at her grandmother's apartment before going to her own half of the duplex they shared.

Six years ago, Candace had moved in at her grandmother's suggestion, to help save money. And, Grandma Woodrow had added, to look after her because she was getting up there in years. Candace suspected it was more that Grandma, who had more energy than Carrot Top on steroids, was a bit lonely.

Candace's father, Grandma's only child, had headed for a permanent tan in Florida years earlier, making occasional seasonal visits on his way up to his summer lake cottage in New Hampshire. Candace's mother, who seemed to be trying to break Elizabeth Taylor's husband record, was always away on one honeymoon or another.

That left just Candace and Grandma Woodrow. Truth be told, Candace liked it that way, despite Grandma's habit of offering quirky advice on everything from buying watermelon—look for one that thumps when you smack it—to kissing men—look for one that doesn't smack you when you thump him.

"So, what are you girls cooking up today?" Grandma asked.

Rebecca gestured toward the trashcan. "A groom's cake. But it refused to stay up. Maybe we should have added some Viagra to the mix."

Grandma shook half a cookie at Candace. "It's a sign."

"I just undercooked it. It's not a sign of anything." Candace recovered the cookies and put them away.

Grandma's face took on a stricken look. She actually pouted.

"Okay, only two more. We need these for orders." She peeled back the lid and held out the container. Grandma grabbed four before Candace snapped the top shut again.

"I'm an old woman," she said. "You have to indulge me."

"You're only old when it's convenient."

Grandma ignored her. "Are you sure Barry is your soul mate?"

They were retreading familiar ground. She'd be glad when the wedding was over and all of them would stop quizzing her. "Grandma, you know I don't believe in signs or soul mates or harbingers of evil. You meet a guy who doesn't have any outrageous fetishes or a criminal record, you marry him and you hope you can hang on for a few years before the lawyers start dividing the toys."

"What about romance? True love? Undying devotion?"

"That only happens in Meg Ryan movies. Not in my life."

Across the room, Maria and Rebecca were mute. As the maid and matron of honor, they supported Candace marrying Barry, but both still held this deep-seated belief in love at first sight, a statistical improbability according to the article Candace had read in *Newsweek* last month.

Candace knew her friends didn't quite agree with her numerical analysis of her future. The other two lived life on the right side of their brains. Rebecca was happily married with a three-year-old. Maria had a new love of her life on a quarterly basis. Right now, it was David, a cute gynecologist who'd moved into Maria's condo last month and pledged his undying devotion with a pearl necklace and one-half the rent.

Candace was too levelheaded to get caught up in that wine and roses stuff. And she was only three years from turning thirty. It was past time to give up on the Cinderella fantasy.

Besides, any woman who had mice for best friends was probably legally insane anyway.

Maria's Favorite Hangover Remedy

1 banana, chopped
½ container chocolate syrup
3 ounces milk
3 ounces rum
2 Tylenol, crushed

Dim the lights and for God's sake, don't open the blinds. Muffle the blender motor with a towel, then blend all ingredients until as frothy as a virgin's prom gown. Don't bother with a glass; drink straight from the damned pitcher.

Repeat as necessary. Then get to a mall and a Krispy Kreme store for further remedial help.

CHAPTER 2

The gnomes inside Candace's head were having a fiesta worthy of Cinco de Mayo, complete with the flashing red jalapeño lights and a band of hammers pounding out the rhythm to "Celebration" in double-time. The sound waved and rolled with her stomach, increasing in volume every time she moved a fraction of an inch in the bed.

A snippet of advice from Grandma Woodrow floated through her mind. Candace latched onto it with every bit of consciousness she could muster. *Put one foot on the floor and you'll get off the hangover Tilt-a-Whirl.*

Candace wasn't sure she could feel her foot, never mind move it.

She pressed her palms against her throbbing temples. Willing the headache away didn't work. Shutting her eyes tighter only made the pounding intensify. She moaned and rolled over, clutching the pillow beside her.

The sheet came loose when she moved and cool air tickled against her skin. Down her spine. Along her belly. Past her legs.

Not against pajamas of any kind.

Candace froze and did a mental inventory. Exquisitely

soft bed linens. No gurgle of the fish tank she had in her bedroom. No Trifecta snoring at the end of the bed. No traffic sounds outside the window.

Without opening her eyes, she ran a tentative hand down her body. She felt a bra. Panties.

Nothing else.

She bolted from the bed, tripping over some shoes and landing in a heap on the floor. Scrambling to a sitting position, she glanced wildly around the room. A room she didn't recognize. Her heart thudded in her throat, threatening to suffocate her.

The gnomes kept up their steady hammering. Maybe they were building a condominium in there. Candace closed her eyes again, but that only intensified her vertigo. She hoped, no prayed, that she was at a friend's apartment. Yes, that was it. She was at Maria's. Who had—Candace scrambled for an explanation—gone on a major redecorating spree in the last twelve hours.

Yeah. That works. Doesn't it?

A pair of Levi 505s lay in a crumpled heap beside her. Jeans she'd never seen before. Jeans that definitely didn't belong to her. Or a woman, for that matter.

Okay. Take a breath. Try to remember.

Maria. Rebecca. The can't-find-a-dress pity party at the restaurant. A few drinks. Okay, a lot of drinks. And a man.

Oh God, a man. She was pretty damned sure his name wasn't Barry, either.

Candace bit her lip to keep from screaming. Nothing else existed in her memory—no name, no conclusion to the night, and especially no memory of how she'd ended up in someone else's bed wearing nothing more than her underwear.

She clung to the sheet, the one sane thing she had in Wonderland. She cradled her head with her other hand, praying for the throbbing to stop so the fog could clear. "Oh Lord, why can't I remember?"

"Because you had too much to drink," a deep voice called from nearby.

Unless Maria had gotten a sex-change operation last night, that was *definitely* not her best friend's voice.

Candace ducked down beside the bed like a SEAL commando and peered over the edge for a glimpse of who had spoken.

The blinds were still drawn, but a tiny sliver of sunlight peeked through the slits. Most of the bedroom remained in shadow. Beside the massive four-poster sat a polished mahogany nightstand holding an empty bottle of German beer and a half-dozen books. Plenty of expensive furniture, but no body to match the voice.

She'd imagined this. A total tequila hallucination.

Behind her, a door creaked open. Candace spun around. Light spilled into the room from a bathroom ten feet away.

A man stood in front of a pedestal sink, shaving.

That was *so not* Maria.

Candace patted the hardwood floor. No luck. No magic rabbit hole to swallow her up so she wouldn't have to deal with this man and anything that might have happened between them last night.

Oh, God—anything that might have happened?

An ocean of nausea rolled through her, threatening to deposit whatever was left in her stomach onto the Oriental rug.

Who was he? And why was she in his bedroom, doing a private Victoria's Secret runway event? The obvious answer was too horrifying for Candace to consider.

He was definitely not the man she had promised to marry in twenty-one days. No, if today was Sunday, twenty days.

Her mouth went dry as she considered the possibilities of who he might be. Serial rapist. Psychotic killer. Deranged kidnapper. Right-wing Republican.

Using the bed as a crutch, she pulled herself to a standing position, ignoring the sudden blast of pain in her head and fighting with the sheet that had tangled around her feet. With a solid yank, she tugged it out from under her and promptly lost her balance. She tumbled to the floor again, losing her grip on the cloth.

She staggered to her feet and prayed the light-colored sheet covered her. It didn't. A quick glance down confirmed the outline of black lace and a Wonderbra.

She didn't even want to *think* about how—or with whose hands—she had gotten undressed.

Her navy sundress was only a few feet away, draped over the arm of a wingback chair. Candace bent to grab it. But she didn't move fast enough.

"Nice view," said a voice from behind her.

She spun around, at the same time wrapping the sheet tighter.

He held nearly a foot's height advantage over her. His hair, still wet from the shower, was slicked back in a dark wave. Deep blue eyes that appeared almost black in the half-light of the room studied her with clear amusement.

Her gaze traveled down, past his bare muscular chest, following the vee of dark hairs to the waistband of a pair of checkered silk boxer shorts. The satiny material stopped mid-thigh along his lean, defined and—okay, she had to admit it—inordinately interesting legs. She jerked her attention back to his face.

He's gorgeous.

He grinned.

And he knows it.

In her experience, which admittedly could fit on the head of a pin and still have room left over, men with that self-satisfied grin used their looks like shark hunters used chum. Bait, hook, use up the good parts, then toss the useless carcass to the seagulls.

"I take it you don't remember anything that happened last

night?" He wiped his chin with a hand towel, then sent it sailing into a corner hamper.

She shook her head, wishing she were anywhere but here, standing in front of a short-haired Adrian Paul doppelganger wearing little more than two hundred-count cotton.

He took a step closer, fingering the tip of the sheet. Even his eyes were rich, flecked with tiny bits of gold among the sapphire. He grinned again, either as a tease or a suggestion, Candace didn't know. Didn't *want* to know. "You had a wonderful time, I can assure you."

The room swayed. Her stomach lurched. Candace smacked his hand away. "That's a matter of opinion."

"Perhaps." He sat on the bed and began to pull on the jeans. "In my opinion, we enjoyed ourselves fully."

She ignored the implications, hoping that's all they were. "But . . . where . . . I mean, how . . ."

"How did you get here?" he finished for her.

She nodded, her cheeks warming.

"In my car, of course."

"And who are you?"

He grinned. "Think of me as your knight in shining armor."

Candace let out a few curses even Grandma had never heard. "I mean, what is your name?"

"Last night, you were content to call me Romeo." A smirk played at his lips, displaying a crescent indent on the right side of his smile. He had a dimple. *That* caused a whole other kind of lurch in her stomach. "I kind of liked it."

"I'm not kidding. Who are you?"

He rubbed his chin, ignoring her question. "Of course, you also called me Loverboy. Oh, and—"

Candace held up her hand. "Stop! Just *stop*. I get the idea. Forget I even asked." She drew in a deep breath and knew she had to ask the question, even if she didn't want to know the answer. "Did I, I mean, did we . . ." Her gaze dropped to the floor. Amidst the plush fibers of the carpet, she saw her shiny red toenails—the pedicure she'd gotten because Barry had this thing about her toes. She gulped. "Did anything happen?"

"Well, that depends on how you define the word 'anything.'"

"Since I'm not packing a dictionary in my back pocket, I'd say anything beyond a handshake."

He got to his feet, which placed him closer, within touching distance. "I was a gentleman, more or less. Your reputation, if you had a good one," he added with a grin, "is still intact."

She didn't rise to the bait. "Who undressed me?"

His gaze swept the room. "There are only two people in this apartment and one of them was a little too drunk last night to do, I mean *undo,* anything."

Heat flooded her face when his gaze settled on the sheet. She clutched it tighter. "I'd like to get dressed now, please."

"Go right ahead." He zipped his fly. The *vrrpp* sound seemed as loud as a bullhorn in the heavy quiet.

"Would you mind leaving the room?"

"It's my room," he pointed out. "I don't have to leave."

He obviously wasn't going to make this easy for her. With a frustrated huff, she reached for her dress. He reached out at the same time, his hands closing over the garment, and over her fingers, before she could get away.

Electricity jolted through her. She stumbled back, trying not to stare at his bare chest, trying desperately not to think about what it would feel like against hers. Had he held her last night? Had he curled himself around her, draped a leg over her hips and pressed his—

She shook her head. The gnomes drummed those traitorous thoughts right out of her head. She was engaged. Three weeks from getting married. She'd leave thoughts like that for the nights when Barry was snoring like a chainsaw and the only sex she could get came with batteries included.

"I'm sure you're enjoying this little game of cat and mouse—" Her hand darted out for the dress. He whisked it behind his back. All she got for her efforts was a smug grin from him and a handful of air. "—but I need to leave. My fiancé expected me hours ago."

A lie, but not a bad one. The only people waiting for her had four paws—well, some had three—and whiskers. Barry was away this weekend.

"Do you always do what people expect you to do?"

"Of course." She held out a hand. "My clothes?"

He leaned closer. "You've never once done something spontaneous, wild and unexpected?" He glanced down at her white-knuckled grip on the sheet. "Except for last night, of course," he added with a mischievous smile.

"If you had so much as a shred of decency, you'd give me my dress and leave me alone."

"If I were any less of a gentleman, you wouldn't be wearing anything at all right now." He rubbed the back of his head. "And I wouldn't have a stiff neck from sleeping on my couch."

Relief surged through her. *Nothing happened. Thank God and Jose Cuervo.* But then, a teeny, tiny part of her felt disappointed. Must be the hangover. It was ridiculous to think she'd actually want to do anything so stupid as a one-night stand. Besides the 20 percent chance of ending up pregnant or with an STD, there was the Barry element to consider.

Oh God, Barry. She needed to leave.

Candace put out her hand. "My dress?" she said again.

But he didn't hand it over. Instead, he placed it beside him on the bed, out of her immediate reach. "Not so fast. We didn't get to know each other very well last night."

"I don't want to get to know you. I'm getting married in three weeks and it's a little late for me to invite any new 'friends.' So, let's just write last night off as a mistake and go our separate ways."

"You keep telling me you're engaged, and yet here you are with me. Is going home with men you don't know something you do regularly?"

She glared at him. How could Maria and Rebecca have left her in the clutches of this maniac? "No, it's not. I have no idea how I ended up here. Besides, you're not my type."

"Oh, *really*. Just what is your type?"

"A man who's responsible, mature and practical." The words rattled out of her mouth before she could stop them.

He mocked a yawn. "In other words, boring." He stood and moved closer. "What about sexy, romantic, humorous?" He took another step. Only a few inches and a Waverly separated them. She could smell the faint scent of his cologne, a mixture of woods and man that sent shivers down her spine.

He reached out and drew the back of his hand slowly down her cheek, tracing the line of her jaw. Her body temperature leaped twenty degrees. For a minute, the room went fuzzy. "Trouble can be so much fun sometimes. Don't you agree?"

"I-I-I wouldn't know," she stammered. A few Tylenol, an ice pack and a hot bath would set her straight. This hangover had to be a king-size whopper. Otherwise, Candace knew a man like him would never make her react like a kangaroo in heat.

And yet, at the same time, she got the distinct feeling she was lying to herself.

His hand stayed along her jaw, one finger beneath her chin. Candace didn't pull away, didn't *want* to pull away. Searing electricity hummed within her, a feeling so foreign it seemed to overtake all five of her senses—a self-made mutiny. She stood there, unable to move, think, or do anything but stare up into the stranger's sapphire eyes.

"Last night, you told me you were tired of being bored," he said, his voice dropping into the lower quadrants.

She swallowed. "I did?"

He nodded, a slow, deliberate nod. "You said you wanted a man who could show you what you'd been missing." His finger tugged her chin closer, inches from his. He leaned down and his breath tickled along her lips.

The room disappeared. Her heart stopped beating; her breath stopped coming. A tingling, twisting yearning brewed within her, making her feel she'd collapse in a heap at his feet if he stopped touching her.

Don't. Don't stop. Don't do this. Don't stop. Don't . . .

"Do you still want to know?"

She opened her mouth to answer but no words came out. Instead, she felt her head, which seemed disconnected from her body and her brain, give a short, quick nod. A hot gush of anticipation rushed through her veins.

Don't. Oh, yes. Do.

He closed the gap between them, his lips a breath away from hers. "Good," he murmured, the word sounding sexier than anything she'd ever heard. And then, the wait was over, his mouth was on hers, hot and insistent, tugging at her to respond, her resistance evaporating in an instant.

He didn't just kiss her—he orchestrated a concert against her lips, his mouth at first tender, seeking, then hot and demanding. She leaned closer, gripping at him, the sheet forgotten, her life outside this room a distant memory. His body was hard—harder in some places than others—and that only fueled what she felt, adding kerosene to the flame.

His tongue slipped into her mouth and she responded with the same, grasping and seeking, and not even knowing why. All she wanted was *more*. More of whatever magic he seemed to possess in his touch.

And then, just as quickly, he ended the kiss, pulling back and inserting distance between them. Candace stood there, stunned and mute. Her entire body pulsated like one giant hormone.

"Does *he* ever kiss you that way?"

She blinked. "Who?"

"Bob Boring." She stood there, drawing a blank. "Your fiancé."

"Oh." Candace swallowed and forced herself back to planet Earth. Engaged women did not kiss other men. They also didn't go home with strange men and wake up in their underwear, but for now, she was just going to deal with the kissing part. Bad idea, bad thing to do . . .

But oh so good for those few seconds.

No, she wasn't going to think about that. This had been an exceedingly bad choice. She would forget about it, move on, and marry Bob B—

Barry. His name was Barry.

"Sure, he's kissed me like that before."

"Uh-huh. Of course he has." The man grinned. His hand dropped away and his demeanor changed back into the teasing one she'd seen earlier.

Teasing she could deal with. Kisses that imprinted themselves on her lips like permanent tattoos, well . . .

"Have you ever read *The Love Song of J. Alfred Prufrock?*"

What? Had he just said what she thought? After what happened a moment ago? The man was crazy. Clearly a flag-waving conservative. "I'm standing here in my underwear and you want to discuss *poetry?*"

He reached over and withdrew the third book from the pile on the nightstand. "Read it sometime," he told her, tossing her the thin volume. "You might realize what you'll be missing if you marry Mr. Boring."

Instinctively, she put out her hands to catch the book. The sheet dropped to the floor, landing in a puddle of cream.

To her surprise, Romeo/Loverboy averted his eyes, glancing up at the ceiling instead of at her underwear. She clutched the book in front of her with one hand and bent to grab the sheet off the floor with the other. "For your information," she continued as if nothing had happened, as if that kiss wasn't still burned into her brain, as if she still had her wits about her and hadn't lost them somewhere between the Oriental carpet and the Casablanca fan, "I'm not missing anything. Barry happens to be a wonderful man."

"If he's so wonderful, why are you here with me?"

Candace wasn't about to answer that question. Not for him and certainly not for herself. She wasn't going to ask herself why she'd kissed him back, why her instincts were screaming at her to drag him back to the bed and see what happened when they went beyond mouths.

Instead, she yanked her dress off the bed. When she turned on her heel, the sheet tangled around her ankles and she lost her balance. Again.

Before she could topple to the floor, a strong arm looped around her waist. He released her an instant later, but not before a blazing heat shot through her midsection, undoing a good portion of her resolve. Her gaze traveled back down to his legs. *Damn.* Those were an unfair advantage over her hormones.

She blamed it on too many *Highlander* episodes and Jose Cuervo's morning-after effect.

"Bathroom's over there, in case you forgot." He pointed to the room on her left, giving her a knowing smirk.

Oh God, he'd caught her looking. Red heat crept up her neck. "Oh, I noticed everything in the room," she said. "I just didn't pay attention to the things that didn't interest me." She passed a quick, dismissing glance over his torso.

There. That should set him straight.

Then she tossed her hair over her shoulder and walked across the room with as much aplomb as was possible for a woman wearing bed linens.

Rebecca's Chuck-the-Guilt Chocolate Chip Cookies

1 cup butter, softened
1 cup granulated sugar
1 cup packed brown sugar
2 eggs
1 teaspoon vanilla
2 ¼ cups all-purpose flour
1 teaspoon baking soda
½ teaspoon salt
1 cup chopped nuts
1 twelve-ounce package of to-die-for semisweet
    chocolate chips

Set the oven to 375 degrees. Take out some of the day's stress by beating together the butter, sugars, vanilla, and eggs. Don't even think about how your time could be better spent cooking dinner, cleaning toilets or walking the dog—these cookies are designed to erase guilt, not add to the total. Quick, before anyone comes in and catches you making cookies, stir in the flour, baking soda and salt. Add the nuts.

Hold a tiny moment of silence before adding the sacred chocolate chips. Ignore your own advice about salmonella poisoning and taste the raw dough. If the kids come in, lie your brains out and tell them it's a new kind of broccoli casserole. These are *your* cookies. You worked hard for them.

Drop by huge spoonfuls onto an ungreased cookie sheet

and bake for ten minutes. Inhale deeply while allowing the cookies to cool (be sure all spouses, children and anyone else of cookie-eating age is upwind). Then gorge on as many as it takes to erase any guilty feelings you might be having. Hide in the bathroom and lock the door if you need privacy for your guilt-fest.

Remember: feeling guilty burns enough calories to cancel out the cookies.

CHAPTER 3

Every block of the trip home compounded Candace's guilt, rolling in her stomach along with the stench of the cabbie and his faux Cuban cigar. How could she have done something so stupid? And if Barry ever found out . . .

He wouldn't. She was going to sweep this momentary lapse of common sense under the rug and leave it there with the Cheetos from last year's Christmas party. The only people who knew were Rebecca, Maria and herself. Surely the three of them could keep a secret for the next, oh, fifty years.

As the cab rounded the corner of her street, a swell of anger rose in her throat as she thought about how she must have ended up in the pickle in the first place. How could her "friends" leave her with that Rudolph Valentino wanna-be? What had they been thinking? Had this been some twisted bachelorette scheme?

He'd claimed she'd asked him to take her for a ride on the wild side. Impossible. He was lying, taking advantage of her hungover state. She wouldn't have. She couldn't have.

Well . . . yeah, but she kind of had with that kiss.

No, that was a pod twin of herself. A temporary fugue

state. Candace tossed the possibility that she'd had anything to do with her own predicament right through the smeared dirty window.

The cab stopped and Candace paid and hopped out, shutting the door silently. She crept into the house, hoping to pass by Grandma's door undetected. It was, after all, only a little after seven. Maybe Grandma had slept in. But since Candace had all the sneakability of an African elephant and Grandma had the hearing of a Navy man in a brothel, that wasn't to be.

"Candace? Is that you?" Grandma Woodrow opened her door and stepped out into the hall the duplexes shared. Dressed head to toe in purple-and-teal Spandex, punctuated with knee pads, elbow pads and a dark purple bicycle helmet, Grandma looked equipped for extreme knitting.

Candace let out a laugh. "Don't tell me. I don't think I want to know."

"Pshaw." Grandma waved a hand at her. "George is teaching me to Rollerblade. We're thinking of going to Venice Beach in January, and everyone who's anyone there Rollerblades."

George was Grandma's sixty-two-year-old boyfriend, though she called him her Latin lover. As far as Candace could tell, George didn't have an ounce of blood in him that had come from anywhere south of the border. Pale and fairhaired, he usually toted SPF 45 everywhere he went. He'd earned his nickname because of his penchant of having sex in public places. God forbid Grandma ever ended up on the front page of the *Herald:* SENILE SENIOR CAUGHT FORNICATING AT FENWAY.

Grandma adjusted her helmet. "Got to keep up with life, you know, or life will catch up with you."

"Well, have fun," Candace said, heading toward her apartment door.

"Not so fast."

Damn.

"You never came home last night." Grandma leaned closer, her gaze searching Candace's face like a human lie detector. "Did you take a different stallion out of the corral? You can tell me."

"Grandma!" Candace put on a properly shocked face and blocked the images of riding Romeo/Loverboy that flashed through her mind like a late-night porno.

But Grandma's sharp blue eyes missed nothing. "You did, didn't you?" She clapped her hands together. "Oh, Candace, I'm so proud of you!"

"Proud of me?"

"Why, for grabbing the bull by the horns, so to speak," she laughed at her pun, "and not just settling for Barry."

"I'm not settling, Grandma. And nothing happened last night."

"Are you sure?"

She'd said "last night," not "this morning." Technically, that wasn't lying. "Of course."

"Pity."

"Grandma, I'm getting married in three weeks. I'm not supposed to be fooling around with other men."

Grandma wagged a finger at her. "It doesn't hurt to taste the other cheeses in the deli before you plunk down good money for the Gouda."

"I've tasted all I want to taste," she said, to herself more than to her grandma. "Barry is the man for me."

"Why?"

"Why?" Candace parroted back. "What do you mean, why?"

"Why is he, of all the men in the world, the one you can't live without?"

"Well, I wouldn't say I couldn't live without him—"

"Ah-ha!" Grandma exclaimed like she'd just hit Megabucks. "Then you aren't really sure!"

"I am sure about Barry. I just don't think love and marriage have to be a do-or-die thing."

Her grandmother waved a disapproving hand. "You young people. What about love, passion? Romance?"

"I have that with Barry." Before her grandmother could say another word, Candace started down the hall. "I have to walk Trifecta and feed Bob before the two of them gang up on my couch cushions." She turned back to Grandma. "Be careful on those Rollerblades. And take your calcium."

"Yes, Mother."

Candace thought Grandma was going to let it go at that. She should have known better.

"Love means never having to settle for second best," she called out before Candace could open her apartment door. "Especially in bed!"

Candace pretended she hadn't heard that, then ducked inside, closed the door and slumped to the floor. Trifecta toddled over and started licking her face. Bob flicked a few cat whiskers in her direction in lieu of his missing tail, then hopped on the sofa, clearly ashamed of his mistress's all-night absence.

"What do you know?" she said to the neutered cat. "You don't even have testicles."

Three more weeks. Then she could forget that last night and this morning had ever happened. She'd get on with her life and the world could finally stop offering their opinions on her sex life.

Three hours and a good dose of Tylenol later, Candace lay on her couch, having a damned fine pity party. The seven gnomes had returned to offer background music while her stomach hosted a rousing rebellion against all four food groups. The only plus—and Candace had to struggle to find anything remotely positive about the day she'd had—was that it was Sunday and she could suffer in peace for a full twenty-four hours.

The doorbell rang. She buried her head in the couch

cushions in a good impression of a dead woman. The doorbell rang again. Then she heard Rebecca's concerned voice. "Candace? You in there?"

With a groan, Candace got to her feet and staggered for the door. She flung it open, grunted a hello and stumbled back to the couch.

Rebecca didn't take offense at the Neanderthal greeting. That was the good thing about best friends—they understood hangovers and PMS. "Hey, what happened to you last night?"

Candace curled into a corner of the sofa, leaving room for Rebecca to sit. "What happened to me? What happened to *you*? You guys abandoned me and now I'm *dying*."

Rebecca laughed and handed her a cup of Starbucks. "Here, drink this. Everything will get a little clearer with some coffee."

"You're a goddess." Candace took the cup and inhaled the aroma of a Vanilla Breve Latte before taking a long sip. The hot java hit her stomach and then, like a domino, her brain. The room came into sharper focus. "Ah . . . I think I'll live."

"I take it you don't remember much about last night?"

"I remember marching through half the bridal shops in Boston, then giving up and stopping off somewhere for dinner and drinks with you two. But everything else after that is pretty fuzzy." Except for the model in boxer shorts she'd woken up to this morning. Candace left that part out for now. If she never mentioned it, maybe it would go away, like a bout of food poisoning.

"We didn't abandon you, Candace. You told us to leave."

"But . . ." Even as she started to protest, a sliver of memory came back. She groaned. "I did, didn't I?"

"It was getting late, Maria had a date, Jeremy had already called twice to find out when I'd be home." A faint blush crept into Rebecca's face and Candace knew exactly why Jeremy had wanted his wife home. "You didn't want to leave. You were sober, though. We never would have left you there drunk. And it was a nice restaurant. You kept insisting you'd be fine, have some dessert and one more drink, then catch a cab home."

"Was there a . . ." Candace paused, bit her lip. *Just spit it out. Like a Band-Aid—yank the words out, even if it stings like hell.* "Was there a guy with me when you left?"

"No. There were a few people in the bar, but the dining room was pretty much empty. When we left, you were sitting in our booth by yourself. Why?"

"I . . . I . . . I need another coffee." Candace got to her feet and stumbled for the kitchen. Her mind was an Oster blender, whirling bits and pieces of disjointed memories into a froth of confusion. She lurched for the coffee canister on her counter, nearly spilling it. When she spooned the beans into the grinder, her hand trembled. A few dozen escaped, skittering across the countertop like roaches in sudden light.

"You okay?" Rebecca's voice behind her made her jump. The rest of the beans in the scoop flew up and landed with a soft clatter on the vinyl.

"No." Candace dropped the scoop and leaned against the counter. "Not at all."

Rebecca put an arm around her shoulders. "Aw, honey, come on. Tell me. What happened last night?"

"I . . . I . . ." Admitting she had all the morals of a wild monkey wasn't easy. Saying the words made them feel and sound so much worse. "I went home with some guy."

"You did?"

"Uh-huh." Candace turned around and faced Rebecca. "And the worst part is, I don't even know his name."

Rebecca blinked twice. Then twice more. "That is *so* not you."

"I know." Candace raised her hands in frustration. "I have no idea what happened or how I ended up there. I just woke up in his apartment and he was there—"

"Was he cute?" Rebecca interrupted.

"Oh, yeah." She nodded.

"Was he good?"

"Rebecca!"

"Well, was he worth it?"

Candace turned back to the coffee and finished shoveling the beans into the grinder. "He said nothing happened, and considering I was still wearing my Wonderbra, I believed him." If there was anything about last night Candace was grateful for, that was it. She didn't mention the kiss. She wanted to bury that particular memory deep in her brain, never to be resurrected again.

"So what are you worried about? It's over; it's in the past. Just think about Barry and it will all go away."

"I am thinking about Barry. And wondering . . ." her voice trailed off.

"Wondering what?" Rebecca prodded.

"How much I really love him if I can go home with a complete stranger less than a month before my wedding." There, it was out. The one thought that had been nagging at her ever since she'd woken up in another man's bed.

All her life she'd been a planner. Or tried to be, because she knew too damned well the consequences of chaos. Things worked out in an orderly manner, if enough forethought was given to each decision. But lately, her life had turned topsy-turvy. It wasn't just disconcerting—it was scary as hell.

"Candace." Rebecca clasped her hands around her friend's. "You wouldn't be human if you didn't have a few doubts. Everyone gets cold feet."

Candace sighed. That was it. Just the patter of cold feet. No reason to doubt her sanity or run to Excel and recalculate the reasons-to-marry-Barry spreadsheet. "I guess you're right." She finished readying the coffeepot and turned it on. Within seconds, the blissful sound of percolating coffee began.

"You know what you need, don't you?" Rebecca said.

"A brain transplant? A hormonal reduction?"

"A large dose of chocolate." She crossed the kitchen and began opening Candace's cupboards, pulling out ingredients and mixing bowls. "Let's make some cookies. Everything looks better after you've had a ridiculously high amount of calories and carbohydrates."

Candace smiled and reached for the bowls. "Rebecca, you're a genius. Ever thought about joining Mensa?"

She laughed. "I lost half my brains when I had Emily. Three years of conversations about what's on Nickelodeon and why Mickey Mouse only has four fingers has pretty much destroyed the few cells I had left."

"Cookies will help with that, too. In fact, I think cookies solve about any problem pretty damned well." Candace put the butter in the microwave, pressed the button and watched the butter become a yellow river.

"My thoughts exactly." Rebecca began measuring and mixing the eggs, vanilla and sugar. She was about as precise as a hippo doing a ballet, but since it was cookies, a few extra ounces of sugar couldn't hurt.

Candace opened the bag of chocolate chips and inhaled deeply. "Ahh . . . I feel better already. Heaven, thy name is Hershey."

"Amen, sister."

"Hello?" A singsong too-happy voice ricocheted through the apartment. "Anybody home? Surprise!"

Damn. Should have locked the door.

The high-pitched, overly joyous voice could only belong to one person. Her mother.

Della was clearly back from honeymoon number six or seven or twenty. Candace had lost track after Davy, Arnold, Reggie and the hairy wolfman—whose name she could never remember—had each been discarded in quickie Reno divorces, then replaced with new-and-improved models.

"Oh! Here you are. And with your friend, too. How sweet!" Her mother bustled into the kitchen, launching air kisses like cluster bombs all around Candace's face. Rebecca managed to busy herself with cookie dough and avoid the Chanel No. 5-scented attack.

Della was a walking testament to Liz Claiborne Sport, her preferred traveling clothes. A teal shell and cardigan was completed by floral print pedal pushers and snazzy rhinestone-studded high-heeled sandals. Her pedicure was flawless, her nails impeccably French and her salon-blond hair neatly twisted high on her head, with two—not three or four, but two—strands loose on either side.

"Hi, Mother," Candace said. "Back so soon from your honeymoon?"

Della's face took on a pained look. "Antonio and I . . ." she cleared her throat. "We had a parting of the ways."

"But you've only been married, what, eight days?"

"Seven." Della pursed her lips and shook her head. "We decided we're hitching rides to the moon on different stars."

Candace knew what that meant. "He turned out to be bankrupt?"

Her mother nodded, shoulders sagging. "Worse. He's not even a Count. He's a"—for this, her mother withdrew a hankie from her Louis Vuitton handbag—"a hot dog vendor at Yankee Stadium."

"I guess when he said he had a lot of gold—"

"He meant mustard." She dabbed at her eyes.

"So what are you doing here?"

"Well," her mother's eyes got bright and perky, *"that's* the surprise."

From the other room came the sound of frantic yip-yip-yipping. Then Trifecta's bark joined in, her nails clacking against the wood floor as she dashed around the room. Bob let out an indignant howl, then streaked through the kitchen, heading straight for the pantry.

Candace recognized the sound of the two-pound ball of fur that had disturbed the hangover peace in her apartment. Her mother had brought along the only male who could make her happy—Percival, the Pomeranian with the personality of an overindulged wolverine.

"Oh, I'm so happy to hear Percy settling in and playing

with his old friends," Della said, clasping her hands. "He just loves it here."

Trifecta let out a yelp, then came barreling into the kitchen. She twined herself around Candace's legs with a whimper. *Coward.* "What do you mean, settling in?"

"Didn't I tell you?"

"Tell me what, Mother?"

Her smile got wide and toothy. "I couldn't let you plan this wedding all by yourself. Especially when I have so much experience with creating the perfect setting for till-death-do-us-part."

Or until the husband no longer passes muster. "Mother, I've got it all under—"

"And you know your father; he won't arrive a minute earlier than necessary. He won't show up until the church bells start ringing. So I thought it would be wonderful if we could spend these last few weeks together, before you become an old married woman," Della barreled on, ignoring Candace's protests. "Planning, shopping, decorating. Percy agreed, and so here we are!" She flung out her hands like Monty Hall.

"What do you mean *here?*"

"With you." She smiled more. "It'll be one great big slumber party. Won't that be fun?"

About as much fun as a leg amputation. Candace lunged for the Hershey's chips, tipped the bag into her mouth and waited until the chocolate had fully assimilated her palate before speaking. "That's exactly what I was thinking."

Candace's My-Life-Sucks Rocky Road Chocolate Fudge

2 cups sugar
⅔ cup milk
2 tablespoons corn syrup
¼ teaspoon salt
2 squares Godiva-worthy unsweetened chocolate
2 tablespoons butter
1 teaspoon vanilla
½ cup chopped peanuts
½ cup mini marshmallows

Smear butter all over a loaf pan and try not to cry in your grease, since we all know tears and butter don't mix. Over medium heat, cook the sugar, milk, corn syrup, salt and chocolate. As it melts, think of it as all your troubles cooking away (okay, that analogy would probably only work on a cheesy talk show).

Once the chocolate is melted and your kitchen smells a hell of a lot better than your life, keep the heat on until your candy thermometer reaches 234 degrees. Add the butter. Remove from heat. Make a list of all the things you want to change about your life while the fudge cools to 120 degrees. Add the vanilla, beat the daylights out of the mixture. Then add the nuts and marshmallows—add extra, depending on how bad your day has been.

Spread in pan and let cool as long as you can possibly stand to wait. Cut into squares just a tad smaller than the opening of your mouth.

CHAPTER 4

With a soup tureen-sized mug of coffee and the rest of the chocolate chip cookies, Candace snuck out of her own apartment, feeling like a teenager who'd missed curfew.

She crept past her mother, prone and snoring on the fold-out couch, looking more like a mummy than a mommy. Under thick cotton tube socks, Candace knew Della had hand cream smeared over her hands and feet. Her eyes were being "rejuvenated" by an aqua blue gel eye mask. On her head she'd twisted a thick terry turban, part of some overnight hair mask treatment she'd bought off the Home Shopping Network, probably getting a few toots from Tootie for her purchase.

As soon as Candace opened the back door, Trifecta and Bob zipped past her, down the stairs and into the yard. Percy took a tentative step forward on pedicured toes, whimpered, then stood in the doorway and whined.

"I'm not carrying you," Candace told him. "Be a man. It's just grass."

Percy plopped his miniature butt on the stoop, wagged his tail and cocked his head to the right, eyes wide and full of dejection. Probably hoping to garner sympathy for his lawn phobia.

"You've got four feet of your own."

Percy whimpered.

"Oh, all right," Candace huffed. "But just this once." With her free arm, she scooped up the dog, padded down the deck stairs and deposited the puffball on the lawn. Percy took three steps forward, lifted his leg and . . .

Peed on the lilacs.

"See if I carry you again, you ungrateful bundle of fur," she muttered, returning to the deck. Percy followed, smartly staying a respectable distance behind. To his credit, he only whimpered twice about the four-step hike.

"Breakfast of champions," she told Trifecta, dunking a cookie into her coffee. The dog barked her disapproval, then headed back through the dog door into the house, with Bob close on her heels. Percy decided going inside was clearly too much effort, and curled into a ball on the deck.

Candace sighed as she put her feet on a second lawn chair, then closed her eyes and inhaled the thick, sweet smell of smog, late spring and fresh-cut grass. Traffic hummed down the street behind her house, the continual drone of people navigating their way into South Boston like a Pac-Man game.

Finally. Peace, quiet and solitude. Maybe, with a proper chocolate-induced high, she could figure out the meaning of life. Or at least why her perfect life had turned into a Fox TV reality show this week.

She'd risked her upcoming marriage and Barry, all for some guy she didn't even know. How stupid could she be? And what the *hell* had she been drinking?

She should call off the wedding. Or disappear into a cave in Guatemala until she could figure out why she had this constant nervous feeling in her stomach. Getting married was supposed to be the happiest time of her life.

Then why did she feel like Marie Antoinette facing the guillotine?

Cold feet, that's all. Even Rebecca had been stressed about

getting married, and look how happy she had been since the "I dos" were over. Clearly, Jeremy Hamilton was the right choice for Rebecca. Just as Barry was the right choice for her. They had the same taste in almost everything, from menus to music. Sometimes they even completed each other's sentences. To her, those moments were proof positive that she and Barry were perfect for each other in every way.

Candace devoured another cookie and felt considerably better.

"Need some company?" Grandma Woodrow poked her head around the short length of fence that separated their two decks. She wore a sunflower yellow towel, the scent of cocoa butter enveloping her like a cloud.

"Grandma, what are you doing?"

"Tanning," she said with a shrug, as if everyone's grandmother laid out at seven in the morning in early June. "George calls me his little brown muffin. And I'm brown *all* over. Not a tan line on this body." Her hands went to the towel, as if she were about to prove her uniform baking job.

"Grandma!"

"What? No one can see me in the yard. And if they do, and get a little thrill out of a naked granny, well, then I haven't lost my touch."

"But at your age—"

"At my age, I can do whatever the hell I want and people just smile and think I'm senile."

Candace laughed. "You have a point."

Grandma settled into the opposite chair, tucking the towel in tighter. "What's troubling you—besides your mother crashing through your front door, expecting food, lodging and sympathy over the loss of yet another husband?"

Between Grandma Woodrow and Della, there were about as many warm fuzzies as between a hyena and a vulture. When Della had left Jacob Woodrow for a trapeze artist with a lisp, she'd gone on Grandma's shit list and stayed there, hovering around number one, right next to the checkout girl at the Stop & Shop who always loudly insisted on giving her the senior's discount.

"I'm fine, Grandma. Really."

"Then why do you look about as happy as Jerry Falwell at a gay bar?"

Candace took a sip of coffee, then sighed. "I miss Barry."

Grandma let out a little snort.

"He's been at his mother's house in Maine all weekend. I won't get to see him until tomorrow night."

"Nothing else bothering you?" Grandma laid a hand on Candace's arm.

For a minute, she considered letting it all pour out—the night in another man's bed, the impending feeling of doom that seemed to follow her around like the Addams family storm cloud. The queasy feeling in her stomach that even Pepto-Bismol couldn't conquer. But she knew, if she said any of that, Grandma would insist it was all a sign that she was courting disaster by becoming Mrs. Barry Borkenstein.

Barry was the right man for her; Candace knew it. Except for his last name and his little obsession with carpet fringe—but she couldn't expect a man with no flaws. And, well, that weird thing he did with his nose when he laughed, but really he didn't laugh all that much. . . .

What was she doing? A mental pros and cons fest on her fiancé? Candace stopped herself, reached for two more cookies and took a bite.

"I'm fine, Grandma," she repeated.

"You sure?"

"Sure as a monkey in a tree."

"Hey, that's my saying."

"It's kind of cute. I think I'll make it my new life motto." Candace dunked a cookie in her coffee and took a bite. "I need to get to work."

"You work too much." She waved at Candace in reprimand. "All that time you spend at those charities, the hours you put in at the shop. You don't have to do it all, you know."

"I like volunteering. And I'm not the only one working at Gift Baskets. Besides, I don't hear you complaining about my hours when I bring home leftovers and samples."

Grandma grabbed two cookies from the container. "True. But I do have to wonder . . ." She tapped a finger to her chin.

"Wonder what?"

"If you're keeping really busy to avoid something."

"What I'm avoiding is bankruptcy." Candace got to her feet. She didn't avoid things. She was a confronter. Sort of. "I've got to hop in the shower. I'll see you later."

"You're looking awfully pale, honey." She put a soft, crinkled palm against Candace's cheek. "Why don't you come over to my deck for a while? George won't mind if you lay out with me. And if you want to do it naked, I'll draw the drapes."

"Uh, thanks, Grandma, but I'm all set."

Grandma shrugged. "Suit yourself. Or don't suit at all," she laughed, gesturing to her towel. She toodled a wave, then disappeared around the corner.

"My life totally and completely sucks," Maria announced, breezing through the door later that Monday morning. She had a clutch of tissues in one hand and a bulging Macy's bag in the other. A bag of Krispy Kremes dangled from a pinky.

"What happened?" Rebecca paused in the assembly of a large wicker basket of cookies, coffee mugs and oversized chocolate bars spelling out "Congratulations Graduate."

"David and I broke up. Can you believe it? He told me all that crap about how he wanted to marry me, how I was the most wonderful woman he'd ever met, how perfect my hips were for birthing his children . . ."

Candace raised an eyebrow.

"What? He's a gynecologist. He thinks about those things."
She dropped the bag of clothes on the floor, tossed the tissue
into the trash, took a seat on one of the stools in the kitchen,
then opened up the Krispy Kremes bag and dove in.

"So why'd you two break up?" Candace asked. She handed
Rebecca a stuffed bear in a miniature cap and gown to tuck
into the right side of the basket.

"Bambi." Maria sighed. "With a heart over the *i*, no less."

"As in the deer?"

"As in the stripper who gave him the lap dance of his life
last weekend when he went to that bachelor party for his
brother. He said he hasn't been able to stop thinking about
her. She came to his office on Wednesday to have him check
her out, if you know what I mean." Maria took a bite of a
jelly-filled, chewed, then swallowed. "I think getting the inside view of her lap pretty much shorted out every decency
cell David had in his brain."

"How did you find out?" Rebecca asked.

"I caught him screwing her. On *our* dining room table. He
was holding onto the chandelier, for God's sake, and whoop-
ing it up like Tarzan on top of a bull elephant." She closed
her eyes, shook her head and dug into her pocket for more
tissues. "We refinished that table together last week. He said
it would be where we'd have our first dinner as Mr. and Mrs.
And now there's this big fat imprint in the polyurethane from
Bambi's butt."

"What did you do?" Candace thanked God she'd never
have to worry about Barry doing something like that. For
one, he wouldn't be caught dead in a strip club. He broke out
in hives whenever he was around too much silicone.

"I threw them both out, then I dragged that table down the
stairs and threw it at David's car." Maria smiled. "I made
quite the impression in his Beemer. He won't forget me, or
our table, any time soon."

"Are you okay?" Rebecca draped an arm around Maria's
shoulders. The anger in Maria's face immediately disappeared.

"No," she cried, swiping at her eyes. "I-I-I loved that god-damned table."

All three of them laughed, then finished the assembly of the baskets, bashing David and cursing his name three hundred different ways. By the time the last bow was attached, Maria had moved on. She had the resiliency of a paddleball when it came to men and breakups.

"Oh, I almost forgot to tell you! I've got good news," Rebecca said. "I think we all could use some, too."

"You have that right," Candace sighed.

"I think we might have landed a huge account with Vogler Advertising. I talked with the president of the company on the phone Friday. They received one of our baskets from a client, and apparently the office staff went nuts over it."

"We're freakin' good," Maria quipped, blowing on the tip of her finger like it was a smoking gun.

Rebecca chuckled. "He sent me an e-mail this morning saying he'd be coming by to talk to all three of us about using our shop for a lot of different projects for his agency. Sounds like it means major business, from what he said."

"When's he coming?"

Rebecca glanced at the clock. "Shit! Now. I totally forgot about it. See what happens when you let me live vicariously through you two? I get all caught up in Bambis with fat butts and Candace's one-night stand with a stranger and I forget—"

"You had a one-night stand and didn't tell me about it? And after I brought in Krispy Kremes and everything?" Maria yanked the bag of donuts away from Candace's vicinity. "Dish, girlfriend, or I'll make you sugar-detox cold turkey."

"You wouldn't."

"Just try me."

Candace started to speak, but then the shop door jingled. She turned around and froze, coffee mug halfway to her mouth. "Oh my God."

"What?" Rebecca asked.

Through the glass, Candace watched the approach of the

man she'd prayed she'd never see again. Only this time dressed in navy Brooks Brothers instead of silk boxers and Levis.

She would have run out the back door if her shoes hadn't suddenly filled with cement. "It's him."

Rebecca tugged on Candace's arm, pulling her toward the door. "Yeah, I told you, we have an appointment with the owner of Vogler."

"No. It's *him.*"

"The one-night stand?" Rebecca whispered.

"Oh my God," Maria echoed. "You went to bed with *him?* Wow. He's cheesecake. With fudge topping. For a guy like that, I'd *build* a dining-room table."

Before Candace could run, hide or enter the Witness Protection Program, Romeo/Loverboy Vogler swung open the glass door to the kitchen and ruined her perfect, planned-out life. Again.

Rebecca's When-Your-Life-is-Upside-Down Chocolate Cherry Cake

1 21-ounce can cherry pie filling
2 ¼ cups all-purpose flour
1 ½ cups white sugar
¾ cup unsweetened cocoa powder (choose brand well)
1 ½ teaspoons baking soda
¾ teaspoon salt
1 ½ cups water
½ cup vegetable oil
¼ cup distilled white vinegar
½ teaspoon vanilla extract

Grease a nine-by-thirteen-inch pan and spread the pie filling evenly in the bottom. When life is crazy, at least get your cake level. Eat any cherries that look bigger than their roommates. In a separate bowl, mix the flour, sugar, cocoa, baking soda and salt. Then take a second bowl (bribe the kids to do the dishes in exchange for a slice of cake), and mix the water, oil, vinegar and vanilla. Dump liquid ingredients into dry. Stir. Faster. Time's a-wasting and the cake won't bake if you dawdle (not to mention, someone's going to need you before you know it, so hurry). Pour over the cherry pie filling. No eggs in this one, so feel free to taste the batter. If you've had an exceptionally bad day, add more chocolate and sugar. Bake at 350 for thirty-five minutes. Invert cooled cake onto a serving dish. Serve with chocolate sauce, whipped cream and more cherries. Or slather the decorations over a good-looking man and satisfy more than your taste buds.

Better yet, take a slice into the tub, lock the door and let the hubby deal with the kids. Sometimes, escape is the only option.

CHAPTER 5

Of all the people Michael Vogler expected to see standing in the kitchen of Gift Baskets to Die For, Candace Woodrow was not one of them. She wouldn't even have made his list of top one hundred possibilities. Not that he hadn't wanted to see her again—in fact, he hadn't thought about much else since he'd kissed her and then watched her storm out of his apartment.

Their kiss had been phenomenal. The kind that wrapped up Christmas and Easter in one huge package, tied it with a bow and sprinkled stardust over the outside.

Not to mention she'd looked damned good in his sheets.

Too damned good. He'd about had to put a leash on himself just to stay away from the bed after he'd woken up and seen her in there, all spread out in black lingerie. Like his own personal *Playboy* centerfold.

Only sweeter. And nicer. And with a hell of a lot of sass.

The night they'd met, Candace had mentioned owning a gift shop somewhere between her third and fourth margarita. She hadn't elaborated, and he hadn't put the pieces together. Boston was, after all, a hell of a big city. Her shop could have been located anywhere.

But, no, it was here.

Damned good luck, if he said so himself.

Apparently, Candace didn't agree. She was staring at him like he was the Antichrist, bringing Armageddon to her neat, organized and gleaming stainless-steel kitchen.

He smiled at her to show he wasn't all bad.

She glared back.

A thin, trim brunette stepped forward. "Hello, Mr. Vogler. It's nice to meet you." She stuck out a hand. "I'm Rebecca Hamilton. We spoke on the phone."

"Michael Vogler," he responded, shaking hers. Out of the corner of his eye he saw Candace take a few steps back, as if she was going to bolt for the door.

"These are my partners at Gift Baskets to Die For." Rebecca gestured toward a smiling woman with chestnut curly hair and wide, interested eyes. "This is Maria Pagliano, our designer." Then she gestured at Candace, who had ducked behind the Kitchen Aid mixer. "And this is—"

"Candace Woodrow," he interjected with a lazy smile. "We've met."

Candace straightened and figured if she couldn't blend in with the kitchen appliances, she'd do a damn good impersonation of Miss America. The glass door reflected back lots of teeth and a face that looked more like a raving lunatic than a beauty queen.

Okay, maybe the mixer had been a more attractive cover.

She scrambled for a businesswoman-type reply. She rejected "Nice to meet you in your clothes," and "Good to see you outside the bedroom" and went with her gut instinct— pretend the night never happened. Claim amnesia. Cop an insanity plea. Grab the first pill bottle she saw and insist she'd missed her last dose.

She thrust out her hand and shook his firmly. "I'm looking forward to doing business with you."

"You left so quickly that morning, I didn't get a chance to

get your phone number. I wasn't sure I'd see you again," he said. "This is a *very* nice surprise."

"I—I—I . . ." *I need a Valium. And a double-thick chocolate shake to help it go down my throat.*

Rebecca stepped forward. "Mr. Vogler, why don't we step into the office and talk about how we can help your agency?"

As soon as this was all over, Candace was nominating Rebecca for a Nobel Peace Prize.

Rebecca led the way through the kitchen and into the office, with Michael following behind. Maria and Candace brought up the rear, Maria's favorite position. She jabbed Candace with her elbow, gesturing with an enthusiastic two thumbs up at Michael's ass.

Okay, it was cute. And tight. Better than some football players. Heck, better than Russell Crowe's. The image of him in the silk boxers came to mind.

All right. Even better than Jean-Claude Van Damme's naked butt scene in *Kickboxer*—which she knew from freeze-framing the scene many times.

Barry's butt was more . . . round. Sort of . . . well, soft. Boyish.

Michael was . . .

All man. And a bag of Oreos.

Maria made an imaginary A in the air, then punched her fist forward as if she'd just stamped him. Approved by the USDA and Maria Pagliano. Candace shot Maria a look of irritation, which her best friend ignored, a "who-me" smile on her face.

Trifecta lay inside the office door, snoozing in the AC. When they entered, she lurched up on three feet, tail wagging with a wild frenzy that said she figured everyone was there to cater to her every whim and throw tennis balls until the fuzz wore off.

Candace gestured to the spaniel-terrier mix to lie back down. Trifecta dropped her head and let out a whine of protest.

"Nice dog," Michael said.

Two words and Trifecta betrayed her mistress like a prostitute tempted by a fifty. She crossed to Michael, brown eyes filled with undying devotion. He laughed and stroked her head. The dog groaned with pleasure. Her eyes lolled back and she flattened her head against his thigh in wanton disregard for her dignity.

Traitor. Candace shot her dog a glare, then tugged her back by her collar. "Leave him alone."

The dog let out a sigh, then plodded back to the corner. Every few feet, she paused to glance over her shoulder at Michael.

He chuckled. "Seems I have a new friend."

"Toss her a compliment and she's yours for life," Candace said.

"Too bad her owner isn't so forgiving." He leveled his sapphire gaze on hers. Her stomach did a flip-flop.

She gulped. "Well, shall we get down to business?"

He stared at her a second longer. "Certainly."

Rebecca bustled around the room, keeping Michael busy with small talk while she doled out cups of coffee and laid a plate of macadamia nut cookies on the table. He leaned back in his chair, an ankle crossed over one knee, looking far more comfortable than Candace felt.

Trifecta let out a couple of sighs, her gaze never leaving Michael. Candace sent a second evil eye toward her morally deficient dog. Trifecta paused, then lowered her head to her paws and snarfled.

Rebecca sat in an opposite chair. "Mr. Vogler, why don't you explain to Candace and Maria what we talked about earlier?"

He leaned forward, slipping into business mode as easily as some men wielded a remote control. "I represent a number of large clients in the Boston area. A few pharmaceutical companies, a couple of tech firms, several law firms, et cetera. Last week, our office received one of your baskets as a thank you from a client." He turned to Candace again. "It was delicious. Very memorable, too."

She got the feeling he was talking about much more than a basket of cookies and homemade chocolates. Oh, God. If she crawled under the table, would her khaki pants blend her into the berber and let her disappear?

"We have a client," he continued, "a baby food manufacturer who is looking for a unique promotion to launch their newest line of formula." The whole time he talked, Michael kept looking at her. A quivering of heat started low in her belly and rumbled through her veins.

She was hot, that was all. She needed a dip in a pool, not another glimpse of his rear profile. She forced herself to focus on the words coming out of his mouth.

But all that did was bring up memories of kissing him. Hot memories. She squirmed in her seat.

Focus on business, not on butt cheeks and blue eyes.

She must be coming down with the flu. Maybe malaria. Possibly typhoid. There had to be a reasonable, medically sound explanation for why she had all the concentration of a cat in a field of catnip.

"The company we represent would like to send a gift basket to all the new mothers in the Boston area," Michael said, looking at each of the women in turn. But his attention kept coming back to Candace. "Sort of a pampering treat. Something for mom, dad, baby. Including coupons and a sample can of the client's baby formula, of course. A major diaper manufacturer has expressed interest in providing a package of diapers to go with the basket, and paying part of the costs for the privilege."

Michael let his gaze hover on Candace's heart-shaped face. She waved her hand at her throat as if she were hot. He paused, watching her fingers flutter at her neck. Such a simple, uninhibited movement, but at the same time damned sexy.

The women he knew were so sophisticated they walked

around like bored China dolls, firm and perfect in everything from their manicures to their breast sizes.

Candace's hair wasn't glued down, her figure was natural and she was unplastic–surgery adorned. Though she tried to hide them, her emotions played on her face like a bad poker player.

She was . . . real. And that had him more intrigued than a slow striptease in perfectly matched Victoria's Secret.

"What a great idea. I would have loved one of those when I had Emily," Rebecca said, interrupting his thoughts and bringing him back to business.

As Rebecca started tossing out ideas such as mini wicker baby buggies and bottle-shaped cookies, Michael reminded himself his priority was the client. He could entertain thoughts of Candace after the meeting.

And maybe entertain more, if he could get her to agree to see him again. What had she said? Three weeks until her wedding?

He was crazy as hell for thinking he should ask her out. She belonged to another man, but . . . only by a promise, not a binding legal document. That meant he was only playing with fire, not launching a five-story inferno by asking her to dinner.

No need to call in the arson squad. Yet.

"I think this will go over really big," Maria said, and Michael had to remind himself she meant the gifts, not his potential invitation of her business partner for a date. "We already do considerable business with people who send our baskets to new mothers. A lot of the moms call us to rave about the gift, and later, they order them for other occasions."

"Great. That's good to know. Maybe we can tie in a follow-up promotion." Michael turned. "Miss Woodrow?"

"Huh?"

"What do you think?"

Candace blinked several times. She'd been thinking about a tropical beach. Hot, sweaty sunshine. A man in a Speedo.

Actually, this particular man in a Speedo. She took a gulp of coffee to clear her head, but only succeeded in choking on the scorching liquid.

Maria gave her a good thwap on the back. She recovered her breathing and felt her face turn red. Michael was staring at her.

"I-I-I." She cleared her throat. "I agree."

"Good." He steepled his fingers, then continued. "We're looking at probably fifteen thousand baskets the first year, delivered to major hospitals in the Boston area. Brigham and Women's Hospital, the biggest birthing center in New England, delivers more than nine thousand babies a year. If this program works out well and sales pick up, then our client may increase the order next year."

"Fifteen . . . fifteen thousand?" Maria stammered.

"Yes. Is that a problem?"

The number was what yanked Candace's reluctant brain back to business. She did the math in her head. It didn't take much to see that this account was a major boost. Tens of thousands of dollars, at a time when orders often slowed down because the rush of weddings and graduations was coming to an end.

"No, no problem at all," she said.

"I was hoping you'd say that." The look in his eyes was heated. Almost electric. Something in her gut melted into a puddle of senseless goo.

"Normally, I'd like to give you time to put together a proposal and budget, then wade through the creative steps. But my client is eager to make a dent in the Boston market. The product roll-out is this week and they'd like to coincide a test run of the baskets with that event."

"Sounds smart to me," Rebecca said.

"Is there any chance you could get two hundred of these together by Friday? I can get you the product if you can coordinate the baskets and the goodies. And assemble them, of course."

"Yes, of course," Rebecca said. "We'd be happy to."

At least one person in the room sounded confident. All Candace could think about was the possibility of seeing him again this week. Not a good thing for a woman who was about to be married. Him being here had already sent her hormones over the edge.

"Great. I look forward to doing business with you," Michael said. He spoke to Rebecca, but his body language was clearly tuned to a different latitude and longitude.

When he rose, Candace jerked up and stood, nearly knocking over her chair. He hadn't said a word about that night. Maybe he'd forgotten about it. Maybe he was going to be a gentleman and never reveal the details, even under Chinese water torture.

Or maybe the night had been so bad, he'd *chosen* not to remember or talk about the rest of the story, like a B-horror movie that wasn't worth the price of admission at the theater.

If so, then why did that thought bother her?

With people milling about the room, Trifecta seized her opportunity. She scrambled up and hobbled to Michael's side, pressing against him again like a lovesick fifteen-year-old.

"You're pathetic," Candace mumbled to the dog.

Michael laughed. He ruffled Trifecta's multicolored coat, then reached into his trousers, withdrawing a small, bone-shaped dog biscuit.

"You keep kibble in your pockets?" Candace blurted out before the sensible businesswoman side of her could kick in with the idiot mouth lock.

"Sometimes I get hungry."

The silence in the room was as heavy as a stone. Even Trifecta paused, ears perked.

Michael patted the dog's head again. "No, I have a springer spaniel named Sam. He doesn't like being left alone so I bring him to work with me sometimes. But what Sam hates more than being home by himself is riding in the car.

Some past life fear of vet visits, I guess." Michael shrugged. "I've learned to carry bribes."

Candace watched her dog lavish her best wags on Michael's navy pants. "So you do have a redeeming quality or two," she muttered under her breath.

He grinned. "Just a couple."

"Then where was your dog that . . . that morning?"

"I have a neighbor who loves to walk Sam. She thinks he's adorable."

"I bet." Had that been a trickle of jealousy in her voice? Where had that come from?

Michael gave Trifecta a final pat, then directed his attention toward Candace. "I'm sorry about . . . well, about giving you a hard time the other morning. I was out of line."

In the background, Rebecca and Maria had busied themselves with clearing the dishes, silent as guerilla fighters trying not to spook the enemy.

"I'd like to make it up to you, if you'll let me," he continued.

Candace opened and closed her mouth. Her senses had gone into overload, assaulting her brain with those Tropicana images again, combining them with some very interesting ways he could make it up to her. "I'm . . . I'm engaged."

Yeah, Barry. Remember him?

"Does that preclude you from having a cup of coffee with a fellow dog lover?"

She'd never known a man who used the word "preclude" in conversation. Or who read poetry. Or who had the ability to make her forget her name. "We're working on a business deal together," she finally said. "It wouldn't be a good idea—"

"To keep the client happy?"

Candace swallowed. "That all depends on your definition of happy."

"Since I'm not carrying a dictionary with me," he said, teasing her with her own words, "I'd say that equals a cup of coffee. Nothing more. No strings. No nudity."

Pity, her mind whispered.

She should say no. She should come up with twenty other excuses why doing anything more than share the air with a guy like this was a bad idea.

From somewhere far off in the background, Candace heard the tinkle of the bell over the shop door. She should get back to work. The general ledger needed to be updated. And if there wasn't enough to do here, she could go home. Scrub the grout on the tub until it was whiter than her teeth. Pick out all the gunk that had accumulated in the sink drain. Change Bob's kitty litter, maybe draw a pattern in the sand for better chi.

Or, she could forget all that for the first time in a long, long time and just say—

"Candace? Are you here?"

Rebecca and Maria jerked to attention. They looked at Candace, eyes wide. *Barry,* they mouthed in panic.

"I'm back early, honey. And I have a surprise for you."

Rebecca sprang into action. "It was very nice to meet you," she told Michael, thrusting out her hand, practically dragging him toward the door. "We'll get back to you with the details on the baskets. Later."

"Candace?" Before anyone could move, the door to the office opened and Barry entered the room. He broke into a wide grin when he saw her. "Hello, sweetheart. I brought you a surprise."

Barry stepped to one side. Behind him stood a bright fuchsia muumuu, or rather, a large woman in a muumuu, with a matching turban wrapped around her gray hair. "Mother has come to help with our wedding plans. Isn't that wonderful?"

Bernadine Borkenstein shouldered her way past her son and into the room. "Nice shop you have here, Candace." She harrumphed and looked around. "Too bad the street you're on is so narrow. Practically needed an FBI agent to find it."

"Now, Mother," Barry soothed. "Candace has a great

business here with her friends. You loved the cookies I brought with me to Maine. She and her friends made them."

Bernadine harrumphed again. "Best chocolate chip cookies I've tasted in months, except for those burned ones."

Candace worked up her Miss America smile again, although it was a bit tougher to do the second time around. Those cookies had been perfectly baked. Bernadine was one of those people who derived a perverse pleasure from giving a compliment and then undermining the nicety in the same breath.

"I'm Michael Vogler," Michael said, sticking out his hand.

Why couldn't the man just leave quietly? Why was he so intent on throwing her life into a tailspin? "You must be Barry. Candace has told me a lot about you."

The two men shook, Barry's arm rising and lowering like a floppy water pump. "Barry Borkenstein. Nice to meet you."

"Mr. Vogler was just leaving," Candace said, ushering him toward the door. If she'd had a bullhorn and a cattle prod, she'd be able to clear the room in double time. But with Bernadine huffing and frowning in place and Michael casting amused glances her way, she could see disaster descending on her faster than a speeding train.

But then, thank God, Michael took three steps toward the door. "You'll be in touch?" he asked. "With the details," he added, almost like an afterthought.

She gave him the full-wattage Miss Universe smile. Damn, she was getting good at that. "Of course. Soon."

"I'm looking forward to it."

Then he was gone, leaving Candace alone with a depressed three-legged dog, an eager fiancé, two dying-to-interrogate-her friends and a muumuu masquerading as a future mother-in-law.

And not a single Hershey bar in sight.

Maria's The-Devil-Made-Me-Do-It Parfait

1 box devil's food cake mix
1 box white cake mix
2 containers frozen whipped topping, thawed
½ cup finely chopped pecans
½ cup mini chocolate chips
Chocolate syrup to taste

This is mindless cooking, girls, the best kind. Whip up the cakes according to the package directions. Bake and cool, then cut into rich, hunky cubes. Put half of the devil's food cake cubes in the bottom of a deep glass serving dish. Remember to leave lots of room for the chocolate syrup and whipped topping.

Add one-fourth of the whipped topping, some of the pecans and chocolate chips, then squeeze the chocolate sauce *all* over. In *every* nook and cranny. No need to make it pretty. This is a parfait, not a work of art. It's a lot like sex—just make it taste good and don't worry about how it looks.

Repeat with the white cake and top again with the same layers. Add more whipped topping and as much chocolate sauce as it takes to satisfy your carnal appetites. Chill until ready to serve. Or, if you don't feel like sharing, get a massive spoon and dig in. If anyone catches you, tell them the Devil made you do it.

CHAPTER 6

"Wait!"

Michael paused in unlocking his Lexus and turned around. Candace ran up to him, nearly out of breath, cheeks aflame, chest heaving, honey-colored hair in wild, windblown disarray. She looked messy and sexy all at once and he thought about kissing her again, until she looked that way because she wanted him, not because she'd been doing the fifty-yard dash. "Change your mind about that cup of coffee?"

"No, I . . ." She grimaced, then let her question tumble out in a rush. "Can I talk to you?"

"Sure." He leaned against the car. He'd hoped she wanted the coffee, maybe more, but it was clear she didn't. She had her priorities—in a five-foot-eight accountant type who barely seemed to have a pulse. Why on earth she was marrying that guy, he didn't know. To Michael, locking lives with a guy like Barry Borkenstein was akin to following a lemming off a cliff.

"No, not here. Not where—"

"Barney might see?"

She didn't correct him on the mangled name and he took that as a good sign. "I don't want him to get the wrong idea."

"I'm just a client, remember? What idea is there to get?" But he unlocked the Lexus, walked around to her side of the car and opened the door for her.

She slid in against the cream-colored leather. Her long khaki pants and beige silky top made her blend with the car, like she was part of the seat. Like she belonged there. The last few women to ride in his car had seemed more like decorations—with beaded dresses and high heels. Somehow, Candace's simplicity fit the lines of the Lexus better.

"Shall we go someplace?" he asked after he'd come around and gotten into the driver's side.

"Here is fine." She cast a glance over her shoulder at the backdoor of the shop, as if she was afraid Bob Boring and his Mommy might come charging through the door. "I have to get back in a minute anyway."

That wasn't what he'd wanted to hear. Like a craving he couldn't shake, he had this overwhelming urge to save her from herself. Or at least from marrying someone who looked about as right for her as a coat on a cantaloupe.

She didn't say anything for a long minute, just sat there, hands in her lap, knitted together so tightly the knuckles nearly turned white.

"Did you want to talk to me or just check out my car?"

She released the grip on her fingers and turned to him. "I wanted to ask you about that night. When you brought me home, to your place." She let out a breath and he got the feeling this was a conversation she'd rather not have. "Why?"

"Why did I take you home?"

"Well, yeah, that's part of it. But more." She paused, then gulped and finished, "Why . . . why did I go?"

To Michael, it was clear why she'd gotten drunk and flirted outrageously with him. Why she'd flopped against him in the booth, murmuring something about wanting to be sure before she tied the knot. But he had a feeling she wasn't quite ready for the whole truth yet. "So, you want to know what happened that night?"

"I don't remember much of it." She flushed slightly. "I don't think I've ever been that drunk before."

"You don't seem the type to get hammered on a regular basis." She didn't ask what type he thought she was, so he went on. "You were sitting alone when I came in. I was supposed to meet a client, but at the last minute, he canceled because his kid got sick. Anyway, you were there alone, and I was alone at the table beside you. And then you spilled your chowder, and that's how we met."

"I spilled my soup? On you?"

"Not all of it. Just the clam and potatoes part."

"Oh God, I'm so sorry. I remember that now." A memory of lurching to her feet, soup bowl in hand, to get a sprinkling of oyster crackers from the buffet table came to mind. She put a hand to her mouth. "The margaritas probably made me a little clumsy. I thought if I ate, I wouldn't feel so drunk."

"It's a good idea to eat *before* you drink, rather than after the fact. It's a little late then."

"Yeah, I know that now."

He smiled at her. "You kept trying to clean the soup off my suit and sort of, well, tumbled into my lap."

"I did?"

His smile widened. "It'll be a hell of a story to tell our grandchildren."

Where on earth had that come from? Grandchildren, hell, marriage, wasn't what he intended here. A few dates to get her out of his system, convince her not to marry the mortician, and that would be it.

Marriage was not in his plans. Not now. Not ever. And not even with her.

Either she hadn't heard the grandchildren comment or she'd chosen to ignore it. "Then what happened?"

"Well, you kept apologizing for spilling chowder on my suit and insisted on paying for my dinner. I asked you to join me, and that's how we ended up together."

He didn't elaborate on why he'd asked her to dine with

him. This lonely, empty feeling he'd been having lately was a temporary glitch, nothing more. Thirty was only a year away and that milestone was making him feel like a racehorse who hadn't hit his stride in a while. That and the string of dates with women who had been about as satisfying as a shot of whipped cream for dinner.

She twisted at the ring on her left hand. "How many margaritas did I have altogether?"

He waggled three fingers at her.

She flopped back against the leather seat. "Plus the two I had with Rebecca and Maria, before you arrived." She closed her eyes. "Did I do anything humiliating?"

He shook his head. "No, not at all," he lied.

She eyed him quizzically, as if she knew he'd held back a few details. "Then how did I end up in your apartment?"

"You were pretty drunk and I thought about bringing you home or putting you in a cab, but—"

"What?"

"You kind of passed out."

"In the cab?"

"In the restaurant. I roused you enough to help you stagger out to my car."

"Oh, God. I'll never eat there again. I probably drooled on the table, too." She closed her eyes again. "Why not look at my license and drive me home?"

"I saw the diamond on your hand." He gestured to the simple, half-carat pear-shaped gem she wore, "and I wasn't sure if you had a jealous, homicidal fiancé waiting at the door." And there'd been something about her, so fragile and vulnerable, that had compelled him to take her home with him. Some deep-rooted sense of chivalry had sprung to life in him, like a latent gene.

"So you kept me *overnight* instead? Wouldn't that have been worse for me when I went home?"

"To be honest, I didn't expect you to sleep so long. I dozed off on the couch waiting for you to wake up." He didn't tell her how he'd first spent a few minutes watching her sleep, curled up against his pillow, seeming so pure and sweet lying there in his four-poster.

So unlike anyone he'd met in a long, long time.

"Thank you." Her quietly uttered gratitude extended like an olive branch between them.

"It was nothing," he muttered. "You just needed someone to take care of you that night."

"No, really, you didn't have to do that. Any other man would have—"

"Taken advantage of you?"

She nodded.

He laughed. "I'm not exactly Sir Galahad, but even *I* wouldn't take advantage of a woman who was drunk. That's not to say I wasn't tempted. It was . . . you were . . ." He shook his head. "Anyway, you had that ring on and you were snoring. Those are pretty good stop signs for a guy."

"Well," she said, letting out a gust of relief, "at least no one knows about that night."

"Except us."

"Yes, and I want it to stay that way." She eyed him like a parent laying down the law.

"Maybe forgetting it isn't such a good idea."

"Are you crazy? I'm getting married soon. I don't need this kind of complication."

He turned to face her fully, draping his arm over the back of the seat. "But you're interested in me."

"I am not."

"I know interest when I see it." He leaned closer to her, close enough to see the flecks of gold in her hazel eyes. "And when I taste it."

The memory of his lips on hers came rocketing back to Candace, hot, fast. "That was a momentary lapse of judgment. It won't happen again."

"Oh, really?"

"Really." Her vocabulary had been reduced to playground level.

"So, if I leaned forward right now"—and he did just that, coming closer to her, within an inch of her mouth—"you wouldn't be the least bit tempted to kiss me again?"

"No, not at all." She managed to say the sentence without stammering.

"It wouldn't make you remember that amazing kiss in my apartment?"

She swallowed, then shrugged. "Already forgotten it."

"And you wouldn't lean forward just a teeny, tiny bit," he drew out each word, making them sound like a slow tease, "wanting to kiss me even as you said you didn't?"

"Are you going to kiss me again?"

"Do you want me to?" he countered.

She thought of Barry and Bernadine back in the shop. Of the diamond on her finger, the wedding she should be planning. In a couple of weeks, she'd be Barry's wife. And Michael Vogler would be nothing but a pleasant memory. That should be enough, but for some reason, she felt like she would be missing out on a part of her life by not kissing him again. Those were crazy, insane, marriage-ruining thoughts, she knew. "Why are you so interested in me?"

He leaned back a little. "You're different."

"Different as in from another planet or different as in a mental asylum escapee?"

He smiled. "Different as in someone who doesn't bullshit their way through life. Who looks at things in black and white. In my field of work, everything's gray. There is no line between truth and fiction. It all gets blurred in the name of advertising and marketing."

"Oh." She wasn't sure how to respond to that.

"And that interests me. But at the same time, it makes me want to tease the hell out of you."

"Why?"

"Because I love the way your eyes get wide and your cheeks flush whenever I get too close."

"They do not."

He invaded her side of the car again. "Oh, but they do." He drew a finger along her cheek and even she could feel the heat in her face. "See?"

Her plan for confronting him, made in a hasty run out the back door of the shop, hadn't extended beyond prying the truth out of him about that night so she could . . .

What?

Candace had no idea. No carefully laid path came to mind. And with him touching her, all her brain activity seemed to have ceased. "I shouldn't be here."

He moved back, resting his arm again on the seat. "You're probably right."

"I'm getting married."

"Why?"

She let out a chuff of frustration. "Why does everyone keep asking me that?"

"It's an important question, don't you think?" When she didn't answer him, he went on. "Just tell me one thing."

"What?"

"If you can sit here and look me in the eye and tell me, honestly, that Barry Borkenstein is the man for you, I'll leave you alone. Forever."

In the passenger mirror, she glimpsed a mushroom cloud of fuchsia exit the back door of the shop. Bernadine. She shut the door, then stood against the brick wall, rooting in her oversized purple purse. Candace slumped down in the seat, hoping she hadn't been seen. Bernadine found what she was looking for—a package of lady's cigars and a floral lighter. She smiled, a big, wide, help-is-here smile, and lit up, smoking the cigar in rapid draws.

How was she going to get out of the car? Bernadine would

undoubtedly see her. She glanced in the mirror again and saw Bernadine drag in nicotine, then release a cloud of smoke. How long did it take to smoke one cigar anyway?

"Candy?" Michael said.

She turned to him. "What did you just call me?"

"Candy. As in short for Candace." He cocked his head and studied her. "Don't you have a nickname?"

"No. I'm not really a nickname kind of person." Well, when she'd been a kid, there'd been the inevitable "Four Eyes," fixed with a pair of contacts, and "Braniac," her peer reward for acing a test. But no one had ever shortened her first name, not even Della.

"I think it fits you. Perfectly." The way he said the words made her feel like she'd slipped into a mink coat. "Candy," he said again, soft, slow, deep. "Sweet, sweet Candy."

That pulsing, twisting need for him began again in her veins, teasing in her chest, tugging at the nether regions of her body. She swallowed, trying very hard not to think about that kiss, telling herself his deep blue eyes did nothing for her, that she didn't want to run her fingers through his ebony hair and forget that Barry ever existed.

It was animal instincts, nothing more. Hormones and a long weekend with Barry out of town. That was all. Once she and Barry got back into their regular routine of dates on Tuesdays and Fridays and reading the Sunday paper together, everything would be fine.

"Candy," he said again, quiet as a caress. "Kiss me."

She opened her mouth to say no, but the word refused to come. It stayed in her throat, a defiant child. The silence stretched between them. One second. Two. With each passing tick, Candace felt her resolve unravel like a thread with too much tension on it.

"I'm marrying Barry," she said finally, then burst out of the car before she forgot why.

When she did, she realized too late that she *had* forgotten something else. Something large and pink and just looking for a reason to hate Candace.

Bernadine turned at the sound of the car door opening. Her mouth dropped open, the cigar dangling from the left side, held in place by saliva. She glanced at Candace, then at the Lexus. Her eyes narrowed, her mouth closed and she harrumphed. She stubbed out the cigar and went back into the shop before Candace could come up with a reasonable excuse.

Behind her, the Lexus—and Michael Vogler—still waited. Ahead of her was the shop and Barry. Candace hesitated for a moment, then ran like hell for the door.

Della's Your-Soul-Mate-Could-Be-Around-the-Next-Corner Fried Bananas

½ cup flour
2 tablespoons cornstarch
¾ teaspoon baking powder
½ cup water
2 bananas
vegetable oil for frying

Chocolate Sauce

¾ cup sugar
1 cup water
⅛ cup cocoa powder, sifted
Pinch of ground cinnamon
½ teaspoon vanilla

Heat 1 ½" of oil in a pan to 350 degrees. Ah. Nothing's better than fried food—except fried food served up by a naked, single and rich guy. Whisk together the dry ingredients, then add the water until smooth. Strip the bananas (ooh lah lah) and slice them into thirds. Coat them with the batter. Carefully drop them into the oil and cook, turning occasionally, until they're Coppertone gold (about two minutes—faster than a spray-on tan). Remove and drain on paper towels. There. You've just made them much healthier and lowered the calorie count. One hearty jaunt in bed should work off a couple of these (just be sure to first check your intended bed partner for a ring. No sense wasting those calories on a man who's already attached).

Fried bananas are all well and good, but fried bananas in chocolate are even better. Be patient—it's almost time to eat. Stir sugar and water over low heat until the sugar has completely dissolved, then bring to a boil and let it rock and roll for one minute. Take the pan off the heat, and add the cocoa, vanilla and cinnamon. Whisk, then reheat.

Now fill your belly—and your soul—until you feel better. If you want, ask your company to spend the night; put on a little mood music; a lacy, see-through negligee; and if he proposes, you'll be *totally* satisfied.

CHAPTER 7

All Candace wanted was to be alone. Retreat into a ball of self-pity in her apartment and nurse the headache that had started radiating out from her left temple about the same time Barry had returned from his trip and Michael Vogler had planted all those doubts in her mind again. How had he managed to do that? No wonder he was in advertising. Those were the kinds of guys who did screaming ads for beards in a spray can, who'd say anything to get you to buy into their spiel.

She lay on her couch and burrowed her head into the pillows. Trifecta came up and placed her paw on Candace's back, as if atoning for her earlier infidelity.

Candace flipped her head and looked into the dog's wide brown eyes. *"Now* you're sorry."

Trifecta whimpered a bit and snuggled closer.

"Barry is a nice guy. Why don't you like him?" The dog had never quite warmed up to Barry, no matter how hard he tried to ply her with baby talk and biscuits.

Trifecta didn't answer. Just closed her eyes and kept her paw on Candace's spine.

"Good choice," Candace told the dog. "I don't want to talk about men right now, either."

Candace decided she'd simply lie here for the rest of her life, overdosing on Ho Hos and *E! True Hollywood Story,* forgetting about the evil eye Bernadine kept throwing her way after she'd returned to the shop, and definitely forgetting that conversation with Michael in the Lexus. All bad moments, best left in the recesses of her memory.

But her watch told her it was only twenty minutes until her scheduled shift at the animal shelter. Once a week, she spent a few hours at the Paws a Minute shelter, helping the staff bathe the animals, tend to the sick ones and design what she hoped were eye-catching ads that would get every stray in the city a good home.

She closed her eyes and sighed. She had enough time for a ten-minute pity-fest if she broke the sound barrier when she drove over there.

There was a flurry of noise at her front door and then her mother burst in, carrying Percy and a slew of shopping bags. "I'm so glad you're home! I went shopping today and got you a proper trousseau."

Candace groaned and rolled into a sitting position. Trifecta shot Percy a glare, then wandered off to the bedroom. *Smart dog.* "What do you mean 'a proper trousseau'? I've got everything I need already."

"Candace, I've seen what you wear to bed. You can't spend your wedding night in a T-shirt and sweat socks."

"Mom, I don't want to shock you or anything, but I'm twenty-seven. I'm not a virgin anymore. Barry and I have had sex. Many times. The wedding night thing isn't exactly a big surprise for him."

"You still need something fancy." She wagged a finger. "Keep his eye on you or his eye will stray."

"Not Barry's eyes, trust me." Candace curled into the corner of the couch.

"Any man can be turned by a pretty face," Della said. "Not to mention a doctored ass and breasts."

Candace shook her head. There were days she didn't think she and her mother were on the same planet, never mind in the same family. "I already bought something for the wedding night."

Her mother dropped Percy to the floor. "Something lacy?"

"Lace irritates Barry's skin. He's very sensitive."

"Oh." She glanced at the bags in her hands. "Are you sure? What about feathers?"

"Feathers?"

"Yes, as in a boa?" Her mother withdrew a hot-pink feather boa from one of the bags and draped it around her neck. "See? Sexy."

"You look like a flamingo on steroids."

Her mother made a face. "What about leather? Does Barry like leather?"

"He's allergic. And he feels it involves unnecessary animal slaughter."

"It also makes most men hot as a team of horses." She peeked in one of the bags. "How about fishnet? Does he have something against fishnet?"

"Uh, I don't—"

"Good. This will be perfect, then." Her mother tugged something long, black and the consistency of dental floss out of her bag. Percy yelped and ran into the kitchen.

"What the hell is that?"

"It's a body stocking." She held it up by the shoulders. Candace could see the very lean shape of a body in it, if she squinted. Della started poking a finger between the legs. "It's even got a convenient opening right—"

"Mother!" But even as she protested Della's show-and-tell, a traitorous part of her mind told her Michael Vogler would like that body stocking—and the convenient opening—

very, very much. He'd probably also like lace. Definitely leather. And if she closed her eyes right now, she knew she'd imagine his reaction to her in the boa. And nothing else. "I'm not wearing that thing. My relationship with Barry isn't based on sex."

Theirs was a relationship she could depend on. Barry was the kind of guy who showed up exactly at the time he said he'd be there, who remembered when her car was due for an oil change, who never let a month lapse without balancing the checkbook. He was all the things she'd never had in her life—security, reliability and quiet.

"Oh really, Candace. Lighten up. How do you expect to keep Barry interested in you?"

"Long conversations about intellectual subjects."

"Bullshit." Della dumped the bags on the kitchen table and let out a sigh. "Honey, you need to live a little before your life gets away from you."

All Candace wanted to do was take a handful of Tylenol and forget that the world—and fishnet body stockings—existed. Her mind, however, kept coming back to Michael, like a dieter who'd been denied cake for months and had accidentally gotten locked inside a bakery. She needed to get back on track, back to Barry and her regular life. "Now you sound like Grandma," she told her mother.

"I doubt she'd be happy to hear that." Della paused in front of the hall mirror and spruced up her hair. "By the way, don't wait up for me. I have a date tonight."

"You just arrived yesterday. You met a man already?" Actually, Candace knew she shouldn't be surprised. In one weekend trip to Reno, Della had been divorced on Saturday and remarried before the sun had set on Sunday.

"I met the nicest man at Lingerie for Lovers." She sighed. "He's a poet."

"Translation—poor."

Her mother took out a tube of Lancôme lipstick and applied cranberry red to her lips. "Maybe. But he's really cute. You should see his—"

"I have to go," Candace interrupted. No way was she going to stay here and discuss the physical attributes of some wanna-be poet who sold garter belts for a living.

She got to her feet, skirting a wide path around the hot-pink lingerie bags on the table. A few minutes later, she had changed into jeans and an old T-shirt and was weaving her way through the streets of Dorchester to the shelter.

Inside Paws a Minute, the scene was sheer chaos. Dogs yapping, cats mewing, fur flying and bits of dog food skittering across the floor. Jeanine, the manager, nearly tackled her in relief when Candace arrived. "My assistant called in sick today," she said. "I've been here alone since nine."

"I need a few hours with four-legged creatures who have no input whatsoever into my love life." Candace grabbed an apron off the wall and tied it around her waist.

Jeanine laughed and kept Candace to her word. For the next four hours, she shampooed and clipped, fed and petted, walked and scooped.

By the time her shift was up, her arms ached and her legs were wobbly with exhaustion. It should be enough to put her to sleep and knock out all thoughts of pink boas and one particular blue-eyed man. She drove home, too tired to even flip on the radio.

Grandma was sitting on the steps of their shared porch, oiling the wheels on a skateboard. Her bike helmet sat beside her, at the ready for a bit of pavement hanging ten. "I see Barry's back," she said, wiping off the excess oil with a rag.

Candace took a seat beside her on the worn wooden steps. "How'd you know?"

"He came by earlier to introduce me to that harpy he's got with him."

"Grandma! That's his mother."

"She's a gargoyle. If you marry him, you better wear battle armor."

"What do you mean *if*? *When* I marry Barry."

Grandma spun the cap back onto the oil container. "There's time to change your mind."

"The invitations already went out."

"Uh, sort of."

"No, Barry told me he and his mother mailed them out last week, when he was visiting her. He thought it would make it easier on me if he took care of that."

Grandma wiped her hands on a rag, then reached into her back pocket and withdrew a cream envelope, blank except for the stamp and Candace's return address. "Here's what came in the mail today, actually for you, but the mailman gave it to me since you weren't here."

"Yeah, the invitation."

"Not exactly." She wagged it. "There's no addressee."

Candace snatched the paper out of Grandma's hands. "How can that be?"

"Seems you've had a label letdown." Grandma fingered the flap. "The innards are there, all neatly addressed in a curly script to 'Eleanor Woodrow and Guest.' Pretty penmanship. But, no one's going to see that if the invitations aren't addressed to anyone." She tapped the envelope. "It's a sign."

"Will you stop saying that? There are no signs of anything here. Just defective labeling products."

"Or a man who can't make it stick."

"Grandma!"

Grandma draped an arm around Candace's shoulders. When she did, Candace could smell the familiar scent of Grandma's vanilla perfume, topped with a bit of wheel oil. "I love you, honey, more than anything. Please, for me, take a minute to think about what you're doing. Figure out if Barry really is your soul mate."

Candace let out a sigh. "How does anyone know what that is? If there even is such a thing, which there isn't."

"How do you know unless you ask?"

"Ask who?"

"Anyone." Grandma cupped Candace's chin in her age-softened palm. "But most of all, ask yourself. And do it fast, before you find yourself exchanging muumuus under the Christmas tree with the gargoyle."

On Tuesday morning, Candace started to panic. She lay in her bed, project planner pad in hand, and created a to-do list that grew frighteningly longer and less doable with every minute.

Two weeks and four days left until her wedding. She had no dress, invitations that were MIA and a grandmother who'd planted a tiny little doubt in Candace's mind, growing like those expandable cockroach-alien things she'd seen once in a *Star Trek* rerun.

"I am a committed person," she said to the ceiling. "I do not run off willy-nilly and make stupid decisions." For the past twenty-seven years, sticking to well-thought-out plans had served her well. No unfortunate surprises. Well, except for one. And she'd learned a very painful lesson from that, never to be repeated, because every time she thought about it the hurt returned anew, like a scar that hadn't quite healed. After that, Candace no longer took chances or veered off the straight and narrow path. Unlike her mother, who lived life by the seat of her designer pants, Candace believed in stability.

All of which was why she should focus today on her wedding. If she poured her energy into that, she could get back to her regularly scheduled life and forget about Michael Vogler. He was an interruption she could do without. She'd ask Rebecca and Maria to handle all the business dealings with him, and that way, she could avoid ever having to see him again.

At that thought, a trickle of disappointment went through her, but she shook it off and picked up her list again.

Today was her day off from the shop. Normally, she'd spend it helping out at the Lincoln Homeless Shelter's soup kitchen and working on this week's ad for Paws a Minute. The ad could wait until Wednesday night; she had until Thursday at noon to get it to the paper. She made a quick call and switched her schedule at the homeless shelter to Saturday afternoon.

This morning, she'd find a dress. No matter what. The invitation problem could be solved with a couple of hundred phone calls.

There, a plan. She felt better already.

A few minutes later, she stood under the hot shower, the water pelting at her face and head like a large-boned Swedish masseuse. She sighed and leaned farther into the spray.

In the back of her mind, she could hear Barry's voice. Seventy-five percent of water usage is sucked down the bathroom drain. Shaving two minutes off a shower could save umpteen gallons a year, reducing water costs by a gazillion dollars over the course of her lifetime. "Every drop counts," he'd say to her in the mornings, after he'd spent the night, while he shaved at the sink using a few tablespoons in the basin for rinsing his razor and cheeks.

But he hadn't been here last night, had he? He hadn't helped set her mind at ease or turn off the nightmares she'd had about facing an empty church in her underwear. Or the recurring dreams that featured a man with blue eyes greeting her at the end of the aisle, not Barry's dependable browns. No, he'd been off with his mother, showing her the town.

Candace switched the water to cold and gave herself a blast of icy water, both to clear her head and get rid of the last vestiges of sleepiness. She shouldn't be mad at Barry for spending the evening with his mother. Or for his commitment to saving money. Those were good qualities in a man.

It was just that today, it all annoyed the hell out of her.

Maybe she needed a donut. Everything looked better after a donut.

The telephone rang. Candace shut off the water, wrapped herself in her terry robe and dashed into the bedroom to grab the cordless phone off the nightstand.

"Good morning," Barry said, his voice clear and crisp. He always talked as if he didn't want to fritter away any syllables. Barry was a man who wasted almost nothing. "After work, would you have dinner with Mother and me?"

Grandma's comment about the gargoyle came to mind and Candace had to bite her lip to keep from laughing. "I get a choice?"

"What did you say, dear?"

She cleared her throat. Bernadine was going to be her mother-in-law, for better or for worse. She'd better start getting used to the idea. She was about to agree, then remembered Bernadine had seen her getting out of Michael's Lexus. "I might be busy at work."

"Mother will be very disappointed if you don't come. She really wants to spend more time with you."

I'll bet. She could avoid Michael Vogler forever but she couldn't avoid her mother-in-law. Surely in the next eight hours she could come up with a reasonable explanation for being in his car.

Unless . . . Bernadine hadn't mentioned it because she'd been *sneaking* those cigars. Barry hated the smell of cigarette smoke and definitely would have mentioned it if his mother had such a habit. Had Bernadine been doing a little lying of her own? If that was the case, then Candace didn't think she had to worry about Bernadine squealing. "I'd love to go to dinner with you two," she said.

"Wonderful. Mother has great ideas for the wedding. You'll love them."

Candace plunked down onto the bed. "Barry, about the invitations . . ."

"Mother and I worked all last week on those. She has such beautiful penmanship."

"Well, there's a problem."

"What do you mean?"

"Did you remember to address the envelopes?"

"Sort of."

"What does that mean?"

"Well, Mother's hand was starting to cramp after we put all the return addresses on there, and you know no one can read my handwriting, so we decided to create our own labels. I did a very nice Excel spreadsheet and mail merge. You should have seen it."

"My grandmother's invitation arrived without a label. What happened?"

Barry paused a second, obviously surprised. "Uh, well, Mother was starting to get a headache from the fumes. That label glue was pretty powerful." He tsk-tsked the manufacturer. "Do you know what they put into glue? It's all animal by-product. I didn't want to get near it, either. Who knows what it would do to my allergies."

"Fumes?" Candace shook her head. "What kind of labels did you use?"

"Oh, we got a great buy on them. Five thousand for two dollars at the dollar store."

"Barry, these were our *wedding* invitations. Tell me you didn't skimp on them."

"We bargain-shopped, not skimped. Every penny counts, you know."

Tension knotted into Candace's shoulders, undoing the shower massage. "You used substandard labels on our *wedding invitations?*" She could hear Grandma's voice in the back of her head: *It's a sign. It's a sign.*

"I had every reason to believe they would stick. The package said 'sticks to anything.' "

"They're not a great bargain, Barry, if they don't stay on the envelope," Candace said, her voice rising in sharpness.

"Why didn't you just run the envelopes themselves through the printer?"

"Oh." Barry paused. "We didn't think of that."

Candace ran a hand through her wet hair and flopped back onto the pillows. "There's not enough time to send out new invitations. We're just going to have to split up the list of guests and call everyone."

He sighed. "I'm sure most of the invitations were fine. You worry too much, Candace." He paused, and the annoyance hummed on the line between them. Then he dropped his voice a few levels, into a soothing tone. "But if it will make you feel better, I'll try to slip in a few calls this week."

"A few? We invited two hundred people. You're going to have to find time for a hundred calls."

"Actually, Candace, many of those people are couples. I think it would be more accurate to say a total of eighty-six calls. And if you subtract Mother, your grandmother, your mother, Rebecca and Maria, since we can tell them in person, it's only eighty-one calls. If I take a few, surely you can handle the rest. Isn't today your day off?"

"I have to shop for a wedding dress."

"You still don't have one? Darling, our wedding is only two-and-a-half weeks away. Mother found her dress last night at Filene's Basement in Downtown Crossing. Oh! I have a brilliant idea!"

"What?"

"Why don't you and Mother shop together? I know she'd love to spend more time with you."

Candace scrambled for an escape route. "Uh . . . I was going to work at the shelter today and shop on my break." She cringed at the lie, but figured it was either that or end up with a Technicolor caftan for a bridal gown.

"Okay." He sounded disappointed. "After dinner, how about I drop Mother off at my place? Then you and I can spend some time alone at your apartment. We could rent a movie, have some popcorn with cheese on it. I've missed you so much. I hate being away from you. You're my anchor, honey."

"I've missed you, too," Candace said, and meant it. When Barry was around, she felt like her keel was back in the water, keeping her on a straight path. She'd known him for two years. Being with Barry was as comfortable as an old pair of slippers. "What should we rent?"

There was a pause, and then both of them said *"Titanic"* at the same time.

Relief flooded through Candace. All was right with the world again. "See, that's why we're perfect for each other. It's like you can read my mind."

"You're the one who's perfect for me, *always,*" Barry said softly. "I'll see you at six."

Candace hung up the phone and smiled. Soul mates and signs were all ridiculous thoughts, the kind of things dreamed up by greeting card salesmen and people vying to get on *Oprah.* She didn't need a soul mate.

Not when she had Barry Borkenstein.

Grandma's Soul-Mate-Worthy Chocolate Biscuits

½ cup butter
¼ cup sugar
1 cup self-raising flour
1 pinch of salt
¼ cup chocolate powder

Get out the mixer and whip that butter and sugar until it's as creamy as a squirt of Ben-Gay. Sift together the flour, chocolate and salt, then stir them into the creamed mixture. Get it good and gooey, like a big brown mess of taffy.

Roll the dough into balls and place with TLC onto a greased cookie sheet. Leave room between them for oven growth. Flatten each ball slightly with a fork dipped in water. Resist the urge to make cute crisscross patterns. You don't have time for that crap, not at your age. Remember, the sooner they bake, the sooner you can indulge.

Bake at 375 degrees for eight minutes. Remove from oven and share a few with your soul mate in front of a roaring fire on a bear rug. Best served with a dinner *he* has cooked. Why? Because he loves you, of course.

And if you want to eat naked, just watch out for hot butter drips.

CHAPTER 8

Twenty minutes and two Boston Kremes from Dunkin' Donuts later, the soul mate thing kept cropping up in Candace's head like brain heartburn. It refused to die a slow death no matter how often she reminded herself that Barry was the ideal mate.

She pulled out from the coffee shop and started heading toward Fannie's Fantasy Bridal Shop in Newton, one of the few stores in the state of Massachusetts left unscathed in her second quest for a dress. As she hit the outskirts of Dorchester, she passed the huge, stained-glass-and-stone Our Lady of Faith cathedral where she and Barry had promised to exchange "I dos."

She banged a quick right, prompting the driver behind her to lay horn in true Boston style, and skidded into the lot. She parked, got out of the car and marched toward the church. She'd put Grandma's soul mate notion to rest once and for all, and be able to dismiss the little doubts that had been planted by Michael Vogler, too.

Father Pete was a no-nonsense, live-by-the-Good-Book kind of guy. He frowned on horoscope reading, fortune telling and Oscar predictions. Surely, he'd be the voice of reason she needed. Certainly a better one than Father Kenny, who'd abandoned the collar for the cross-gender church secretary.

After her eyes adjusted to the darkened church, she headed back to Father Pete's office. Surrounded by a clutter of books and papers, he sat behind his desk working on something—a sermon, she supposed. He was doing double duty until a replacement could be found for Father Kenny.

Father Pete was given to extemporaneous biblical exposition, if the mood struck him and an unwitting parishioner stumbled in at the wrong time. Candace breathed a quick prayer that Father Pete was not in a gabby mood today. The last thing she needed to add to her list of worries was a trip down Fire-and-Brimstone Lane.

Father Pete looked up when she entered and smiled, half rising out of his chair to gesture her into the room. He was a bald man with a youthful face, which made it nearly impossible to place his age. He wasn't handsome, but he wasn't ugly, either. For a second, she wondered what made a healthy, male human choose celibacy. Had girls recoiled from him in high school? Did he have some fetish for wearing black? Or worse, did he have a thing for seeing other men in black?

Or maybe he simply liked the ordered structure of priesthood. The no surprises, no broken hearts, no soul mates life of self-deprivation. Actually, put that way, it sounded like a pretty sensible choice.

"Candace," he said. "How nice to see you. Please, have a seat." He gestured to the cranberry leather chair across from his desk.

Candace sat. Above the chair, a three-foot crucified Jesus looked down at her, almost as if in sympathy. A Madonna on the opposite wall stared back in painted smugness. She, after all, had chosen the right man and had been glorified for it for centuries. Had Mary ever wondered about Joseph? Had she pondered her fate with a different man? One who had more than a donkey to offer?

Candace swallowed. Now that she was here, she wasn't

quite sure how to phrase the question . . . or if asking it was even wise.

Ticktock. Ticktock. The wall clock loudly broadcast her hesitation.

"Candace? Was there some reason you came to see me?"

She rose halfway out of the chair. "This is a crazy idea. I'll come back another time."

"You look as if something is troubling you, my child. Why don't you tell me about it?" He pushed a silver-plated bowl of Hershey kisses her way.

Well, now that he'd added chocolate into the mix, refusing to stay would be rude. Not to mention the mutiny her taste buds would launch if she left without gobbling a few pieces.

She plopped back into the seat, picked a kiss out of the bowl, removed the foil wrapper and popped it into her mouth. The sweet chocolate melted against her tongue with the grace of a ballet. She swallowed. "I think the church should nominate Milton Hershey for sainthood."

Father Pete gave her a beatific smile, but didn't answer. Clearly, he didn't think chocolatiers ranked as high as St. Patrick and St. Francis.

Ticktock. Ticktock. Candace grabbed a second kiss for fortification. "This is going to sound crazy."

"Nothing sounds crazy when you're in the house of the Lord, Candace."

She ate the second candy and grabbed up a third. "Well, my grandmother, you know how she is . . ."

Father Pete nodded and gave his noncommittal smile again.

"Well, she has this insane idea that I should marry my soul mate. Somehow, she's got it in her head that Barry isn't it." A small, slightly hysterical laugh escaped her. She ate the third kiss quickly to silence herself.

"Do you think Barry is your soul mate?"

Ah, the twenty-million dollar question. "Well, yeah, I guess. I mean, we like the same movies, the same foods. We even own the same car, a gray Honda Civic. What are the chances of meeting a guy who drives the same car as you do?" Candace devoured a fourth Hershey kiss. She reached forward and scooped up numbers five, six and seven for good measure. "We aced that compatibility test in the pre-cana classes. We had the highest score out of everyone. That's good, right?"

"Candace, those compatibility profiles are not graded. They're meant as a guideline, not a competition."

"But it goes to show Barry and I are meant for each other. Don't you agree?"

Father Pete gave a tiny nod. "Perhaps. Romans twelve says 'Be of the same mind toward one another.' "

Ah ha. Even God backed up her choice.

"But," Father Pete added, putting up a finger. Candace winced. There was a *but?* "First John says 'There is no fear in love.' Are you experiencing fears about marrying Barry?"

Candace toyed with the little Hershey flag. "I'm just wondering if there's such a thing as a perfect person for each of us."

"Sort of a match made in heaven?"

"Well, I wouldn't go that far. I don't really believe God is up there with his own version of the Together dating service." And if He was, He'd screwed up royally by introducing Michael Vogler into the mix.

Father Pete laughed. "No, not quite. But He does steer us in the direction of what's best. You just have to listen to His wisdom." Father Pete pressed his hands together and rested his chin on the tips of his fingers. "As far as I know, the Bible doesn't say anything directly about soul mates, but it does say a lot about trusting in the Lord. He will provide, if you let Him."

"What He's provided me is a big huge mess." She thought of the soup, the night in Michael's bed, the way her hormones kept attacking her and driving her toward him like some self-induced attempt at premarital suicide. How half of her wanted validation for her choice of Barry and the other half wanted—

She wasn't going to think about that half. Not with the Madonna and Christ watching her.

She reached for more kisses. Father Pete leaned forward and with one quick movement, yanked the candy bowl out of her reach. Apparently she'd indulged enough. "Maybe you should read the fourth chapter of Song of Solomon."

Candace paused in unwrapping the silver foil on the kisses she already had in her hand. "What's that?"

"Ah, that's the song of true love." He closed his eyes and began to recite. 'Behold, thou art fair, my love; behold . . .' "

Father Pete continued, but not in the monotone he usually reserved for Mass. Instead, he became Mel Gibson in *Hamlet,* delivering the words with a gusto she'd never seen before. His hands waved, his voice boomed, his chest heaved with passion.

Finally, he finished and opened his eyes. He blinked several times, then cleared his throat. "Well. That's what the Bible says."

"So basically, it doesn't say soul mates exist."

"Well, no, not really. Only that true love is a wonderful thing that should be celebrated and glorified."

"Just what I thought." Barry was her true love. Soul mates weren't even a real thing. She got to her feet. Now she could shop for her wedding dress in peace.

"Wait a minute," Father Pete said. Candace paused. "Think long and hard about the choice you are making. 'Better is a dinner of herbs where love is than a fatted ox and hatred with it.' Proverbs fifteen," he explained. "The wrong choice can put your heart . . . and your soul in jeopardy."

"Gee, nothing like a little pressure."

Father Pete got to his feet, too, and came around the desk, laying a hand on her shoulder. "It will all be fine. Listen to your heart. And if you need to talk again, I'm here."

She thanked Father Pete, resisting the urge to grab the

bowl of chocolate, stuff it under her shirt and run like hell for the door. Instead, she left sedately, feeling as if she had fewer answers than when she walked in there. "Lot of help he was," she muttered.

When she got back in her car, she studied her to-do list. Focus on the plan, she reminded herself. Plans made her feel calm. In control.

Number four reminded her to stop off at Doctor Card's to pick up some heartworm pills for Trifecta. And while she was there, beg for some more donated services for Paws a Minute. The vet's office was two blocks away from the church, so she decided to make a detour for shameless pleading.

A few minutes later, she was walking across the parking lot to Doctor Card's office. A springer spaniel came bounding through the door, leashless and clearly on the lam. Candace stepped to the right and caught the little brown-and-white dog in her arms.

"Sam!" a male voice hollered from inside the vet's.

The dog's ears perked up and he pressed himself to her. Candace closed her eyes and prayed the Sam in her arms was not the Sam she thought it was. And that the voice she'd heard belonged to Hugh Jackman or George Clooney or even Macaulay Culkin. Anyone but—

Michael Vogler came running out of the office, waving a dog biscuit in one hand and a broken leash in the other. "Sam? Come here, boy." He skidded to a stop when he saw Candace holding his dog. "It's you." Surprise pitched his voice up a few levels. "And Sam."

"I caught him trying to make a break for it."

"Thanks." Michael smiled and gestured with the biscuit. "He hates going to the vet. Especially when he's up for a flea dip."

Candace got to her feet, still holding the little dog. She stroked Sam's head and his stumpy tail began wagging like a crazed thumb. "I'm not too fond of those myself."

He laughed and handed the biscuit to Sam. "What are you doing here?"

"Heartworm pills. For your new best friend." She tried to keep her gaze on the dog, but found that his master eclipsed her attention. Today he wore a button-down shirt with stripes that perfectly matched the blue of his eyes. The cuffs were rolled up, exposing lean, defined wrists. Strong hands. Fingers long enough to—

Candace cleared her throat. She'd just left a church, for Pete's sake. Maybe she needed a return visit for a few Hail Marys. Or a bit of cane-induced penance from the nuns who'd taught elementary school. She gave Sam a final pat, then deposited the dog in Michael's arms. "Well. I should get in there and get the . . . ah . . . the . . ."

"Heartworm pills," he reminded her with a grin that said he knew her thoughts hadn't been on four-legged creatures.

"Yeah. Those." She started to walk past him, trying to ignore the tantalizing smell of his cologne. Geez, if Bloomingdale's was selling that scent, it was no wonder they made so much money.

"Do you like Italian?"

"Huh?"

"Want to get some manicotti with me?"

Her stomach began to rumble with the anxious pleading of a four-year-old outside a toy store. Italian food ranked a close second to chocolate in Candace's life. "I really shouldn't —" she began.

"I know this great place down the street. Run by fourth-generation Italians. Food so authentic, you'd think you were on the set of *The Sopranos*."

"Really?" Her stomach started chanting *"Go, go, go."*

"Would I lie to you?" His voice was low and dark, implying more than lunch recommendations.

She shook her head. "I need to go buy a wedding dress. I don't have time for lunch." She didn't add that this morning, she'd vowed never to see him again. Having lunch with Michael wasn't part of the plan.

"Come on, stop living your life by a clock. Do something spontaneous." He tied the broken leash onto Sam's collar and lowered the spaniel to the ground.

"I'm spontaneous."

"Tell me the last thing you did for the hell of it."

"I . . ." she scrambled for an answer. "I bought a pair of shoes I really didn't need."

"Whoo, that's living on the edge." He grinned. "Eating lunch with me isn't dangerous."

"Oh, yeah?"

"Yeah." He stepped closer, so that he was inches from her. His cologne seemed to pull at her senses, like a spiderweb drawing her into a sticky situation. Everything about this man was wrong. He was so clearly a man who thought with everything *but* the left side of his brain. But still, she didn't leave. "If you kissed me, now that would be very, very risky, Candy."

His use of the nickname sent her memory careening back to the car, to the closeness of him then, to the way she'd leaned forward, betraying her own better judgment. Her breath began to come in short gasps. "How so?"

"Because you might enjoy it." He inched closer still.

She knew she would, from experience. And damn her plan to hell, she wanted him to kiss her anyway. Around her, the city buzzed and hummed. But Candace barely heard it. Every molecule in her body was pinging on him like a sonar system run amok. "I think you're right," she admitted.

He reached up a hand and for a second, she thought—no, hoped—he was going to put actions behind his words. Her eyes opened wider and her lips parted, all of their own volition. Certainly not because the anticipation of his lips on hers was racing through her like a hungry greyhound after a rabbit. "Then I won't kiss you."

"You . . . you won't?" Had she heard him right? And why did she feel so disappointed?

"No." He pulled back and a draft of air brushed against her. "Besides, you're engaged to Barney."

"Barry," she corrected. But her fiancé had never seemed so far away as he did right now. So dependable. So predictable. So . . .

Boring.

"Yeah. Him." Michael reached into his pocket, pulled out a biscuit and handed it to Sam. "Let me drop Sam off for his dip and then we can get some manicotti."

"I should go—"

"Are you afraid of me?"

"Certainly not." But she knew she was. And he knew it, too.

"Don't you like Italian?"

"I love it."

"Then what's the problem?"

She gestured at him, then herself. "You're a guy. I'm a woman."

"I noticed that. More than once."

"Having lunch with you—"

"Is not automatically a date," he finished. "It's a meal. Sustenance. People do it every day." He leaned down and mocked whispering in her ear. "I hear some people even do it *three* times a day."

"Some do it more," she squeaked.

"Help me convince Sam that a flea dip is in his best interests and I'll repay you with a lunch you'll never forget."

She *did* need to eat. Shopping on an empty stomach resulted in bad impulse purchases. Like the purple suede skirt hanging in her closet. Oh, and that awful orange faux linen shirt. Both were purchases made on lunch hours when she'd chosen Macy's over McDonald's. Clearly, it made both smart financial and dress-shopping sense to have lunch with him.

Right. That's exactly why she said, "Okay."

As she followed Michael Vogler and Sam into Doctor Card's office, she wondered whether Father Pete would approve of her choice. Then again, the priest was celibate. When was the last time he'd felt passion for anything other than a tuna melt?

Maybe there was an opening at the convent. She could ask the nuns to lock her up, throw away the key, and keep her from masochistically destroying her life, just when it was weeks from being exactly what she'd planned it to be.

Because right now, she had all the self-control of a sugar junkie about to enter Willy Wonka's chocolate factory.

Maria's Better-Than-Sex Cake

1 box devil's food cake mix
1 jar caramel topping (or if you're feeling especially
    sinful, use chocolate topping)
1 8-oz. container of whipped topping
4 candy bars (chopped into small pieces), any kind, as
    long as they're high in calories and chocolate
a few maraschino cherries, for extra sex appeal

Girls, this is one of those recipes that has less muss and fuss than real sex, and satisfies your craving for a man *almost* as well. Bake the cake according to the directions on the package, then let it cool for ten minutes. Blow on it to speed up the process.

Using the end of a wooden spoon, make small holes all over the surface of the cake. Draw erotic dot-to-dot pictures if you want, or just make a handsome smiley face (it's going to be hidden, so it's one of those secrets only you will know). Heat the caramel topping, then pour it into the holes. After it's nice and cool, top the cake with whipped topping, then sprinkle the candy and cherries on top. It tastes better cold, so if you can stand the wait, put it in the fridge for a couple of hours.

This is a dessert best served with friends, so send out the invitations, rent a Keanu Reeves movie, and then dish up the gossip and the chocolate.

CHAPTER 9

The minute Michael opened the door to Casa D'Antonio, he knew he'd made a bad choice. The food was excellent, but the service—

"Mr. Vogler! How nice to see you again, and with *another* lovely lady, too." Johnny, the maitre d', came forward, clasping both his hands around one of Michael's. Short and round, Johnny had a way with a tailored suit that hid his penchant for pasta. As Antonio's son he got away with a lot—and kept his job.

Michael cocked his head toward Candace, hoping Johnny would get the hint.

He did. Too well. "Ooh, I shouldn't have said that, should I?" he whispered. "Ah, no harm done, I'm sure. A little jealousy can turn a lady into a real wildcat." He winked. "And we both know how fun a wildcat is to tame."

The food was so damned good, though, Michael could usually forgive Johnny's loose lips.

Michael squeezed Johnny's hands. Hard. "We'd like *just* a table, please."

"Oh, oh. Yes. I understand you." He squeezed off a wink that the crew of the space shuttle could have seen. "Sorry,

Mr. Vogler. Right this way." He led them toward the rear of the room, waving them into a secluded booth tucked away in the back corner. "Your favorite table for a meal with a special lady, I presume?"

Candace quirked an eyebrow at Michael. "Come here often? And rarely alone?"

Johnny had the presence of mind to blush and back away fast, leaving a couple of leather-bound menus onto the table.

"I'm sorry about him," Michael said after they were seated. "He gets carried away sometimes."

"He seems to know you quite well."

"I, ah, eat here sometimes."

"Really?" Candace trailed a finger down the menu. "So, what do you recommend for wildcats?"

Michael swallowed. "You heard that?"

"Johnny's about as quiet as Gilbert Gottfried in a monastery."

Michael chuckled, then laid his menu on the table and caught her gaze. "For the record, I don't take that many——"

She flipped her menu up, blocking his sentence and his eyes. "For the record, I don't care. I'm engaged to someone else, remember?"

"You've only reminded me five times."

She peeked over the top of the brown leather. "You're the kind of man who needs reminding."

"What, you think I can't behave myself?"

"I doubt it. Very much." She put her menu down on the table again and crossed her arms over it. "I think you're interested in me for one reason only, Casanova."

"And what would that be?"

She flashed her diamond at him. "Because you can't have me."

"Who says I can't?"

"This does." She tapped the ring. "It's a promise. To another man. A man I love. A man I'm promising to love, cherish and honor forever."

A tremor ran through her, as if the words terrified her. He doubted even she was aware she'd just let out a reaction worthy of the Richter scale. But it was enough to open the door and let him in.

"Before you walk off into a romance novel with *Barry*"—he drew the name out into a yawn—"why not live a little? Go parachuting. Learn to fly a plane. Climb a mountain." He leaned forward, lowering his voice. "Share a plate of manicotti with a man who tempts you."

"I don't need to. I'm not that kind of person."

"Oh, yeah? Then why were you crying into your margaritas about how boring your life was just three days ago?"

"That was a momentary glitch. Nothing more."

"Okay. Fine." He flipped up his menu again.

"That's it?"

"Yep. I believe you." He didn't, but he didn't tell her that. He'd *prove* he was right instead. That would be much more fun. And if there was anything Michael loved, it was a challenge that seemed insurmountable.

"Well . . . good." Her menu wavered on its way back up in front of her face.

For a second there, she'd almost turned the tables on him, but now he'd regained control of the situation. If he could just keep a leash on Johnny, this meal would work out perfectly.

A waiter appeared at their table. He took their order and left a moment later, retreating into the darkness like a ghost.

Soft instrumental music started streaming through the speakers. *Love* songs. Candace quirked another brow at him and rolled her eyes.

Damn Johnny. The man should have been the host at a brothel instead of at a restaurant. Just when Michael thought he had the upper hand, someone else screwed with his plans.

"Has Ricardo come to take your order?" Johnny came over to their table, as if the mere thought of him made him materialize, like a cough in a hypochondriac.

"Yes, thank you," Candace said.

"Good." Johnny clapped his hands together and took a step back.

Michael sighed, then bit back his relief when Johnny moved forward again. "I have to tell you, miss, that Mr. Vogler is *such* a wonderful man. Quite the catch, you know."

"Johnny, she doesn't need—"

"He owns his own business, has a dog he loves, doesn't live with his mother"—Johnny ticked the reasons off on his fingers—"is always nice to the ladies, and never fails to leave a generous tip."

The waiter slipped in with their wine order, making himself nearly invisible as he poured two glasses then retreated again, as if he didn't want to get stuck in the middle.

Candace shook her head. "I'm sure Michael's great," she told the maitre d'. "But I'm not dating him. This is just a . . . a . . . friendly lunch."

Johnny looked at Michael. Then at Candace. He raised one eyebrow, then the other. "Uh-huh."

"She's engaged to someone else," Michael explained.

Johnny's jaw dropped open. "And you bring her here? To your little dinner love nest? How could you?" The maitre d' tsk-tsked, his hands waving in wild indignation. He shook his head, his face dour. "And I thought you were such a good man."

"Johnny, I—"

"I take it back," he said to Candace, reaching down to touch her arm. "He's not such a good catch. If you ever want a man, you come see Johnny. I have a cousin who will treat you right. He owns his own hubcap store. He's a man with morals." Then he was gone, huffing toward the front desk.

Surely strangling Johnny would be considered self-defense, Michael thought.

Candace sat back against the booth and crossed her arms over her chest. A smug smile teased at her lips. The ball had just been spiked into her half of the court. "Gee, it's nice to have friends who care so much, isn't it?"

"Johnny is not a friend," he muttered.

Her smile became a full-fledged grin.

"Where's our food?" Michael looked around the restaurant but no waiter appeared to bail him out of a very sticky situation.

"It will come when it's ready." Her voice held a high, delighted-to-have-caught-him pitch to it. "So, tell me. How many women *have* you brought here? Ten? Twenty? A thousand?"

"It's not like that at all."

"Oh, really?"

"I date . . . regularly, but I'm not a gigolo or anything."

She waved a hand at him. "Give me a ballpark. Just throw out a number."

He'd never been at a loss of words before with a woman. Clearly, his first impressions of Candace hadn't been entirely accurate. She'd not just put him—but also kept him—on his toes. "Numbers aren't important."

"Tell that to the Census Bureau."

He grinned. "Point taken. Either way, my past is not an issue because you aren't dating me, right? You're just here for a—what'd you call it?—a friendly lunch. And friends don't keep tallies on each other's dating history."

"True." She picked up her wineglass and took a sip. "Then I don't care. Not one bit."

"Good." He picked up his glass and gulped down the Chianti. The full-bodied wine settled in his stomach with a hefty flavoring of disappointment.

When was the last time he'd been so bothered by a woman's refusal to engage with him in the dating dance? She was promised to someone else, he reminded himself.

Again.

But something . . . something had intrigued him about Candace Woodrow. And he had no intentions of letting her ride off into the sunset on the back of a mule with Bob Boring. Not without a teeny taste of what life could be like.

"Your order, ma'am," the waiter said, laying a plate teeming with stuffed manicotti before Candace. He turned and laid a plate of spinach ravioli before Michael, asked if they needed anything else, then disappeared. Clearly, he had yet to learn the Casa D'Antonio rule about interjecting personal opinions before the tip.

"This looks delicious," Candace said. "I probably shouldn't have all these calories just before I go shopping for a dress, but—"

"But you only live once. Indulge."

She inhaled the fragrance of the manicotti, her fork hovering over the plate. "Okay. You talked me into it."

Watching Candace eat was almost as erotic as watching her sleep. It was clear she loved food, especially Italian food, by the way she caressed it with her mouth before swallowing. It was all he could do to keep himself from lunging across the table and taking her right there, among the manicotti and raviolis.

Most of the other women he knew ate like wary birds, picking here and there at the meal, using their fork like a divining rod to find the least fattening ingredients. They rarely finished a plate of anything, even salad.

He wondered if *Cosmo* had done some survey that said men found an appetite unsexy.

If so, they were sure as hell wrong.

He watched her cut a piece off a bulging manicotti, swirl it in the red sauce, then put it in her mouth, smiling almost reverently when the cheese and pasta hit her palate. A tiny glob of ricotta clung to the corner of her mouth and before he could stop himself, Michael had leaned forward and wiped it off with his finger.

Her eyes widened. "What are you doing?"

He placed his finger against her lips. "You, ah, had a little cheese right there."

Instinctively, her tongue flicked out and caught the dab. He bit back a groan.

"Is it gone?"

"Yeah." But he didn't move his hand. She took a breath and he felt his lungs expand to match hers. In. Out. As if they were breathing in tandem. The restaurant dropped away, the booth became a private island. The tension between them pulsed with unmet desire. If she tasted his finger again, he swore he'd have a bigger problem than Johnny to deal with in the tight confines of the booth. "You have amazing eyes."

Her cheeks flushed. "Rather ordinary, I think."

"Don't." He shook his head. "Don't do that."

"What?"

"Deflect the compliment. I'm telling you that you have amazing eyes. The kind that can take a man in and make him forget everything." He drew his thumb along her jaw.

"My . . . my . . . my manicotti's getting cold." She dipped her head and attacked her plate in earnest.

Michael's hand dropped away. The tension between them fizzled like a balloon that had suddenly sprung a leak. He cursed a few times under his breath and felt a whole lot better.

The meal ended too quickly and had Michael wishing he'd suggested something slower, like a fondue bar. He could just imagine her dipping all those little bits of fruit into the chocolate. . . .

"You're staring at me," Candace said.

"I was thinking how fun it would be to do fondue with you."

"Do fondue? As in on the food . . . or on me?"

"Whichever you prefer."

She swallowed. "I really like bananas in mine. Not body parts."

"Have you tried body parts?"

"Uh, no. Not unless you count licking my fingers after I frost a cake."

"Then someday I'll have to show you what you're missing."

A long moment of silence ticked between them as she digested his words. Then she took in a quick breath and glanced at her watch. The escape route.

"Oh gee, look at the time," she said. "I need to shop for a dress. Barry and I are having dinner tonight with his mother."

"Why don't I come with you?"

"Help me shop for my wedding dress? Are you crazy?"

"Would you rather be asking the opinion of the little old lady who runs the shop and sees profit margins in her eyes? Or a man who knows what looks good on a woman?"

"You have a point," she allowed.

"If you want your groom to keel over at the sight of you, then let me go with you."

She put her hands on her hips. "And you don't have an ulterior motive for this, right?"

"No, not at all."

"Liar."

He shrugged. "Polygraph me."

"I can tell you're lying."

"How's that?"

"Your face. You get these dimples beside your smile when you lie. Like it's a joke only you know."

Damned if she wasn't right. Quickly, he thought of another lie to cover his first lie. "You're right. I do have an ulterior motive."

"I knew it."

"I have a client—a big-name client—that I'm trying to land. She's a wedding dress designer and it would really help me if I could get inside the mind of a bride, see what they think about during the selection process. I want to *be* the bride when I go into my meeting with the designer next week."

"Be the bride? Are you shopping for yourself, too?"

"I don't think I'll go that far. It'll be more fun to study you."

Candace propped her chin in her hands and considered him. "I don't think you're being completely honest, but I don't know you well enough to tell how much of a liar you really are." She paused, chewing on her bottom lip. He watched her teeth nip at the dark pink skin and wondered what it would feel like to have her lips under his own teeth. "Okay," she said finally. "I'm going to drag you to every dress shop in town. You're going to regret signing on for this."

"Oh, I doubt that. Very, very much."

Candace's Chocolate-Orange Bad-Decisions-Are-Tart Cake

Crust:

1 ¾ cups crushed chocolate cookie crumbs
½ cup finely chopped peanuts
⅓ cup sugar
7 tablespoons butter, melted

Cake:

12 ounces semisweet chocolate chips
1 cup heavy cream
3 tablespoons Grand Marnier
⅔ cup orange marmalade

Liken the cookie crumbs to the crumble you've made of your well-planned-out life. Then mix them well with the butter, peanuts and sugar and press them into a nine-inch tart pan with a removable bottom. Bake the crust for fifteen minutes at 350 degrees and try not to regret anything you've done in the last few days. Bad for the digestion and all that.

To keep your mind off things, heat the chocolate chips and cream in a saucepan on low heat. Imagine your problems dissolving into the melting chocolate. Stir until the whole mixture becomes smooth as a blank calendar. Add the Grand Marnier. Life's about to get much better. Let it cool for twenty minutes. Caution: drinking the leftover Grand Marnier can be a dangerous choice right now.

Spread the marmalade over the crust. Pour on the chocolate mixture. Taste it with your finger. Yummy enough? Good.

Let it refrigerate overnight. Can't stand to wait that long? Try freezing it for half an hour to get it icy cold fast. Then, when it's firmer than your resolve, remove the tart pan and eat as much as it takes to make you forget you ever made a bad decision in your life.

Better yet, bake two cakes. One for yesterday's choices and one for tomorrow's.

CHAPTER 10

They had elected to take one car—his car—and Candace already regretted the decision. Regardless of whether it saved time, gas or money, the space was altogether too enticing to be comfortable. The Bose stereo, the leather seats, the soft purr of the engine—it was like being inside of *him*.

She shook her head and concentrated on the road. "You're going the wrong way. Denny's Discount Bridal is south, not north. You need to take a left—"

"We're not going there."

"But I told you, it has the best bargains. *And* they're having a samples sale. I'm running out of time. I can't be choosy."

"If you're going to hunt for a wedding dress, then do it right." He banged a right, traveled a few blocks, then took a left. A few blocks later they pulled up in front of a series of converted brownstones fashioned into boutiques. Each had been restored with precision, down to the last brick. Wrought-iron railings lined the granite staircases, planters centered by hanging globe lanterns dotted the sidewalks. Reverie Bridal Shop, located between a day spa and a men's clothing store, displayed its wares in the front window.

It screamed expensive. Elegant. Out of Candace's league.

"Oh, no. I'm not going in there. I can't even afford to walk in the door."

Michael shut off the engine. "A wedding's nothing more than a fantasy, right?"

"I guess."

"Then let yourself live the fantasy. Try on a few gowns." He grinned. "It's like test-driving the Mercedes before you buy the Honda."

Candace glanced at the pristine, elaborate gown that commanded the view in the window. It was clearly designer. And clearly out of her price range. Barry would have a coronary if she spent that kind of money on a dress, especially when there were so many other more sensible options for her dollars. It was, after all, just a dress, as he'd said a hundred times before.

"But what if I don't want the Honda after I drive the Benz?"

"Carpe diem. Live for today and worry about tomorrow later." He got out of his side of the car and came around to open her door.

She shook her head. If she walked in that door, she'd find a dress she loved and before she knew it, she'd be hanging out in alleys and smoky bars, looking for a loan shark. Her Visa couldn't handle the weight of the longing that was already churning in her gut, just from a glimpse in that window. "I still think I should go to Denny's store. I really—"

"I really think you should shut up now. And I mean that in the nicest way." He put out his hand, took hers and tugged her out of the car. He didn't let go all the way up the granite steps and into the shop.

The air-conditioned interior provided welcome relief from the June sun. Muted classical music drifted from the sound system. The carpets were thick, dark cranberry, the walls covered with cream silk. A huge chandelier lit the shop instead of fluorescent bulbs.

Denny's Discount this was not.

"Good afternoon. I'm Francesca." A tall, thin woman approached them, her hand extended in a drooping society handshake. Her face had that tight, pinched look that came from too much BOTOX. Her tailored emerald suit was decorated with a single gold brooch—of wedding bells. "Welcome to Reverie Bridal." She gave them a smile that barely moved. "Where every bride can look like a dream."

"We're here to look at bridal gowns," Michael said.

The woman clasped her hands together. "Delightful. And when's the happy event?"

"In two weeks." Candace smiled to soften the blow.

To her credit, Francesca only blanched two shades. "We'll do our best to make the two of you happy. Even if the time frame is . . . short."

"Oh, I'm not marrying—"

Michael gave her hand a squeeze, cutting off her sentence. "We will be." He smiled at her. "Very happy."

"Delightful. Well, shall we get started then?" Francesca turned and gave them a petite wave, signaling them to follow her into an adjoining room.

"Why did you say that?" Candace whispered to Michael as they trailed behind Francesca's measured stride.

"Do you want to explain this unusual arrangement?" He paused a beat. When she didn't answer, he went on. "Besides, I'm here on a sort of research mission, remember? I don't think Francesca would appreciate that."

Candace frowned. "She doesn't even look European."

He grinned. "But she looks *delightful.*"

Candace reached over and gave him a jab in the arm with her free hand. If she'd been smart, she'd have let go of his other hand, but she hadn't even tried to pull away. Like she was enjoying the contact.

Am not.

Are, too.

Holding hands was just part of the act, put on for shopping purposes.

Yeah, right.

It sounded a lot like the cow manure Grandma used to get the geraniums to bloom, too.

Francesca paused in the center of a fitting room where gold molding bordered the silk-covered walls and a second, even more elaborate chandelier dominated the ceiling. A circular dais stood in front of a massive 270-degree mirror, also trimmed in gold.

Candace didn't need to turn on *E!* to get a view of Elizabeth Taylor's dressing room. She'd just stepped into it.

"What style of gown were you seeking?" Francesca asked.

"Cheap" wouldn't be the kind of answer to give in a place like this. "Tasteful."

"Elegant," Michael supplied. "Yet with a hint of allure."

"Careful, your day job is showing," she said to him. "You're making my dress into a commercial."

"I know the exact gown." Francesca turned, and with the homing instincts of a heat-seeking missile, zeroed in on one dress among the sea of white that was hanging against the wall. She grasped the pink satin hanger. "Close your eyes."

Candace glanced at Michael. He shrugged and grinned. Candace let out a sigh, but did as she was told.

There was a soft drum roll of fabric. "You may open them now."

Cinderella would have been envious. Hell, she might have sued the fairy godmother for substandard services if she'd seen this dress.

The dress had a princess silhouette with a basque waistline. Thin, beaded spaghetti straps connected the bodice in a swirling pattern of diamond-like beads that curved across the front, then swooped down the center of the bodice like a tree of tiny gems. The skirt was made of the same pristine off-white silk shantung, dropping down to the floor with sleek precision, then swirling outward with a gentle swoosh. The beading picked up again across the hemline, curving around the base of the gown and trailing back down to the train.

"It's . . . oh, God . . . it's beautiful," she managed.

"Would you like to try it on?" Francesca held it closer, within touching distance.

Candace shook her head. "If I do, I'm going to want it."

"That's the point," Michael whispered in her ear.

"No, no it's not." Candace put up her hands as if she could ward off the want churning in her stomach. "I could never afford something like this. If I put it on, I'm going to love it. This is the Mercedes. I can't get a Honda after this."

Francesca took a step back, lips pursed, brows raised. Clearly lunatics didn't come into Reverie Bridal looking for dreams. She glanced at Michael for help.

"Try it on," he said. "It won't bite."

"But . . ."

He took the gown out of Francesca's hands and pushed it into Candace's arms. The fabric whispered against her arms. *Buy me. Buy me.* "But nothing. Who knows? You might hate it."

"And I might hate *you* for making me fall in love."

The air between them stilled. A heartbeat passed, then another, before Candace realized what she had said and why it seemed to weigh so much. "Uh, with the dress, I mean."

"Uh-huh." He gave her a gentle shove toward the fitting room, his hand against the small of her back. Just before she ducked into the room, he leaned down, breath warm against her neck. Teasing. Tempting. *Take me. Take me.* "Let me see how you'd look if you were my bride instead of his."

She shut the door with a shaky hand, never looking back. Because if she did, she knew she'd be searching his eyes for clues as to whether he was merely playing the game . . . or being sincere.

Candace hung the dress on a hook and hesitated. What would it be like to be marrying Michael instead of Barry? To be wearing this dress for him—and no one else?

Yeah, and what would it be like to throw herself off a cliff without a parachute into shark-infested waters?

Insane, that's what.

She tore off her T-shirt, determined not to think about Michael anymore.

There was a double knock at the door. "Dear, do you need some help?" Francesca called.

"Uh, no. I'm okay."

"The dresses can be quite difficult to maneuver on your own. If you need some assistance, I'm right here."

After all the dress shopping she'd done with Maria and Rebecca, Candace knew her way in and out of a wedding gown. A handy skill for her wedding night, too.

She slipped off her capris, unzipped the back of the elaborate dress, puddled it at her feet, then stepped into the white pool and pulled it up. She turned toward the door to ensure there was no lurking Francesca, then slipped off her bra and slid the bodice up, putting her arms through the delicate straps. With minor contorting, she managed to zip the back.

"Dear, your groom is anxiously awaiting." Francesca's voice sang through the door.

"He's not—" Candace stopped. Michael was right; the explanation was more complicated than a Hollywood divorce agreement.

"What do you think, dear?"

Candace pivoted toward the wall mirror, expecting to look like an exploded white mushroom, as so many other dresses had made her appear. "I . . ."

This dress didn't look like anything she'd tried on before. Not even the dress she'd originally chosen, lost in the shop fire. It fell perfectly against her hips, the slight scallop of the bodice lifted, giving her breasts a swell that was both provocative and sweet.

With one hand, she twisted her honey-blond hair on top of her head in a crunch of curls. *This* was how she could look. Like a princess.

"I look like a freaking fairy tale," Candace whispered. "I . . . I love it. I want to buy it."

She lowered her arm and it brushed against the price tag, reflecting the number in the mirror. A single digit followed by a lot of zeroes. More zeroes than had attended her senior prom.

Candace stumbled back two steps. Prince Charming would have needed a second mortgage on the castle to afford this dress. Probably would have had to auction off the white horse, too.

Candace stuck a hand against the door for stability and sucked in a breath, then another.

"Let me help you with that zipper," Francesca said, jerking open the door and spilling Candace into the hallway. "Oh, dear, you are a vision! Absolutely delightful!" She clasped her hands together and took a step back, assessing. She reached forward, adjusted here and there. "Perfect. Now, when you walk out there, do it slow, with drama. You're the bride, darling. Let it show."

"I can't." This was getting ridiculous. She wasn't here for the Academy Awards. Just a dress. At this point, she'd settle for a sheet with lace edging. And in this store, that was probably all she could afford. "I don't think I can go out there like that. This dress—"

"You're right! You don't have shoes. You can't walk properly without shoes." Francesca turned to a shelf outside the fitting room. "I'd say a seven?" she withdrew a box, removed the lid and unveiled a pair of strappy white sandals studded with rhinestones at each juncture.

"Oh, no. You don't have to—. Oh. *Oh!*"

Now those were shoes.

She let out a half-squeak of protest when Francesca pushed her into a Louis XV-style chair and slid the sandals onto

Candace's pedicured feet. After the straps were fastened, the saleswoman held her foot up for display.

"Delightful, aren't they?"

"Delightful," Candace agreed. They probably cost as much as the national debt, she thought. Now she'd gone and fallen in love with a Mercedes *and* a Beemer. Big mistake. Huge, terrifying, stupid mistake. She pressed a hand to her chest. "Oh God, I can't breathe."

Francesca patted her hand. "It's jitters, dear. Now go on out there and dazzle your groom. He's insisting on seeing you, even though I told him it's bad luck. Says he doesn't have to worry about that with you." She smiled. "He's a keeper, all right. I'm sure once you see the joy in his eyes, everything will be right again."

"I shouldn't . . ." Breathe. "I . . ." Breathe, breathe. "I . . ."

"Of course you can." Francesca took advantage of her weakened state, helped her to her feet and guided her out of the fitting area. She slid a veil into Candace's hair, tugging out a few curly strands, then turned her toward Michael. "Remember, be the bride," she whispered, then stepped away, leaving Candace to walk the last few feet alone.

Michael had his cell phone to his ear and was talking when he saw Candace. Their gazes met and he paused in midsentence. His jaw dropped. He clicked the phone shut without a good-bye.

She took a step forward and the skirt swooshed around her legs in a white cloud. Another step, and a second cloud of fabric swirled into the first. The lights above twinkled in the rhinestones, like stars in a midnight sky.

Michael's gaze swept over her like a slow, tender touch. He started at the top, drifting past her hair, along her bare shoulders, trailing along the scoop of the bodice, down the leafy rhinestone pattern.

Candace breathed in and her breasts heaved upward, along with Michael's eyes. An odd rush of power surged through her. She slowed her pace a tiny bit more and stepped with deliberate movement. Another breath and Michael's pupils dilated.

This control over a man was heady stuff. She inhaled and like a puppet on a string, he responded with another glance at her breasts.

And she'd thought the shoes had been exciting.

"Don't forget these!" Francesca stuttered forward on her high heels to thrust a bouquet of silk flowers into Candace's hands. "There. That's exactly what you need to be a complete bride."

"No, it's not." Michael moved forward, took the bouquet from her and tossed it back to Francesca, whose jaw dropped all the way to the carpet. She sputtered something unintelligible that was probably the opposite of "delightful."

"Every bride needs flowers," Candace said.

The shop phone rang and Francesca disappeared out front to answer it.

"Not you." His sapphire eyes met hers and once again, her breath began to come in hitches, but this time for a whole other reason than the price of the dress. "You're perfect already."

"It's the dress. It costs—"

"It doesn't matter what it costs. It's perfect for you. Buy it."

She laughed. "Are you nuts? I don't make this much in a *month.* I can't waste this kind of money on my dress. I've got a budget all set in my planner." She stepped to the side, to get the ubiquitous organizer out of her purse and prove the numbers to him, but he held her hands.

"Indulge yourself."

"The way you say that, it sounds sinful."

He grinned. "Sometimes it is." He ran the back of one finger along the slim strap, then down the bare skin of her arm. Shivers of delight tingled along her skin, begging for more. "You are exquisite. Any man who saw you in this would marry you on the spot."

"Even you?" Where did that come from?

"I'm a confirmed bachelor," he said, his finger still traveling along her arm, as if it had miles to go before he could sleep, "but if I wasn't . . ."

The implications in his voice were enough to make her wonder what kind of game she was playing this afternoon between the lunch and the shopping. It sure as hell wasn't Parcheesi.

"It may be a beautiful dress, but it's too expensive." Her grin wobbled on her face. "I'm a girl from Dorchester. I'm kitsch, not couture."

"Have you looked in the mirror? Have you really *seen* yourself in that dress?"

"Listen, it doesn't matter what I wear for the wedding. Barry doesn't care. He probably won't even notice the dress. He's not that kind of guy."

"He *should* notice your dress. He should notice everything about you." Michael lowered his face to hers. "Because I sure as hell do. If you came down the aisle in that dress, and *I* was standing at the other end, I'd notice and you'd *know* I had noticed."

She drew in a breath and saw his gaze dip to her neckline, then back to her face again. "Well, Mr. Confirmed Bachelor, that isn't going to happen. And neither is this dress. It's a fantasy. And I don't have time for those."

She turned on her heel and headed back to the fitting room before she could fall any farther in love with the dress. Or the shoes.

Or anything else in Reverie Bridal Shop.

Rebecca's Get-Yourself-out-of-a-Jam Cookies

4 ounces bittersweet chocolate
3 cups flour
½ teaspoon baking soda
½ teaspoon salt
⅔ cup butter, softened
¾ cup sugar
2 eggs
2 teaspoons vanilla
raspberry jam to taste

Whatever you've done, the best way to get out of it is to bake cookies. They make good peace offerings, as well as help you forget bad choices. Start by melting the chocolate. Don't let the kids anywhere near it. This is *your* chocolate.

Combine the flour, baking soda and salt. In another bowl (don't worry, that's what dishwashers are for), beat the butter and sugar until it's as fluffy as a clear conscience. Add the eggs, one at a time, then the lovely vanilla and chocolate. Turn on the ceiling fan or burn a pine candle to mask the scent of goodies. Beat until blended.

Divide dough, wrap in plastic wrap and refrigerate for two hours. Yeah, that's the hard part. The waiting. If need be, get to the mall and do some shoe shopping therapy in the meantime.

When the dough is firm and cold, roll it out to a quarter-inch thickness on a lightly floured surface and cut into dainty two-inch circles. Take half the circles and cut center circles out (like donuts, only better, since you don't have to fry them). Bake the cookies for nine or ten minutes at 350 degrees. Wave the pine scent around the house to throw uninvited cookie gobblers off the scent.

When the cookies are cool, assemble them by putting one whole cookie circle on the bottom, spreading the top with jam, then topping with a cut-out cookie. Voila! Cookie sandwiches. Sounds healthy enough for lunch.

CHAPTER 11

The spaghetti slithered across the plate, zipped up into the air and slurped down Bernadine's throat like a snake on a string. "This is great food," she said. "These Boston people really know how to cook Eye-talian. Too bad the lighting in here is so bad I can barely see what I'm eating."

"Mother, it's mood lighting. Adds a little romance to our dinner." Barry reached across the table at Fazo's Fast Italian Food and grasped Candace's hand. "Don't you agree?"

"Uh, what'd you say?"

"I said, the lighting is perfect for a little romance before the wedding."

"Oh yes, it is." Dinner out with Bernadine was about as romantic as playing with Play-Doh in the nude. Candace stirred at her rigatoni and meat sauce with her fork.

"What's the matter? Didn't you find a dress today?"

She shook her head. "Not exactly."

"Good," Barry said.

"Good?"

He was grinning. "Because Mother and I have a surprise for you."

She swallowed the bite in her mouth. It settled in her stomach like a ball of lead. "You do?"

"We took the liberty of doing a little shopping today and—" he looked at his mother, then back at Candace, his smile broad—"we bought you a dress."

"Barry, you didn't. Tell me you didn't."

"I know, I know. I'm already paying for half the wedding, but this gown was wonderful and Mother thought it would fit you perfectly, so we had to buy it. When I saw it"—he gripped her hand—"I knew it was you."

"Where . . ." Candace swallowed. "Where is it?"

"Hanging up in my apartment. We were going to surprise you after dinner. But you seemed so glum; I couldn't keep it to myself."

He was more excited than Percy with a new sweater. Candace glanced at Bernadine, who gave her a satisfied Cheshire cat smile.

This was all about the back alley. Bernadine had made her first preemptive strike.

She gave Candace a second beam of victory, then very smartly avoided her future daughter-in-law's horrified face. She slurped up more spaghetti, the pasta strands slapping at her housedress on their way up to her mouth, leaving little red pathways amid the tropical floral print.

Candace picked up her drink and gulped down some diet soda. "Is it . . ." She glanced again at Bernadine's florid dress. "White?"

"Of course it is." Barry raised a brow and gestured behind his hand toward his mother. "You're a virgin, so you should wear white."

The soda sputtered out of Candace's mouth. Bernadine stopped chewing and looked over at her. Barry kneed Candace under the table.

"You haven't been doing the hokey-pokey with anyone, have you?" Bernadine asked.

"The hokey-pokey?" Candace managed. "Uh, not exactly."

Although, she had done a damned good electric slide in Michael's living room. And Barry himself had been known to like dancing with Candace, but apparently his mother was under a different impression.

"Good." Another strand snaked its way up her dress and into her mouth. "My Barry deserves a pure woman."

"And that's my Candace," Barry said, clasping her hand with his.

"I need some air." Candace shoved back her chair and got to her feet, yanking her hand out of his and dashing for the door of the restaurant. Once she reached the cool night air, she sucked in oxygen like a thirsty horse at a trough.

Barry caught up to her a moment later. "Are you okay?"

"A *virgin,* Barry? Why on earth would you say that?"

He shrugged. "My mother doesn't like loose women."

"I'm not loose! I can count on one hand the number of men I've been to bed with."

His face pinched up like a rotten tomato. "I know all about your past. The minute the gold band goes on your finger, all that will be erased."

"All what? It's not like I was working the streets in the combat zone. Barry, you knew this when you met me." Candace paced the sidewalk, expending some of her anger before she punched it into Barry. She paused in front of him, hands on her hips. This had never been an issue between them before. He'd never said a word about her wanting to put on this show of virginal innocence for his mother. In fact, he'd been seeking the exact opposite when he'd met her. "I thought you liked being with a woman with a little more experience than you."

His lips tightened into a thin line and for the first time, Candace worried about spending her life with a man who did *that* with his face. "Well, now that we've been together for two years, I'd say we're about even in that department, aren't we? I know how to make you happy in bed."

Why did thoughts of Michael Vogler pop up at the most

inappropriate times like R-rated previews before a kiddie movie? Her evil, traitorous mind replayed snippets of the kiss in his apartment, as if taunting her with the thought that another man hadn't just made her happy—he'd practically made her scream with just one kiss.

But those kinds of kisses came at a high price. With a man who was fickle and an admitted playboy. If she allowed herself to get swept up in passion, she'd end up like her mother, married more times than Larry King.

She'd been down that path once before. No need for a return trip.

"Aren't you satisfied, Candace?" Barry asked.

"Of course I am." The answer zipped from her mouth too quickly, like a piece of gum she'd spat out. Was she satisfied? As satisfied as she'd been last week? Last month? Last year?

"Listen, I don't want to fight with you," Barry said. "I'm sorry I told my mother you were a virgin. I don't know what I was thinking. Just trying to head off an argument. I was wrong. I apologize." He took her hands and drew her to him. *"I* know you're perfect for me. I can't help it if I want everyone else to think so, too."

She looked up into Barry's steady brown eyes. They didn't tease her or make her question anything at all. They were there, day in and day out, as reliable as sun rises. "You're right, Barry," she said. "We're made for each other."

"And after the wedding, my mother will be going back to Maine. It'll be just you and me again. Everything will go back to normal."

Candace laid her head against his chest and let out a sigh. "I can't wait."

Of everything she'd said in the last few days to Barry, those words were the closest to the truth.

*   *   *

"You better like this dress," Bernadine said. "Shopping for it had my corns popping like a bag of Orville Redenbacher. Do you want to see them?" She thrust her foot into the front seat of Barry's Honda Civic. The smell of sweaty leather overpowered the tiny pine tree dangling bravely from Barry's rearview mirror.

"Uh, no, that's okay." Candace forced herself not to gag until Bernadine had withdrawn her Naturalizer. "I'm sure I'll love the gown."

"Well, if you don't, I'm not returning it. Not without a soak in some Epsom salts."

Three weeks until she leaves. Three long weeks.

Barry pulled up in front of his apartment building, parked the car, set the emergency brake, installed his Club, got out, checked that his LoJack was on, then finally opened the doors for Candace and his mother. After they exited the car, he thumbed the lock on the remote, listened for the double beep, then did it again.

"Barry, the car is locked," Candace said. "It's more secure than Fort Knox."

"You can't be too careful in a city like this," Bernadine said. "The Boston Strangler came from Boston, you know."

"That was decades—"

"And Son of Sam. And the Zodiac Killer."

"Neither one of them came from Boston," Candace said.

"Not to mention the mafia has big ties to this area," Bernadine barreled on, ignoring the serial killer location argument. "My boy is just being smart, like I taught him." She patted Barry's shoulders.

He put a hand over hers. "Exactly."

Candace took a long, hard look at the two of them. Hadn't Della said a hundred times, "Marry the man and you marry his mother, too"? Could she really stand to be tied to Bernadine for the next fifty or so years?

Bernadine lived in Maine, two states away. Surely that was enough distance.

"Lord, I need a Tums," Bernadine said, letting out a belch. "That Eye-talian food tore my stomach to shreds. Barry, you better step on it. I think I'm going to need your powder room."

Maybe two states away wasn't enough. Especially not since they'd raised the speed limit on the trans-state highway system.

To help her think about *anything* but what was going on inside Bernadine's intestines, Candace reached into her shoulder bag, pulled out her planner and flipped the purple tabs to the current day. "Barry, we have a few wedding details to talk about tonight. I have to finalize some numbers with you."

"Speaking of which, I met with our photographer," Barry said, leading the way up the two flights of stairs to his apartment. "She has great ideas for making the most out of the parking lot at the hall for some outdoor shots. You're really going to like working with her. She thinks just like we do."

"Parking lot photos? I thought we were thinking of stopping off at a lake or a park."

"No time for that. Marcy knows. She's very efficient, has everything planned down to the last minute. Carries the nicest organizer. Leather bound. And her handwriting—very precise. You have to admire someone with nice handwriting." Barry nodded. "Say, did you make the calls I asked you to make?" He paused in unlocking the first lock on his door. "I got all mine done this afternoon. Mother helped me."

"Calls?" Then she remembered. The invitations. The cheap labels. "Oh, God, no, I completely forgot."

Barry inserted the key into the second lock, then turned to look at her. "That is completely unlike you. You're normally so together. So organized." He paused and turned to her, laying a palm against her cheek. For a moment, his caring gaze connected with hers and reminded her of why

Barry was the one she'd chosen. "You're too stressed, honey. Don't worry so much. It'll all come together."

"You're right." But images of another man's blue eyes popped into her mind like stubborn bumblebees trying to squeeze their way into a closed rose.

Barry turned back to the door, undid a third lock, then a fourth. "Well, this will make you feel better." He flung open the door and flicked on the light switch. "Ta da!"

"Oh, it's . . . it's . . ." Candace struggled to find a word. Any word. Something that wouldn't alienate her soon-to-be husband and mother-in-law in three syllables or less. "Delightful."

"I knew you'd like it," Bernadine crowed. "When I saw it, I thought of you."

Which said a lot about Bernadine's opinion of her. The dress bloomed off the hanger in a shower of bright white tulle, trimmed with thick white lines that curlicued around the bell-shaped base. The V-necked bodice opened in a gush of ruffles, like a Dolly Parton costume gone horribly awry.

Candace took a few steps closer. "Is that *suede* on the skirt?"

"Genu-wine imitation," Bernadine said. "Since my Barry is allergic to leather."

"Gee, I didn't know they made that kind of thing in white."

"The veil is trimmed to match. Wait till you see it."

"Oh, wow, there's a veil, too?" She tried to work up some measure of enthusiasm into her voice.

"Try it on, honey. See how it fits."

Candace hovered in the doorway, her planner still in her hands. The etiquette section in the back definitely didn't have any advice for getting out of this situation with tact. "It's, ah, bad luck to see me in my dress before the wedding."

"Oh, I know you. You don't believe in superstitions. And neither do I. Nothing's going to ruin our wedding." He kissed her cheek. "Nothing at all."

This dress just might. "It looks a little . . . big."

Bernadine heaved herself onto the couch and propped her corns on the maple coffee table. "I knew she wouldn't try it on, Barry. I told you she wouldn't like what I picked out." Bernadine withdrew a handkerchief from her bosom and pressed it to her nose. "I've never had a daughter to dress, and shop for pretty things with, and I'd so hoped Candace would be that daughter. But now"—sniffle—"I'm already being rejected."

"Oh, Mother, it's not like that at all. Candace loves the dress, don't you?" Barry turned and gave her a help-me smile.

There were certain times in life when lying was good form. When it became a peace offering, not a sin. "Of course I do. I . . . I can't imagine walking down the aisle in anything else."

The dress wasn't even a Honda. It was an Edsel. She tried not to think of the Mercedes back at Reverie Bridal. Maybe if she squinted she could pretend they were the same dress.

Nope; she'd have to poke her eyes out to come close. Here comes the bride—Oedipus.

Bernadine sniffled. "Are you sure you like it?"

"Of course." *But I hope like hell it doesn't fit and I have to return it.*

"Try it on, honey, and show Mother." Barry grabbed the gown, pressed it into her arms and gave her a gentle push toward the bedroom.

Two minutes later, Candace had stepped into the dress from hell. If there was ever a dress that would make a bride want to commit suicide, this was it. The bodice pressed against her breasts, flattening them into pancakes while the skirt flared out at the hips and butt, giving "Baby Got Back" a whole new meaning. The sleeves poofed up like mutton-chops on steroids, obstructing her peripheral vision.

And the faux suede had something in it that caused it to attract lint like a magnet. Every time she turned, little flecks

of Barry's navy carpeting seemed to pop up and adhere themselves to the curlicues.

And worst of all, the damn thing fit like a glove.

"How is it?" Barry called through the door.

Hideous. "Wonderful."

"Can I see it?"

Only on my dead body. "In a minute."

Her cell phone rang and she dove for her handbag, hoping it was Spider-Man with a plan for escaping Barry's bedroom wearing anything but this dress. Hell, she'd swing
nude from the window if it meant not having to wear Psycho
Cowgirl Gets Married in public.

"Candace?" Rebecca said. "We have trouble. You better
get down to the shop right away."

Not a Marvel Comics hero, but close enough. She let out
a sigh of relief. "I'm on my way. Soon as I figure a way out
of this fashion emergency."

Candace's Looks-Like-a-Ladder Chocolate Lattice with Berries

2 cups strawberries
1 cup raspberries
3 tablespoons Grand Marnier
2 tablespoons brown sugar
10 ounces semisweet chocolate
10 ounces white chocolate
As much ice cream as you need

If you need an escape route, what's better than one made of chocolate? First, start with the serious stuff. Marinate the berries in the Grand Marnier and brown sugar. Let sit while you're getting the rest assembled.

Then melt the chocolates in separate double boilers until they're smooth as a clean getaway. Place them into a piping bag (improvise with Ziploc, if need be) and pipe out a criss-cross lattice pattern over a large glass bowl. Allow to cool, then remove from the dish. Careful—you don't want to break your best chance for escape!

Take your chocolate cup, invert it into a bigger bowl or on a plate, spoon in some berries, top with ice cream and more berries. If there's any melted chocolate left over, well, don't let it sit there—put it on top. Though, remember, if you're trying to make a fast escape, eating too much might slow you down.

Solution? Take it in a leak-proof to-go bag.

CHAPTER 12

"They're orange," Maria said. "Orange doesn't go with babies. Especially not Day-Glo."

"I know. And we ordered two hundred of them." Rebecca let out a sigh.

"Did you specify pink and blue?"

"Yep. But the lady who took our order over the phone had the handwriting of a chimpanzee." Rebecca held up the scribbled invoice that had been packed in the box. "Either that or the brains of one."

"Now that's an insult to primates. They're actually smarter than most men." Maria snagged a cookie out of the jar on the counter. "They *are*. I read it in *Cosmo*."

Candace picked up one of the wicker containers. "Aren't these supposed to be shaped like baby bassinets?"

Rebecca nodded. "Hey, maybe we could paint them—"

"Paint isn't going to help this. They're not just the wrong color; they're the wrong shape, too. Look at this. They're kind of long and thin and . . ." She paused as the shape began to connect in her brain. "Oh, my. They look a lot like—"

"Penises." Maria wagged a cookie in emphasis.

Candace sunk onto a stool and cradled her head in her

hands. Her heart began to race, her breath coming in gasps again. Would this Tuesday never end? "This is terrible. We're supposed to send our first shipment of 'Welcome to the World' baby baskets to Brigham and Women's Hospital Friday afternoon for Vogler Advertising. We've got two hundred cans of formula and packages of diapers. Then tomorrow, we're making two hundred baby-bottle-shaped chocolates and two hundred dozen pink-and-blue frosted cookies. Not to mention the hundreds of candy cigars we bought for accents." She moaned. "I don't think new mothers want a glow-in-the-dark genitals basket."

"At least not until after the six-week checkup," Maria said.

Rebecca shot her a glare. "Even that's pushing it."

"We're in a peck of trouble," Maria said, hooting with laughter. "Sorry, I couldn't resist."

"Maybe we could paint them. Glue some wheels on the outside," Candace said, her voice rising a couple of octaves. The room began to close in on her. "No one would know the difference if we put a big bow over th-th-the tip."

"No bow is going to mask *that*." Rebecca pointed to the end of the basket.

"Sure it can!" Candace yanked a yellow ribbon off the wall and jabbed it onto the end of one of the baskets. It drooped to one side, trailing against the counter, looking more like spent sperm than satin. "See?"

It hadn't worked. Even a chimpanzee could see that.

Oh, God. This was awful. A total disaster. Worse than anything that had happened thus far.

Candace yanked a small paper bag off the shelf behind her, shook it open, then placed it over her mouth and started to breathe into the sack. In. Out. Until the world stopped spinning and her heartbeat reached a nonlethal range.

"Candace, honey, you need to calm down," Maria said, placing a hand on her shoulder. "Here, have a chocolate."

She plucked a mini Hershey's bar from a bowl on the counter, unwrapped it and handed it to Candace.

She raised her head out of the bag and stuffed the candy into her mouth, then let out a sigh when the endorphins hit her brain. Ah, a much better solution than the sack. "Mmmm. More."

Maria sailed a couple more down the counter.

Candace ate them in two bites. The suede bell-bottom dress flashed through her mind. Then the manicotti with Michael. Then Della, sleeping on her couch. Then fishnet body stockings draped all over her apartment. "More. More. More."

"Are you okay, honey?" Maria asked. "They're just penis baskets. We've dealt with worse."

"I'm fine," Candace said, trying not to sob. She stuffed another chocolate into her mouth. "I'm fine. I'm just fine."

"You said that three times," Rebecca said. "Fine people only say it once."

Candace shook her head so fast, her hair whipped at her face. "I'm a little stressed about the wedding, that's all. There's so much to do. . . ."

"Did you find a dress today?"

"Yes." She dropped her chin into her hands. "And yes."

"What's that mean?"

"I found one I loved. And then Barry bought me one *he* loved, too."

"Your fiancé bought your wedding gown for you?" Maria shook her head. "Girlfriend, this is worse than I thought." She grabbed her purse, flicked up the clasp and pulled out a box of Godiva. "Here. You need it more than I do."

Candace sniffled and took the box. "Thank you."

"I take it you hate the dress?" Rebecca asked.

"You know that section in the back of *Glamour* where they put all the fashion don'ts?"

"The women who think polka dots go with plaid and cotton briefs look sexy sticking out of too-tight Guess?"

"This dress is so bad, they couldn't put it on that page. It's a fashion 'Don't Even *Bury* Me in That.'"

"Oh, honey, you need to do something about it."

"What?" She sighed. "Barry thinks I love it. Bernadine laid a guilt trip the size of Rhode Island on me when I hesitated to try it on."

"Your mother-in-law was there?" Rebecca shook her head. "This may be unrepairable."

"Nothing's unfixable." Maria dug in her purse, produced a second box of Godiva chocolates and handed it over to Candace.

"And if that fails," Rebecca said, picking up one of the glow-in-the-dark baskets and handing it to Candace, "use one of these to hold your bridal bouquet." She put on a bright smile. "At least then no one will be looking at your dress."

One box of Godiva and twenty minutes later, the Three Musketeers split up, divvying up the chocolate supply and the greater Boston area, each taking a section of the city to scour. They left no craft store unturned, no Wal-Mart untouched in their quest for anything wicker and baby.

Maria found basket number two hundred shortly after nine that night, setting off a jubilee of cell phone rings. Candace headed home, her Honda Civic loaded to the gills with wicker.

One disaster averted.

A flicker of light from the backyard caught her eye. It was too big to be a firefly, and too little to be firefighter training. Which left only one answer.

"Let me guess," Candace said as she came around to the back. "You had a late-night craving for s'mores?"

Grandma Woodrow shook her head. "I can't stand graham crackers. The crumbs get all in between my breasts and gum up the friction, if you know what I mean." She tossed another log onto the campfire. "I'm practicing."

"For what?"

"For my Appalachian hike with George. We're going to camp under the stars." Grandma grinned and spiked her brows. *"Au naturale."*

"You'll scare the bears."

"Maybe we'll teach them something about the birds and the bees." Grandma rustled in a cooler beside her. "Want a weenie?" She waggled a hot dog at her.

"No thanks. I've had enough of those for one day." Candace sighed and laid her head on her knees.

"I don't think I want to ask. And for me, that's saying something."

Candace plucked at a few sprigs of grass. "Trust me, you don't want to know."

Grandma laid a hand on her arm. "Is everything okay, sweetie?"

The fire flickered, fending off the mosquitoes and sending out a steady blanket of warmth. Either Grandma's hand on her wrist or the smoke had gotten to her eyes, because they suddenly filled with tears again.

And the nearest chocolate was in her car.

"My mother's living with me, my mother-in-law has picked out my wedding dress, my fiancé thinks I'm Polly Perfect, and . . . and I'm almost out of Godiva." She shook her head. "No, I'm not okay."

"Brunhilde picked out your dress?"

"Uh-huh."

"It's a sign."

Candace let out a chuff of frustration and got to her feet. "There are no signs, Grandma! None at all. I'm marrying Barry in two and a half weeks, even if I have to wear a faux suede bell to do it."

"I really think you could use a weenie." She shook a sticked hotdog at Candace. "The nitrates can cloud your brain. Makes everything look better."

Candace plopped back on the grass again. "I'm sorry. I

didn't mean to take that out on you. I'm just . . . frustrated and worried and scared."

"And typical." Grandma patted her arm again. "All brides feel that way at some point. Frankly, I'd be worried about you if you didn't."

As always, Grandma was right. These feelings were normal. Part of the process of getting married. Hadn't she read that 82 percent of all brides have at least one panic attack before the wedding? Maybe it had been 72 percent. The number, for once, didn't matter. All she knew was that she was in good company.

Candace leaned forward and drew her grandmother into a tight hug. "I love you, Grandma."

"Oh now, what was that for?"

"For always knowing what will make me feel better." She pressed a kiss to Grandma's cheek, then got to her feet. "I'm off to bed. Be sure to douse that fire—"

"With some water. I know, honey. I'm old, not senile."

"Sorry. I guess I tend to be a bit of a worrier."

"You do it out of love, so I forgive you." She wagged the wiener again. "This time."

Candace laughed all the way back into the house. With a fire burning in her backyard and a crazy grandmother who always had a ready weenie and a hug, what more could she ask for?

Della's When-Your-Family-Is-Dippy Fondue

1 teaspoon cinnamon
⅔ cup whipping cream
6 ounces semisweet chocolate (or more, if you want it
    really chocolaty)
¼ cup Kahlúa
Sliced bananas, strawberries, apples, etc., and cubes of
    pound cake or even better, cookies

If you simply must be with family, particularly your crazy
in-laws, then making a fondue with a bit of a kick to it is the
only way to survive the evening. Trust me, I have experience
at in-law business. Bring the cream and cinnamon to a boil
in a small saucepan (sort of like what happens when you
combine dear Aunt Martha with belching Uncle Lester).
Remove from heat, cover, let stand fifteen minutes.

Put the chocolate into a bowl. Bring the cream back up to
a boil, then pour it over the chocolate. *That's* the way to get a
mixer going. Now make it perfect by stirring in the Kahlúa.
Serve it warm, with extra Kahlúa if the in-laws make you
nuts. Remember to keep Uncle Lester away from the sharp
implements.

Or better yet, find a rich, single guy who comes equipped
with a family you can stand *without* the Kahlúa.

CHAPTER 13

Michael stretched out on his couch, Sam at his side. On any other Thursday night, there'd be someplace to go. A networking meeting. A client event. A date with another of what seemed to have become an endless stream of identical women.

But not tonight. In the two days since his lunch and the trip to the bridal shop with Candace, he'd barely been able to work. Finally, after three today, he'd admitted to himself that he'd left his concentration back with her.

He'd closed his appointment book, told his administrative assistant he was unavailable the rest of the day, stopped off to pick up Sam at the neighbor's apartment, and played hooky for the first time in seven years.

A banging started on his door—loud, insistent and mad. Sam jumped off the couch and dashed into the corner. "Some guard dog you are," Michael said.

Sam whimpered in response, then lay down and feigned sleep.

"Open up, Michael, I know you're in there. You can't avoid me forever."

Rachel. If he tried playing possum, he knew she'd probably pick the lock and let herself in anyway. As far as kid sisters went, Rachel took the cake for being innovative and stubborn.

He got to his feet and opened the door. "Hey, Rach. What brings you to this side of town?"

"You, you big dork. What's this 'Mr. Vogler is unavailable to everyone' crap your assistant pulled on me today? Is that some new way of avoiding the invitation to the family dinner next weekend?"

"Why hello, Michael. So nice to see you, big brother," he mocked.

"Cut the shit, Michael." Rachel brushed past him and into his apartment. She flopped onto his couch, kicked off her Keds and put her feet on his cherry coffee table. "I'm not in the mood to play nice."

"Let me guess. Mother? Or Father this time?"

"Both." She let out a sigh and tucked the ends of her pixie cut behind her ears. "How you lived with them for eighteen years I'll never know. I'm having trouble making it through seventeen."

"What'd they do?"

"Signed me up for some all-girls finishing school. They think it will 'feminize' me."

"Well, Rach, you are a little rough around the edges."

"So are uncut diamonds, so shut up."

"Is that why you were trying to find me today?"

"Yeah. I was hoping you could talk some sense into them." Rachel popped forward and grabbed one of his hands. "If you have any love at all for your baby sister, you'll tell Mother and Father to get the hell out of my life."

Michael laughed. "See, that's why they're sending you to a girls' school. So you stop saying things like 'shit' and 'hell.' "

She shrugged. "It gives me color."

"Fall foliage has color. You, my dear sibling, are already pretty without the extra syllables."

Rachel jabbed at his arm. "You're such a jerk." But the words were softer than her punch.

"At least look into it, okay? It'll make them happy and who knows? Maybe you'll like it."

"Being around a bunch of girls all day? I think not. Ugh. I'd rather join the circus." She snagged a walnut out of the dish on his coffee table and cracked it with the silver nutcracker. "So where were you? You never, *ever* miss work. You're like Mr. Perfect."

"I had a date. Sort of."

"Sort of? What the hell kind of date is that?"

Michael arched a brow at her.

"Sorry." She affected a haughty look, peering down her nose at him. "Whatever kind of date is that, darling?"

He laughed. "You are from a different gene pool, I swear."

"You're avoiding my question."

Ever since she'd hit her teen years, Rachel had gotten too smart for his old tricks. "You're right. Did you ever think it's because parts of my life are personal?"

"Nope, I'm your kid sister. Nothing's too personal for me." She leaned forward, chin in her hands. "Give me the four-one-one."

"Four-one-one?"

"Oh, God. You really are old, aren't you? Information? As in calling information."

"Sorry if twenty-nine is ancient to you."

"Just about."

"Hey, don't insult me if you want me to tell you about my date."

Rachel smiled at him and patted his arm. "Do go on, dear brother."

"I met this woman in a restaurant a few days ago," he began, deciding to censor out a few details about what happened after he'd met her, "and I really liked her. Turns out she's engaged to someone else."

"Oooh. This is better than *The Young and the Restless*."

He let out a frustrated sigh. "Why am I telling you this?"

"Because you're dying to tell someone. I can see it in your face. And I"—she patted her chest, right across the "Angel" emblazoned on her camouflage T-shirt—"just happen to be here. Right time, right place."

"Well, it turns out she's part owner of the gift basket company that's putting together some baskets for one of my clients. So we ran into each other a couple more times. I ended up asking her to lunch today and then—" He stopped.

"And then what?"

"Nothing."

"Oh no, you're not stopping there." She wagged a finger at him. "I told you my horrible girls' school story. The least you can do is share back. If you don't, I'll . . ." She paused a minute, thinking of a suitable torture. "Sing Metallica's greatest hits at the top of my lungs."

"You wouldn't."

She grinned. "You know I would."

"You drive a hard bargain. Ever think of going into corporate raiding?"

"I don't think they offer that after embroidery and tea lessons." She waved a floppy mock-socialite hand his way. "Now tell or I start singing." She opened her mouth, one eye on him.

"Okay, okay. I went shopping with her for her wedding dress."

Rachel's mouth shut with a soft plop. She blinked twice. "You did what?"

"You heard me."

"Michael Vogler, son of Nigel and Rebecca Vogler, owner of the third largest advertising firm in the city of Boston, and the most confirmed bachelor I know, helped the woman he likes pick out her wedding gown? To marry another man?"

He shrugged. "It was something to do."

"I could think of a hundred other ways to spend an afternoon. And you, having twelve more years of experience over me, could surely think of a thousand."

"You need to be in a convent. I better call Mother."

"Don't you dare."

"Just behave yourself. Don't use drugs and never, ever get in the backseat of a car."

"God, you sound like my P.E. teacher." Rachel rolled her eyes. "So why'd you do it? For real."

"I don't know." He leaned against the leather sofa. "It seemed like a good idea at the time."

Rachel gave him a dubious look.

"I wanted to show her what it could be like if she thought outside the box a little. I get the feeling she's not so happy with the man she's marrying and I wanted to give her a taste of what it could be like if—"

"If she married you?"

"Hell, no!" He jerked to his feet.

"Oh, come on, it's not a terminal disease. It's romantic."

"This from the girl who asked for combat boots for Christmas?"

"Hey, even I believe in happily ever after. You should, too."

Michael crossed to the window and looked out at the twinkling Boston skylight. "Maybe."

He heard Rachel go into the kitchen, grab a soda out of the fridge and pop the top. She joined him at the window a second later. "Are you going to go after her? Rescue her from Mr. Not So Charming?"

"I'd like to. But—"

"Then do it! Geesh, are *you* indecisive today! You're normally . . ." She paused, waving a hand in the air, searching for the word. "Focused. To the point. You must really like this chick."

"She's not a chick. She happens to be a smart, sassy and very nice woman."

Rachel pointed at him. "See? You're defending her. I say it's love."

"I don't fall in love."

Rachel left him and flounced to the couch. "And why is that, big brother? Tell me what complex Mother and Father have given you. I've got a nice long list of my own, so I'm sure you have a few, too."

"It's not them." He turned to face her. "Not really."

"Dish." She waved a hand at him.

"None of your beeswax," he said, using his favorite childhood tease.

She chuckled. "What are you, ten? Come on, no one says that anymore anyway. Tell me what's wrong with you so I can help get it straightened out."

"You, my darling sister, are seventeen. You barely have enough life experience to drive on the Mass Pike, never mind figure out my problems."

"Well, riddle me this, Batman. Do you think she should marry bachelor number one?"

"No. He's all wrong for her."

"There. Now we're getting somewhere." She drained her soda can and put it on the coffee table. "So, do you think she should marry you?"

"No."

"And why not? Aren't you marriage material?"

"Aren't you out past your bedtime?"

"Since when have you known Mother and Father to care when I get home at night? As long as my picture doesn't make it into the gossip column of *The Herald,* they're happy."

True enough. Michael and Rachel's childhoods had been pretty much free rein. Whatever the nanny didn't catch them doing was fair game, and whenever they came home was fine, as long as the family name was untarnished.

"Either way, I have work to do. I'm not going to discuss my love life with someone who still wonders why Britney broke up with Justin."

"Oh, please. I am so over that." Rachel got to her feet, her shoes making a soft plop against the carpet. "Suit yourself. I'm still the cheapest psychiatric help in Beantown."

He ruffled her hair as they walked to the door. "Hey, I love you for caring."

"See, you do love."

"Yeah, people I'm related to."

Rachel paused in the doorway. "If you like this girl, and you think she shouldn't marry Mr. Mistake, you owe it to womankind to do something about it."

He laughed. "Womankind?"

"Hey, I may not want to go to a finishing school, but that doesn't mean I don't have ovaries." She gave Michael a jab in the shoulder. "And, you might find out you're capable of loving more than a hypochondriac dog and a debutante-challenged sister."

A few minutes later she was gone, humming Metallica under her breath and stomping as loud as she could down his quiet, almost middle-aged hallway.

Grandma's Star-Crossed-Lovers Cinnamon-Chocolate Cookies

2 ounces unsweetened chocolate
½ cup butter, softened
1 cup sugar
1 egg
1 teaspoon vanilla
3 cups all-purpose flour
2 teaspoons ground cinnamon
½ teaspoon baking soda
¼ teaspoon salt
½ cup sour cream

Romeo and Juliet made it work, well, except for that death thing getting in the way. But you'll be smarter than those two flighty kids and take a few lessons from a lady who's seen a few more birthdays than you, won't you? Then you'll see that opposites can attract—in cookies and in life.

Start by melting the chocolate in a double boiler. Remove from heat and cool. Cream together the butter, melted chocolate, sugar, egg and vanilla until it's as light and airy as your heart when you're hiking in the hills with a guy who knows how to get your bushes shaking. Add the dry ingredients, then the sour cream. (See how we're making all these different flavors come together? You might think that sexy hunk of a man is wrong for you, but mix him up with a little midnight madness and see what you get.) Cover and let the dough sit in the fridge for a while. Cool your own jets, too, and open your mind to the possibilities.

Roll out the dough in batches to one-quarter-inch thickness, then cut out in playful shapes. Put on greased cookie sheets, remembering to leave some space between them for growth, and bake at 400 degrees for ten minutes. Cool them on a wire rack until ready to eat.

And then take some to your Romeo/Loverboy. Let him feed you, or you feed him. Just watch that the crumbs don't gum up the friction between you.

CHAPTER 14

Candace was the first one into the shop on Friday morning, undoubtedly due to her Cocoa Krispies and Ho Hos breakfast. Combined with a Starbucks White Chocolate Mocha, she was running faster than J. Lo from the paparazzi.

She headed out to her car, for her third trip for baskets. Maria and Rebecca would arrive in an hour or so, but for now, it was just Speedy Gonzalez Candace and her sugar high.

"Need some help?"

Her head jerked up, nearly colliding with the trunk lid. "Michael! What are you doing here?"

Something in her gut turned into hot, melted fudge at the sight of him. Despite all that had happened, and despite her own better judgment, he'd been on her mind ever since yesterday. She didn't need sugar for fuel—not when he was around.

"I was looking for you." He grinned. "I happened to be in this part of town, dropping off a file to one of our freelance graphic designers. Thought I'd stop by and see how the baskets were going. I wasn't sure if you'd even be in this early."

He was here to check on the job. Not her. She shouldn't be disappointed. Not one bit.

She piled more wicker into her arms. "We'll be getting them out today. No problem."

"Glad to hear it." He gestured toward the remaining baskets. "You want a hand?"

"Sure." She dumped her own load of baskets into his arms, then grabbed several more handfuls.

"That's the easiest sale I've ever made," he said around the wicker.

"Hey, I'm no glutton for punishment. A good-looking guy offers me help, I take it."

He smirked between the wheels of a baby carriage. "You think I'm good-looking?"

"Oh, come on, you know you are."

"I only care what you think." He put a hip against the door to hold it open for her.

"Well, I'm not telling you twice. You'll get a big ego and then you'll be too busy admiring yourself to help me."

"Never."

"Bullshit."

He leaned back. "You don't know me as well as you think."

No, she didn't. And a big part of her—scrambling to get a toehold as the majority—wanted to know him much better. Much, *much* better.

The instant she saw Michael, Trifecta scrambled to her feet and Velcroed herself to his leg all the way into the kitchen, before being shooed back out by Candace. Trifecta whined outside the glass, protesting her banishment from her new object of affection. Her dog clearly had no reservations about overstroking Michael's ego.

Work. She'd think about work. Not about him or about their lunch and that moment in the dress store.

Candace put the bulk of the baskets on the side counter, leaving a few on the main workspace, then started laying out the contents assembly-line fashion. Tissue paper, cookies in little cardboard boxes, baby bottle-shaped chocolates, candy cigars and signs proclaiming "It's a Boy" or "It's a Girl," along with the cans of formula and diaper packages.

And then she realized she was alone. With Michael. Separated by nothing but some baskets and a few newborn-sized extra-absorbent baby bottom protectors.

Stick to work. No extracurricular activities.

Michael waggled a piece of pale pink tissue paper. "How do we do this?"

"Hand me one of each thing and I'll do all the hard stuff." She picked up some tissue paper and laid a soft bed of it in the base of the first basket, a pink bassinet. "Formula first, since it's the heaviest."

"Smart thinking." He picked up a can and laid it in her hands. She nestled it into the center of the basket, then reached for a package of diapers.

His fingers pressed against the back of her hand, like fire on ice. "That's my job, remember?"

"Sorry, I forgot."

Sticking to work wasn't going to be as easy as she'd hoped. Heck, she'd be lucky if she could stick to the subject with him around, keeping her mind on everything but what she was supposed to be doing.

He placed the package in her hand. "Am I distracting you?"

"Not at all." *A lie a day keeps the temptation away.*

I hope.

Michael only harrumphed and gave her a couple of baby bottle–shaped chocolates. "Have you read that poem yet?"

"I've been busy."

"Too busy for a poem?"

"I used to love poetry in college," Candace said, adding tissue paper moorings around each item to secure it in place. "I took a couple of classes in it, and even thought of minoring in poetry, or English lit."

"Why didn't you?"

She cocked her head at him. "It's not very practical, is it?"

"Does everything have to be practical?"

"Come on, you own a business. You tell me. How much of your time do you waste on things that aren't practical?"

"Not nearly enough."

"See?"

"But spending some time is better than none, don't you agree?"

She shook her head. "Too many tastes of the dessert and before you know it, you've eaten the whole damned pie."

"Oh, come on, you can't seriously believe that. All work and no play makes Candy a very unhappy girl."

The way he said the words made it sound awfully tempting to go play—any game he suggested. A vision of a very sexy game of Twister popped into her mind. Oh, that would be so wrong right now. Wrong at *any* time. "I'm a girl with a goal."

"And what is your goal?"

"To make this shop successful."

Michael looked around the kitchen. "I'd say you've done that already."

"Well, I'd like to keep it that way."

"So is that what you want out of life?" He arched a brow, handed her another formula can. "Status quo?"

"More or less, yes." She seated the can in the basket and avoided his gaze.

"Where's the fun in that?"

"What do you mean, fun?"

"Change is what makes the world go round. A little would do you good." He tossed a package of diapers at her, forcing her to jerk up and catch them in midair. She didn't respond to his teasing grin.

"Change is dangerous. It leads to mistakes." She didn't bother waiting for him to help; merely reached past him for the rest of the ingredients and started shoving them into the next wicker bassinet.

"Sometimes. But mistakes are learning opportunities, don't you think?"

She paused, her whole body going silent. "Not all mistakes," she said softly.

"And what mistakes have you made?"

She pushed the finished basket to the side and reached for another. "If you keep talking to me, I'll never get your order done in time."

When she put out a palm for the next can of formula, he held it back. " 'I have measured out my life with coffee spoons; I know the voices dying with a dying fall beneath the music from a farther room.' "

"What are you talking about?"

"T. S. Eliot. And a life spent wondering would it have been worthwhile to take a chance and dare a little."

"That poem was written almost a hundred years ago. It has nothing to do with my life in the twenty-first century."

But she'd lied. In the last few weeks, how many times had she wondered the same thing? She remembered the Eliot poem now. The message about watching the biggest excitements in life pass by and never having the courage to grab them. Of settling for less than all she wanted because it was easier.

Was that what she was doing? Settling for Barry because it was easier than being brave and taking a chance on the unknown?

Michael laid the formula on the counter, out of her reach, and took her hands in his. She tried to withdraw, but he held firm. His grip was warm, tough and soothing all at once. She wanted to run away from it and yet at the same time, lay her troubles in his palms. "I'm a workaholic. We're a lot alike that way, you and me. Go to work often enough and you can avoid the black hole in your heart pretty damned well."

"I'm not doing that."

"You are. And you know it underneath." He ran his thumbs over the back of her hands. "So was I, until you came along. In that restaurant the night we met, what you said really hit a nerve with me. And it made me remember what I'd learned when I read that poem years ago. That not living your life fully is a waste."

"I *am* living my life." Her chin raised a notch. "And who the hell are you to decide I'm not?"

"The night I met you, you were miserable."

"I was drunk." She yanked her hands away.

"You told me you were sick of being in a rut. You said you wanted a little bit of adventure again. What did you mean by that—*again?"*

She pivoted toward the sink, grabbing a cup off the shelf and filling it with water. "Nothing."

"Bullshit."

Candace wheeled toward him. "You have no right to question my love life, my choices or my past. I'm not *yours."*

His cobalt eyes met hers, deep and vibrant and swimming with everything that had yet to be said. The thread between them tightened. Like a noose. "I wish like hell you were."

"No, you don't. Because that would mean a commitment, and as far along as you say you've come, you're not ready for that yet, are you?"

"I'm not good at settling down."

"Well, you know what?" She leaned in closer to him, confronting him with the same truths he'd thrown at her. "You're letting that part of life pass by then, too. It takes courage to make a commitment. And to stick with it, too."

Neither of them said anything for a long time. The clock on the wall ticked away the seconds. "I need to get these baskets finished," Candace said finally.

"Always work first, huh?"

She inhaled and laid the cup in the sink. "I like things orderly. Neat and planned down to the last detail. That's exactly how Barry is, too. That's why I'm marrying him—because he's like me."

"And I'm the opposite, aren't I?"

She let out a laugh. "You? You are chaos to me. And that's the one thing I can't deal with."

"They say opposites attract."

Candace sighed, and for the first time that morning, allowed herself a good look at him. "Attraction is not the problem." Then she pushed off from the counter and went back to work. "Life is not based on sex, though."

He grinned and joined her at the worktable, again handing her things and forming their assembly line. She was ten times more aware of him now. Why on earth had she said anything about being attracted to him? "If the world revolved around sex, we'd have a lot less wars and a whole lot more smiles."

"Men are all the same," she said. "Don't you want to be with a woman who does more than have hot, sweaty monkey sex with you?"

He chuckled as he placed a box of cookies in her hand. "Sure I do. I want someone I can talk to. Preferably a woman who knows her poets."

Candace shot him a look of disdain.

"And one who has superior organizational skills. So she can help keep me on track. Because lately, I can't seem to get to work on time. Or concentrate on a damn thing." He placed a chocolate in her hands and leaned down to whisper in her ear. "I keep getting distracted by thoughts of monkey sex."

Her breath lodged in her windpipe. "You are incorrigible."

He grinned. "My mother's pride and joy."

"I-I-I need more baskets from the other counter."

Michael moved to the left; Candace moved to the right. The two of them collided like a pair of lead-foot preschoolers on the bumper-car track.

"Excuse me," she said.

"For what?"

"For nearly running you over." She hadn't stepped back.

Neither had he. "It might be the biggest thrill I get today, so I should be thanking you."

"I'm sure some beautiful woman is waiting by the phone for you to call."

"No."

"Come on. You're a good-looking guy. Unmarried. Rich. At that prime age when the clock starts ticking for a lot of women." She shook her head. "There are women waiting by the phone for you."

"I only want—" And then he was cut off. By the ring of his cellphone.

She gave him a smug grin.

He flipped it out and answered it. "I'm . . . in a meeting right now. No, tonight won't work." He paused, listening. "I'll have to get back to you on that. I want my evenings free"— his gaze connected with Candace's—"for an indefinite period of time." Then he clicked off the phone and slipped it back into his pocket.

"See. I told you so."

"That was a woman, all right." His smile had a bit of devil in it. "My secretary. Calling to see if I wanted to schedule a dinner meeting."

"Oh."

"But, you were right on one count. It was a dinner meeting with a woman, someone who has expressed more than a business interest in me. I turned it down. I told you, I don't want any other woman."

"Why not?"

"Because you intrigue me more than anyone I've ever met." He closed the gap, his eyes locking with hers, seeking whatever secrets she might be hiding behind her own retinas. "What makes you tick, Candace Woodrow?"

"A . . . a heart." She swallowed. "I think."

What was that gibberish she'd said earlier about commitment? And courage? Maybe the Cowardly Lion had absconded with all of hers, because she sure as heck wasn't feeling brave right now.

"Tsk, tsk." He reached up with his free hand and trailed a finger along her left breast, tracing a very sexy cardiac outline. "Your biology teacher would be very disappointed that you've forgotten your anatomy."

"I'm . . . I'm having a bit of trouble"—she watched his finger slowly circling her breast—"concentrating right now."

"Me, too."

Her eyes went to his anatomy. His breaths went in. Out. Pectoral muscles went up. Down. The rhythm of her breaths synchronized to his, because she couldn't tear her gaze away from his torso. The memory of him from that first morning, wearing nothing more than boxers, flooded her senses.

"We, ah, should be making baskets."

"Baskets are not what I want to make right now." Michael leaned forward and brushed his lower lip against hers, a tease of a kiss. Not enough. Not nearly enough to satisfy the aching need in her gut.

Despite everything she'd said, she wanted him. She wanted so badly to open her mouth and devour him, taking him with the same relish she had the chocolates, letting him assimilate her palate until she forgot her own name.

"I shouldn't—"

"No, you shouldn't." He teased at her mouth again, grinning. "If you did kiss me—oh, that would make you a very, *very* bad girl."

Maybe it was the double adverb. Or the sight of his smile, so sure and sexy. Or quite possibly the scent of him—so masculine and strong, right there, right now. Available for the taking.

Candace didn't quibble with why; she just surged forward, opening her lips against his, darting her tongue in and tasting the man she had been denying herself for a week.

Oh. God. Oh God. Oh God. Oh God.

Kissing Michael was better than an all-you-can-eat buffet at the Godiva plant. More satisfying than a clearance sale at Bloomingdale's. More intense than the ancient wooden roller-coaster at Nantasket Beach. And so damn good, she forgot for a minute she was any other man's but his.

Michael's fingers played at the nape of her neck, edging upward with the precision of Arthur Fiedler. His thumbs traced slow erotic circles along the outer edge of her ears, swooping past the gold hoops she wore and then down to the tender flesh that met her jaw.

She pressed her pelvis to his, feeling his erection and wanting only to grind into the steel of him until the throbbing longing inside her went away. Her hands roamed his back, up and down that damn white shirt, feeling the ridges beneath it and resisting the urge to tear the whole thing off so she could see his bare, muscled chest again.

Her hands went to the waistband of his pants and she had the Van Huesen half out of his Dockers before she realized what was happening.

I've become a hussy. Oh my Lord, I'm worse than Kim Cattrall on Sex in the City.

"I can't do this," she said, stepping back, breaking the contact, as if putting a few inches of distance between them could turn her body off.

It didn't. The longing for him still pounded in her body.

You crazy woman, get back over there and finish this. One quickie on the counter and I could be screaming—

"I think you should go," she blurted. "Now."

He backed up several steps, tucking in his shirt as he did. "And I think you should decide what you want. You can't keep tasting the food and never finish the meal."

"You caught me at a weak moment, that's all."

"And if I come back tomorrow?"

She lowered her head, then raised it again. She knew the

answer. It filled her with a deep, achy emptiness. "Don't come back tomorrow."

"Oh, Candy." He cupped her chin. "Don't let your life come and go like a sunset you never got to watch," he said softly. "You deserve more."

And then he was gone.

Maria's Something's-Up Frozen
Chocolate-Covered Bananas

2 ripe bananas
4 popsicle sticks
¼ cup peanuts, chopped
⅓ cup hot fudge sauce, at room temperature

These work as terrific bribes for people who are covering up a little rendezvous in the kitchen, and for those of us who haven't had a date in a while and need something satisfying. Start by putting waxed paper on a baking sheet. Then peel the bananas, cut them in half and put a stick in the end of each half piece. Place on the baking sheet and freeze those babies until they're firm as a cover model.

Then take the frozen bananas and dip them into the fudge sauce, spreading it *all over* with a spatula. Here comes the fun part—roll them in the peanuts. When you're done, freeze them again until the fudge sauce is as firm as your fruit. Now you're ready for a little temptation—or fudgesicles that'll get the neighbors talking.

CHAPTER 15

Maria was the first to notice something was up. "Lipstick's smeared. Face is flushed. Counter's a mess." She eyed Candace. "Either you had a visitor or you were attacked by a pack of rabid raccoons when you opened the shop."

"Michael came by." She shoved a can of formula into another basket.

"And? Don't leave us hanging, girl. I don't have a love life to speak of right now so I have to live through yours. It's either that or watch reruns of *Love Chain* on E! and frankly, it's too depressing to see women with better boobs than mine get dumped by men with toothy grins."

"And I'm married," Rebecca said. "The words 'love life' left my vocabulary as soon as I said, 'We're having a baby.'"

Candace wrapped a basket in shiny pale blue cellophane, tied a robin's egg–colored bow and an "It's a Boy" sign on the top and slid it to the side. "There's not much to talk about."

"Liar." Maria laid a hand on the next basket. "I'll hold the chocolate hostage."

"Won't work. I already have my own stash."

"I'll . . ." Maria thought a minute. "I'll get Bernadine to go shopping for your trousseau."

Candace shuddered. "You wouldn't."

"Nah, I wouldn't." Maria grinned. "But it is an evil thought."

"Maybe one of your best." Rebecca finished up her own basket, then reached for another.

Candace stepped back from the counter and looked at her two best friends. She could use someone to talk to, even if Maria and Rebecca weren't exactly an impartial jury. They'd take her side no matter what she said. Still, that could go a long way toward making the guilt that was weighing on her chest ebb a little.

She sighed, pushed the basket she was working on away from her and took a seat on one of the barstools. "Michael stopped by early this morning and offered to help with the baskets. I didn't say no."

"Because?"

"Because I haven't been able to stop thinking about him. And when I went to sleep last night, it wasn't Barry I was dreaming about."

Maria laid a hand on hers. "Oh, honey, it's okay. He's a hunk of sizzling hot man. I don't blame you."

"But then I . . ." She paused, bit her lip, then let the rest out: "Kissed him again."

"You owe me ten bucks," Maria whispered to Rebecca.

"You guys are *betting* I'll cheat on Barry?"

"No, just wagering Michael is way too sexy to resist. Hey, I'd screw him if he wasn't interested in you."

"Maria!"

"Come on. You can't tell me you don't look at that guy and think sex. He makes the men in *Playgirl* look like shaved chimpanzees."

"And how would you know what the guys in *Playgirl* look like?" Rebecca asked.

"I said I didn't have a man. I didn't say my vagina had shriveled up and died."

Rebecca sighed. "I think I should pay a visit to the gyno. Mine might have."

"You two are taking this way too lightly." Candace started to pace the length of the kitchen. "This is huge. I *cheated* on Barry. All he's done is trust me."

Rebecca came up, drawing Candace into a shoulder hug and leading her back to the worktable. "Let me tell you something I've never told anyone before."

Maria swiveled around. "You've been keeping a secret from us?"

She lowered her head. "At the time, it was easier than admitting the truth. What happened was—"

"Wait! Don't say anything yet. This is a big moment. It calls for dessert and some coffee." Maria bustled over to the opposite side of the kitchen, set the Capresso coffeemaker to work, then got out a container of iced ginger cookies. A few minutes later, the three of them were seated around the table in the office, dunking and dishing.

"About three months before I married Jeremy," Rebecca began, "I went up to Wisconsin to visit my mom for the weekend. And while I was there, I met someone."

"They have men in Wisconsin?" Maria piped up. "Who don't wear the cheese hats?"

Rebecca laughed. "They have some very cute men in Wisconsin, believe me. Some who are . . . irresistible."

"I see a road trip in my future," Maria said. "I love *anything* dipped in cheese."

Rebecca rolled her eyes at Maria, then went on. "I met this cowboy who worked the farm down the road from my mom's place."

Candace wagged a cookie at her. "And we all know what they say about cowboys."

Maria nodded. "There's a reason they get a starring role in romance novels."

"Well, he was better than a novel. Tall, sexy and damned good at everything he did." A faint blush crept into Rebecca's cheeks. "And I mean everything."

Maria's jaw dropped. "You . . . you slept with him?"

Rebecca gave a little nod, then dipped her head, as if even now, it still embarrassed her. For a long moment, she said nothing. The office was silent, save for the steady hum of traffic outside and the occasional drone of an airplane overhead. "We ran into each other at this bar," she began quietly. "I swear, it was the Travis Tritt that made me do it."

"Wow," Candace sat back in her chair. "I'd never think you, of all people—"

"I know, I know. That's why I never said anything." She toyed with her mug, spinning the ceramic container from side to side. She stilled the coffee cup and looked up, meeting Candace's eyes. "But what I can tell you is that being with that guy told me a lot about why I was marrying Jeremy."

"Was the cowboy that bad?" Maria asked.

"Oh no, he was good. *Very* good." She blushed again.

"But . . . if he was so good, why did you still marry Jeremy?"

"Because what I have with Jeremy is real. And true. The kind of thing you can count on for a lifetime. His spurs are there to stay." She smiled, a soft smile that spoke volumes about how much she loved the man she'd married. "The cowboy was gone before the end of the night and off with another woman the next time I saw him. He was only good at sex. He had no sticking power, just a lot of sex appeal. Still, I'd do what I did that night again in a heartbeat, because if I hadn't, I'd always have those doubts. And the last thing I need in my marriage is doubt."

"So, are you telling me being with Michael might be *good* for me? And my marriage?"

Rebecca shrugged. "I don't know. Hell, I don't have any answers. I sure hope I find some before my daughter is dating." She laughed. "All I know is this—if you have any questions at all about whether you're doing the right thing by marrying Barry, a few nights with Michael might clear those questions up."

Maria slumped her chin into her hand. "It'll also give you a taste of the fun, fun world of dating that awaits you if you stay single."

"But . . ." Candace grabbed another cookie and dunked it in her coffee, but didn't eat it. "What if I find out that Barry isn't the right one for me?"

"Then you've saved yourself—and him—a lot of heartache." Rebecca clasped Candace's hand with her own. "If your love is true, it will withstand anything."

"And if it's not, well, Tornado Michael is one hell of a good storm to tangle with." Maria popped half a gingersnap into her mouth, then pointed at Candace. "I bet he'd wear a cowboy hat in bed if you asked him to. And don't forget to bring some Cheez Whiz along."

Silence. The house was empty when Candace returned to her duplex on Friday night. Della must have been out again with her lingerie salesman/poet.

Barry had left two messages, the last one very apologetic, saying he was taking his mother out to Springfield to visit a sick aunt and would be back by Sunday morning. Before Bernadine had arrived, Barry had always been around on the weekends, regular as rain in the spring. Once the wedding was over and Bernadine was gone, they could get back to normalcy. Soon, she told herself. Soon her life would be back on track.

"Don't worry," Barry said at the end of the message, "I'll be home in time to help with all the wedding details. Twenty-one thousand, six hundred minutes until you're my bride!" His guffawing laughter squawked through the phone. Leave it to Barry the accountant to count down to the last minute. "Love you, darling. See you soon."

Candace erased the message, pulled up a chair at her desk, put the half-empty box of Godiva chocolates to her right, then set about paying her bills. Just because her whole life was falling apart was no reason not to stick to her regular schedule. And since it was Friday, she was paying bills.

Concentrating on writing checks, paying bills and updating her budget spreadsheet helped take her mind off that kiss.

Barely.

When she'd finished the bills, she got out her wedding planner and flipped to the to-do list. At the top, she wrote "Barry" and underlined it. That's where her thoughts should be. On her fiancé and her wedding.

First item on the to-do list: buy a wedding dress.

She picked up a pen, then switched it to a number-two pencil and colored in the box. She was, unfortunately, done with that.

The Godiva was in her mouth before she started to sob at the injustice of it all.

"Hello, darling," Della called as she burst through the door. "I'm home." She released Percy to the floor. Trifecta gave him a glare and the Pomeranian let out a whimper and scooted into the corner. Apparently, the alpha dog had been established—a three-legged female who had a good twenty pounds over Percy.

Good for you. Candace patted Trifecta and shared a smile of victory with her pooch.

"What are you doing on Saturday night?" her mother asked, checking her manicure. "I thought maybe we'd, ah, go shopping."

"Mother, I already know."

"Know what?"

"That it's my shower." Candace grinned. "I've known for weeks. Rebecca and Maria can't keep a secret to save their lives."

"Oh, you always have to spoil everything. I've never been

able to surprise you. Every Christmas, you had the gifts figured out before Christmas morning."

"That's because 'Santa' never remembered to close the closet door."

"You peeked."

"I was hanging up my coat."

"Oh." Della put a finger to her lips. "I probably should have had a better hiding place."

"Mother, it's fine. I'm not one for surprises anyway. They just make it harder to plan ahead." Candace flipped the planner to the budget section. With a heavy sigh, she added back in the amount she'd set aside to buy a dress. Having more money to spend on her wedding didn't make her happy, not when it meant dressing like Jessie from *Toy Story 2* on steroids.

"That's the point, dear. Honestly, whatever happened to your sense of humor?"

"I have one."

Della reached into her Liz Claiborne handbag and withdrew an emery board. "You are exactly like your father. Too sensible for your own good."

"Dad has a retirement account and a diversified stock portfolio. He's smart, Mother, not crazy."

Della sighed. "He's boring."

"Is that why you left him?"

Della started filing her nails, slipping the board along the sides, then checking her progress by holding her fingers up to the light every few seconds. "How did this become a conversation about me instead of you?"

Candace shut her planner and reached for the last piece of Godiva. "Since when is there anything about me that we need to discuss?"

Della brightened, pasting on her brightest smile, the one she reserved for family gatherings where she was forced to be in the same room as Grandma Woodrow. "Let's just talk about the wedding plans, dear. That will make you happy. Did you find a dress today?"

"Why does everyone ask me that question?" She bit off half a piece of chocolate, saving the last sacred bit in the box.

"Because the wedding *is* the dress."

"It is not."

"You're not trying on the right dresses, then. The perfect wedding gown makes you feel like a Hollywood celebrity. Like the belle of the ball."

"I'm becoming Mrs. Barry Borkenstein. There's no need for a star in front of the Mann Theater."

Della rolled her eyes. "Honest to God, if I hadn't seen you emerge from my loins with my own two eyes, I'd swear we weren't related."

"Mother, don't worry about the wedding." Candace headed into the kitchen to feed the animals. And avoid her mother. "Everything is under control."

"Have you rented a hall?" Della followed, taking a stance against the counter.

"The Sons of Italy."

Her mother made a face akin to someone undergoing electroshock therapy. "Don't you think the Marriott—"

"Don't go there, Mother." Bob curled his body around Candace's leg in gratitude for the Friskies.

She sighed. "A band?"

"I have a DJ all set." Candace flaked some designer doggy food into a ceramic dish and laid it on the floor for Percy. He took one look at the bowl, turned up his nose and walked away. Apparently, he'd selected Prima Donna from the menu today.

"A *DJ?*" Della bit off the rest of her comment. "What about the menu?"

"Chicken. It's the white meat of choice."

Della stifled a yawn, clearly showing her displeasure with such a predictable entrée choice. "Flowers?"

"Carnations and roses." She busied herself with the water bowls. Why hadn't she brought the damn Godiva into the kitchen with her? Already she could feel the need for chocolate coming on again, as if the last dose had worn off.

"Carnations?" Della shook her head and pressed a hand to her forehead. "Candace, I can't let you go through with this."

"Mother, please don't try to talk me out of marrying Barry." Desperate now, Candace foraged in the refrigerator until she came up with a lone instant-pudding snack, tucked behind the eggs. She turned and reached to grab a spoon out of the drawer, but her mother stopped her, taking one of Candace's hands in both her own.

"Are you sure about him, dear?" she asked. "You *have* heard the way he laughs, haven't you?"

"Mother . . ."

She threw up her hands. "All right. Far be it from me to question someone's choice in men. But I can't let you have carnations at your wedding. For God's sake, Candace, what are you thinking?"

"That they're less expensive than lilies."

"You, my daughter, are the complete opposite of me. Which means you'll probably only get married once. Twice at the most. Do it up right." She grabbed her arms and gave her a little shake. "Get the good flowers."

"Mother, they're just—" Candace stopped when she caught the look in Della's hazel eyes. Just as Candace needed the chocolate to deal with her ever-mounting stress level, her mother needed to shop. How could she deny Della this one little thing? Especially now that there was a bit of extra money in her budget to spend. "You know what? You're right. Why don't you take over the floral arrangements for me?"

"Oh, honey, are you sure? I'm so thrilled!" Della clapped

her hands together. "Let's see; we'll need to get you a bouquet that has some calla lilies and some orchids, oh, and for accents . . ."

For a few hundred dollars, Candace had bought a second peace treaty. If only solving the problems of the Middle East were this easy, the world would be a much safer—and prettier—place.

Rebecca's Taste-the-Temptation Rum Chocolate Truffles

8 ounces cream cheese, softened
3 cups powdered sugar
12 ounces semisweet chocolate, melted
1 ½ teaspoons rum
Toppings: use your imagination

Oh, you can taste it already, can't you? That's what you get for going too long without indulging. Get to it quick and don't dillydally or you'll be like the Poky Little Puppy and miss all the fun. Beat that cream cheese until it's smooth, then add in the sugar. Once that's all blended, mix in the chocolate and the rum. Ah, you're almost there.

Refrigerate for one hour (tell your husband it's a new meatloaf recipe and he'll stay away from the bowl). Shape into one-inch balls and roll in the topping of your choice. Choose topping based on temptation need—the more chocolate, the worse the situation is.

The best part? They're ready to eat now. And they're so small, you can stuff one in your mouth and be done with it before anyone catches you indulging.

CHAPTER 16

Candace sat at the counter at Gift Baskets on Saturday morning, once again flipping through the pages of her wedding planner. She made lists and checked them, zipping down the different little square boxes, coloring them in a percentage of the way for each portion of the job that had been done. Flowers—60 percent now that Della was in charge. Invitations were erased back to 50 percent.

Oh, shit. She still hadn't called her half of the guests yet. Why was she delaying? Normally, she'd be chop-chop about a job like that. Get it out of the way in one afternoon.

I'm distracted, that's all. I need to clear my head, get a little air.

She stared at the box beside "buy wedding dress." She'd filled it in yesterday, but now it felt like she'd marked it with the wrong color—suede instead of Reverie.

She made out her list of calls and double checks to make today, then finally closed the planner.

Order had been restored. That was much better. Goals were stacked in a pile, ready to be accomplished—just the way she liked it. The last few chaotic days had been unnerving. She'd had to start carrying a paper bag in her purse for when she hyperventilated, for Pete's sake.

Not to mention the two pounds she'd gained in two days from eating more chocolate than real food. Not exactly a balanced diet. Tomorrow, she resolved. Tomorrow she'd opt for bananas over Mars bars, salads over Godiva, oatmeal instead of a brownie for breakfast.

She only had fifteen days until the wedding. There were so many things to do and so little time. The pressures mounted again on her chest, tightening around her aorta. Much more of this and she'd need a heart transplant to get through the ceremony.

"That's it. I'm looking for an agent," Maria said, entering the office. She dumped her purse on the counter and grabbed a cup of coffee from the Capresso.

"An agent?"

"My life is a soap opera. I might as well sell the rights to it and make some money." She took a sip, then settled into a chair. "Might give some people at ABC a few chuckles."

"Hey, it does provide good entertainment for us." Candace grinned. "What happened to get you thinking about selling movie rights?"

"Well, David and his Bambi chick sent a lawyer out to threaten me with a lawsuit for the damage to the Beemer. Something about 'malicious destruction of property.' "

"What'd you tell the lawyer?"

"I told him, 'You bet your ass it was malicious. So was what David and Bambi were doing on that table five minutes before.' When I showed him my evidence, a.k.a. Bambi's ass imprint in my table, the lawyer backed off."

"He gave up, just like that?"

"Not exactly." She smiled, toying with the rim of the coffee cup. "He took a little convincing."

"You *bribed* a lawyer?"

"Hell, no. I merely flirted with a very cute member of the American Bar Association."

"Oh, well, that's different." Candace shook her head. "Not."

Maria batted her eyelashes and gave a mockery of a coy smile. "Five minutes with me and James Nesbitt, Esquire decided he had a conflict of interest representing David, so he dumped the two-timer and made a date with me for Saturday night."

"My, don't you have a powerful gift of persuasion."

"I'd rather think of it as ovaries on a mission." She grinned. "He was hot. Damned hot, especially for a guy carrying briefs." She winked.

"You're irredeemable." Candace laughed and went back to her lists.

Maria waved a hand at her. "Look at you and that planner. You two are glued at the hip."

Candace shrugged and traced the outline of the black vinyl cover. "I like to keep on top of things."

"Candace, you're not only on top of things, you're mounting them with a vengeance. You have a planner for the wedding, another one for the business, and a calendar on your refrigerator. You cross-reference and cross-check them with all the precision of Tommy Franks planning a military invasion." Maria laid a hand on hers. "Honey, I think you need to go to Planners Anonymous."

"Being organized is a good trait."

"I'm saying this as your friend," Maria said softly, her gaze meeting Candace's. "You're obsessive. You need to loosen up a little. Let go. Then when the little things go wrong, it won't bother you so much."

"You call two hundred penis baskets a little thing?"

"Hey, it was hilarious. How often does that happen to us? If we tack one of those on our display board, we'll be a hit at the gift baskets convention next year."

Candace's jaw dropped to her chest. "We can't do that!"

"Live a little. Stop being so damn good."

They were the exact same words Michael Vogler had been saying to her over the past week. What no one seemed to understand was that order gave Candace comfort, like a warm blanket on a cold winter night. She needed it like an addict craved the next high. Her satisfaction came from neat little rows and checked boxes.

Although, if she thought about it hard, it sounded sick. An organizational sickness. God, who got something like that?

Someone terrified of chaos, that's who.

The clock on the wall chimed the noon hour. "That reminds me; I'm supposed to be at my shift at the shelter in half an hour." Candace slipped off the stool and tucked her planner into her tote bag. "I'd better get going. I'll be back in a couple of hours."

"See, that's what I mean." Maria pointed a finger at her. "You're like Mother Theresa, except you're not marrying God. You're marrying Dilbert."

"Maria!"

Her friend drew her into a hug. "Sorry. I shouldn't have said that. It's not nice to poke fun at dead saints."

Candace gave her a jab, then drew back. "Hold down the fort."

"I will." Maria smirked. "But if the Calvin Klein underwear model comes in wanting a special treat, I'm hanging up the CLOSED sign."

Candace shook her head. "I really think we got switched at birth. You and Grandma Woodrow could be twins."

"You may have more of Grandma in you than you realize, girlfriend. Unleash the dog and see where he leads you."

"I know exactly where. To a big pile of crap." Candace grabbed her tote bag and headed for the door.

On Thursday night, Rachel had bummed twenty bucks before leaving. Michael had given her fifty, figuring her advice would have cost him at least that in a shrink's office.

How could a seventeen-year-old get so smart—and he be so dumb?

On Saturday afternoon, he found himself heading across Boston to Gift Baskets. He should be going into the office to get caught up on the work he'd missed the past few days, but this time he was going to take Rachel's advice. He wasn't going to get a damn thing done until he saw Candace again anyway. She'd invaded his thoughts and wasn't leaving anytime soon.

Especially after that kiss. Their first kiss had been a sweet, spicy taste. But when *she'd* taken the lead . . .

Hell, he might as well get out a fire hose and give himself a bracing cold shower. Because if she did that again, he wasn't sure he'd be able to walk away. Hobble maybe, but certainly not walk.

And, he was beginning to realize, he wasn't so sure he'd want to.

Yet seeing her again only complicated things on her end. And on his. He was treading in water he'd vowed never to swim in. What kind of game was he playing?

Before he could answer that for himself, Candace exited the shop, wearing a simple yellow sundress and short-heeled sandals. Summery and buttery.

Yummy.

Michael parked the Lexus and hopped out. "Hi."

She paused, giving him a curious look. "In the neighborhood? Again?"

He leaned against the car. "No. This time I came by because I wanted to see you."

"Michael, I—"

"I know what you're going to say. You've said it a hundred times already." He pushed off from the car and stepped in front of her. "There are two weeks until you marry another man." He reached up and trailed a finger along her jaw. "Forever is a really long time, Candy."

She swallowed. "I know that."

"Then why not be a hundred percent sure?"

"I already am."

He tipped her chin with his finger and lowered his mouth within kissing distance. Holding himself back from her lips was like stopping a tidal wave from crashing over a beach. But he wouldn't kiss her. Not yet. Not until she wanted it as much as he did. "Oh, yeah? Then why do you tremble when I get close? Why did you kiss me that morning in my apartment? And yesterday? What was that about?"

And why hadn't he been able to get her out of his mind?

Seconds stretched between them, their gazes locked, the tension simmering. "I was curious," she said finally, in a quiet whisper.

"So was I. Is that a bad thing?"

"It could be. It could be very bad."

"And it could not be, too." He stroked her jaw with his thumb. Such soft, delicate skin. Like silk beneath his fingers. Made for touching. Caressing. Tasting. "I'm not asking you to call off your wedding or to break up with Barry or to hightail it to Vegas with me. I just want to spend some time with you."

"You mean, date?"

If Rachel were here, she'd punch him if he didn't admit the truth. "Yeah, that's exactly what I mean."

"I shouldn't date someone else when I'm engaged to another man. It's—"

"It's called being sure before you make the biggest step of your life," he interrupted. "You're a woman who plans everything, who doesn't make a decision without making a pro-and-con list. Why are you not being smart about this?"

And then he saw the answer in her eyes. Because it scared the hell out of her. She didn't want to know that her choice was wrong. That she shouldn't marry Barry. For whatever reason, Candace Woodrow was dead-set on marrying the most boring man on the planet.

He couldn't let her do that. There was so much of her simmering under the surface, and marriage to a man like Barry would push that other side away. Michael knew he should walk away. But something in him—the same something that had been brought to life when he'd seen her sleeping in his bed—kept him rooted to the spot.

He picked up her hand. "Let's start with today. Cross the rest of the bridges later," he said. "Just deal with now."

"I can't." She pulled her hand out of his and gestured down the sidewalk. "I'm on my way someplace."

Don't leave yet. Don't walk away from me.

"Then I'll go with you," Michael said.

"I doubt you'd want to go where I'm going. It's not exactly exciting."

"Hey, I went dress shopping with you. I can handle whatever you throw my way."

She smirked, as if she was in on a joke he didn't know. "Are you sure?"

"I'm game if you are." He didn't care if she was on her way to get her nails painted pink and purple. As long as it meant being with her, he would go along for the ride.

She was such a contradiction, this woman who said she wanted one thing and so clearly wanted another. He could see the other side of her lurking under that teasing smile, itching to get out.

"You asked for it." She started walking, her heels making little clicks against the concrete.

He pointed to the Lexus. "Don't you want to take my car?"

"Nope." She grinned again. "It's not far."

He fell into step beside her. "What isn't?"

"It's a surprise."

"I like surprises. And I like how you are right now."

"What do you mean?"

"The way you're smiling. Having fun. It's like the first day of spring." When she turned to look at him, he touched the dimple in her cheek. "And I like it."

"Plenty of women smile. Laugh. Have fun."

The lunchtime crowd skirted them, parting like a school of fish around an anchor. He stared into her hazel eyes. "You're *not* plenty of other women. You're smart yet vulnerable. Sassy"—he touched the tip of her nose—"but genuine. You're a jigsaw puzzle waiting for someone to align the pieces right."

"And you think *you* are that person?"

His hand trailed down to toy with her fingers. "I'd like the chance to find out."

She didn't respond. Instead, she started walking again, glancing at him as they rounded a corner. "You know an awful lot about me, but I know almost nothing about you. It's your turn to share."

He fingered the buttons on his shirt, grinning. "Do you want a show-and-tell?"

"Just the tell will be fine, thank you very much."

"Pity."

A teenager with an orange Mohawk came striding down the sidewalk in combat boots. His head jiggled along with the MP3 player in his ears, little silver hoops shaking in his brows and nose. "Dude," he said, then brushed right between them.

"Is that teen for 'Excuse me'?" Candace asked.

"Not where I grew up."

"And where was that, Mr. Strong-and-silent type?"

"I thought women liked that. You know, men who don't talk much, but listen well to shopping woes."

"Maybe other women, but not me. I'm a fan of two-way conversations."

"That's refreshing," he said. "Okay, my résumé's short and sweet. I grew up in the Berkshires. I'm the older of two children. My parents are wealthy and bored unless they're buying something. My kid sister is seventeen, smart as hell, and a rebel with too many causes to keep straight. Me, I've owned my advertising agency for nine years and have built it from a one-man firm to a company with about seventy employees."

"A rich kid, huh?"

"Believe me, in the ways that count, I'm not rich." He ran a hand through his hair.

"What does that mean?"

"Nothing."

"Oh, I see. You can analyze my life, but when it comes to yours, it's another story."

"There's not much to analyze. I live alone with a dog for company. No kids, no wife, no mortgage. I have a few fine things, but not the closets-full my parents have. To me, it doesn't matter how many Mercedes you can park in the garage."

She paused and glanced at him. "Then why are you a confirmed bachelor?"

"Ah, there's the conflict." He grinned. "Gotta have one; everybody does."

"That doesn't answer the question."

He let out a gust. "I want what I'm not good at."

"You should meet my mother. Although she's the opposite—a serial marrier."

"You make it sound like a crime."

"In her case, I think it should be."

He chuckled. "Maybe she hasn't found Mr. Right yet."

"And maybe you haven't found Ms. Right." She circumvented a mother with a baby carriage. "What makes you think you're so bad at commitment and relationships?"

"I've been there. And I'm good for a while, then I start to get this . . . penned-in feeling, like I'm stuck in a coffin. And I undermine my own good thing."

"Well, that's pretty stupid."

"Easy for you to say."

"Why don't you try to tough it out? Stick with a woman long enough to see if that feeling goes away? Or is there more to your fear than you realize?"

She'd hit close to the mark. It was exactly what he'd been asking himself lately. He didn't have any answers for himself, either. "How much Dr. Phil are you watching?"

She laughed. "I'm a girl. We love to analyze guys."

"Well, guys just like to watch girls."

Maybe it was the sunshine, or the conversation, but suddenly Candace didn't feel like playing it safe anymore. He'd opened up a little to her and she felt a little more open, too, as if a door between them had been unlocked.

"Then watch this." She sashayed in front of him, hips swinging, exaggerating the movement. She whirled around, her hair swinging around her face. The surprise in his eyes was worth every step. "Get a good enough view?"

"Almost. Could you do that again?"

"Not on your life." She fell into step beside him again. "That's a once-in-a-lifetime view." And probably a big mistake, but it had felt very, very good. Like something a whole other Candace would do.

Something *Candy* would do.

He reached over and took her hand in his, the touch coming as a surprise, and yet feeling as comfortable as a warm shower at the end of a long day. "What are you doing?"

"Holding your hand."

"Why?"

"Because I want to. And because I'm afraid you might run off on me."

"I'm not going anywhere."

"Because you've decided to try this dating thing with me?"

She laughed. "No, because we're here." She gestured to a small steel door on the narrow, shadowed side street. Above it was a sign that read LINCOLN HOMELESS SHELTER. Beneath that was another sign categorizing the building as a men's residence shelter. A tacked-on paper sign noted a free lunch several afternoons a week. Candace reached for the handle and twisted the knob.

His hand covered hers. "You want to go in here?"

She turned a sweet smile on him. "Oh yes, very much."

"With me?" Michael surveyed their surroundings. A dumpster sat a few feet from the door, trash bags spilling past the lid. The odor of garbage and molding concrete hung heavy in the air. Twenty feet away, a man slept on the sidewalk, balled up against the brickwork, missing a shoe but clutching an empty wine bottle. "Are you sure you have the right place?"

Candace smiled and put her hand on the small of his back, pulling him closer to the battered door. "This is *exactly* where I want to be with you right now."

"But . . . what are we doing *here?*"

"Working. You said you wanted to be with me, and this is where I was going. I didn't think you'd mind volunteering some of your time to help me."

He reached past her, putting a hand on the door, preventing her from opening it yet. "Let's get one thing clear," he said, grinning. "I don't mind helping you and I don't mind being here. What I do mind . . ." He leaned down, closing the gap between them. "What I do mind," he repeated, "is being tempted and then not finishing what we started."

"I never said—"

"You didn't have to."

"I was only teasing you."

"I'm not a man who's happy with only a taste of ecstasy." He leaned forward, touching his lips briefly to her forehead, then again to her mouth, before pulling back. "I want more, Candy. Much more. I have a feeling you'd like to try the whole entree as much as I would."

She blinked, but not before he saw the war between desire and conscience in her gaze. "I . . . I already ate today."

He trailed a finger down her cheek. "Doesn't look like it was anything of substance."

She shook her head. "Just chocolate."

"That's no way to live." He picked up her left hand, holding the diamond in front of them. Slivers of light glinted off the pear-shaped stone in a hundred directions. "A little stressed?"

"Wouldn't you be?"

He chuckled. "I'd have already run for the hills."

"I bet you would have." She removed his hand from the door. "I think that means we've come to an impasse. Time to get to work." She turned, opened the door and stepped inside the building.

Grandma's Taste-of-Love Chocolate Syrup

2 squares unsweetened chocolate
⅓ cup water
½ cup sugar
3 tablespoons butter
¼ teaspoon vanilla

Microwave the chocolate and water in a microwaveable bowl on high for 1 1/2 minutes. Why? Because you sure as hell don't have all day to stand around and wait for love, that's why. When chocolate is melted, add the sugar and microwave for one more minute. Stir. Pop it back into the nuke machine for another two minutes, then add the butter and vanilla. *Voila!* Chocolate sauce is done.

You *could* serve this over ice cream like boring people do. Me, I prefer to serve it over a sexy guy. Make *him* dessert and you'll know why I call it my taste of love syrup.

CHAPTER 17

Candace clearly wasn't going to continue the conversation about them finishing what they'd started. And if Michael did, he'd be going down a road he'd done a damn good job of avoiding most of his life.

He told himself to be grateful for the change in topic. He wasn't a man who liked attachments. So why was he fighting Candace's determination not to have anything between them? He should have been happy as a humpback whale in the middle of the Atlantic.

What did he want? Hell, he was as bad as she was. He'd accused Candy of choosing the wrong path, and yet he seemed hell-bent on staying on the same rutted one himself.

So he took the bachelor male's favorite course—dropped the subject and followed her. But a little twinge of disappointment churned in his stomach all the same.

They went down three steps and into a room buzzing with activity. The room had green walls, pale tile, and a long line of people holding plastic bowls and spoons, all winding along in a zigzag to a set of tables. Steaming pots of soup sat inside chafing dishes while stacks of sandwiches filled nearby platters.

Despite the warm June weather, most of the people were dressed in layers of threadbare, ill-fitting clothes. They waited with patience, some chatting with others they knew, some quiet and sullen. A few were having a rousing debate with themselves.

He noticed two men missing legs; another missing an arm; and a few with glazed, lost looks in their eyes and emaciated bodies that spoke of drug abuse and lives of despair. Everyone's story was different. But the one thing they all had in common was that none had a home.

The adults didn't bother him as much as the children. One thin blond girl—she couldn't have been more than six—held tight to her mother's hand, her green eyes wide and round. In her other hand, she clutched a stuffed bear. Most of its fur had worn away, leaving great empty patches of pale cloth where brown tufts had once been.

Part of him wanted to run across the room, scoop up that little girl and take her to every store in the city, showering her with toys, clothes and food. He watched her move along in the line with her mother and thought of all the experiences she must be missing: playing in a schoolyard, opening presents on Christmas morning, making French toast on Sunday mornings. All the things normal children's lives included. And yet, he'd grown up wealthy, and without any of those traditional family joys, too.

He'd never used the wealth that had come attached to the Vogler name. He'd made a living on his own, without the benefit of a trust fund. But for the past nine years, most of the money he'd earned had been sitting in a bank somewhere, collecting interest and not doing anyone a damn bit of good.

That was going to change.

"It's a pretty gruesome sight, isn't it?" Candace said, leading him over to the tables. "I've been volunteering here for two years, and you know what? Every time I walk in here, it tears my heart out."

Before Michael could answer, a short man with a white beard trailing down nearly to his waist hurried up to them. *"Shalom,* Candace!" He gathered her up in both his arms, giving her a warm, tight hug that she returned with equal affection. His battered brown cloak flowed behind him with the movement.

Candace laughed. "You taking care of yourself, Rabbi?"

"As best I can. The Lord's been good to me this week." He gave her a broad smile.

"You always say that."

"Because I always see the bright side of life." He gave her hand a squeeze. "Thanks for coming to help." Then he bustled away, humming to himself.

"I've never seen a guy so cheerful, especially living like this."

"Jerry was a rabbi, until he lost his way, as he says, and became an alcoholic. He lost his synagogue and his home. For a while, he was a resident at the shelter until he got himself back on his feet. Now he works here, helping other people and counseling some of the residents," Candace explained. "People listen to him because he's been down their road before, and still stays positive. And sober."

Hell, that could be almost anyone Michael knew, he realized. For a lot of people, only a few paychecks, a breakdown or an addiction separated them from those who filled this room. It was a scary thought.

"For some people, having nothing isn't as depressing as it seems," she continued. "To them, just seeing a friend is a gift." Candace reached for an apron off the pile on the table and began fastening it around her waist. "I like to work here because it reminds me of what's important."

"And what's that?"

"Family. Friends." She shrugged. "Not material possessions."

"Sounds like a damn good philosophy to me."

"It's the one I try to stick to, anyway." She turned away and called over to a group of people she knew.

Seeing Candace among these people, the ones whom everyone else seemed to ignore—hugging them, greeting them, asking about their pets, their friends and their lives—was a galaxy away from the world he'd always known.

At that moment, Michael's interest in Candace went from garden-variety attraction into something much, much more. She wasn't just bright and pretty. She was someone who put actions behind her words, who knew what was truly important. A woman whose heart was her most attractive asset.

No wonder she was engaged. She was the kind of woman a man married. Had kids with. Planned trips to Disney and Myrtle Beach with. Not a woman a man slept with and walked away from.

That was the kind of commitment he'd avoided all his life. In his circle of friends, and in his screwed-up family, he'd never seen a relationship that had worked. Most of the marriages were more business matches, it seemed, than lifetime love matches. He wasn't sure that kind of thing existed—or if he even knew how to make a relationship like that work.

He could run a business, but making a life with someone—well, that was another story. And yet, for the first time, he found himself wondering what it would be like to be the man who had put that ring on Candace's finger.

Damn, his sister could read him like a book. She'd known before he did.

Want for Candace—a very deep, visceral kind of longing, started to grow inside. But, oh, he was treading on some very dangerous ground. To have her might risk breaking her heart.

What the hell kind of man did that?

"Are you ready to get your hands dirty?" She'd left the group and now returned to wave him over to the table where the other volunteers were serving up bowls of chicken noodle, vegetable, and beef and barley soup. A little farther down the table were heaps of peanut butter sandwiches. Candace stepped back and gave him an appraising glance. "I think the pink will fit you just fine."

"Pink what?"

Candace grinned. "Apron. Wouldn't want you ruining that nice three-piece suit." She patted the breast pocket of his Brooks Brothers jacket, then reached into the pile of aprons behind him, pulled out a hot-pink apron and tied it around his waist before he could protest.

He leaned over to whisper in her ear, close enough to taste the delicate lobe. He wanted so much more of her. But not now, not here. "Revenge can be very sweet."

She fumbled with the bow. "You're making me mess it up."

"Oh, that's too bad."

She gave him a look that said she knew he was about as contrite as a cabbie playing highway Frogger on I-93. "Now, hold—"

"Well, hello. Who do we have here?" A redheaded woman strode over to them. She was tall, but not overly thin, and her green apron strained against her chest. "Hi, Candace."

Candace gave up on the bow and came around him to introduce them. "Denise, this is Michael Vogler. Michael, this is Denise Meyers. She's in charge of the shelter and coordinates the volunteers." She turned to the other woman. "Michael is here to help today."

"Oh, wonderful!" Denise smiled and pressed a hand to her hair. "I'm sure we can find *something* for you to do. Maybe you could help me move those big, heavy bowls over to the table."

"I'd be glad to," Michael said. "Just point me in the right direction."

Denise did, with a little flourish and a big smile. Michael

dutifully headed toward the kitchen. Denise followed his every step with her gaze, like a little laser beam right on his butt.

Candace withdrew a barrette from her pocket and slipped it around her hair, pulling the long strands back from her face. She didn't care that Denise had eyed Michael with all the greedy interest of the Red Sox general manager at the first round draft picks.

Not one bit.

As soon as Michael was out of sight, Denise turned to Candace. "Whoo! I can see why you're marrying *him*. Lord, he's hot."

"He's not my fiancé." Barry had never come to the shelter with her. He'd always found one excuse after another not to be here when it came time to dole out the soup. He supported the shelter with regular tax-deductible donations. But Michael . . . he had donned the pink apron and pitched in without a complaint. *It's a sign,* Grandma's voice sang in her head.

It's a sign I'm going crazy, that's what it is.

"So, who is he?" Denise asked.

"He's . . ." Candace dug in her pocket and managed to find a chocolate mint. "Just a friend." She unwrapped the candy and shoved it into her mouth before she could explain anything more. "Friend" didn't define Michael, but she wasn't about to get out a thesaurus for Denise.

"Oh, *really?*"

Michael had exited the kitchen and stopped to put on a pair of gloves that had been offered to him by one of the staff members.

Denise took a second, much more appraising, look at him. She puffed up the ends of her hair and licked her lips. "Is he available?"

Candace could lie. Give him a wife, two kids, a pet iguana, a house in Somerville, a Range Rover . . . "No, he's single."

Damn her conscience anyway.

"Well then, I should make him feel welcome!" Denise darted to Michael's side, and within seconds, had her hands on his hips, ostensibly tying his apron for him.

Candace crossed to the tureen of chicken noodle and tried not to stare. But it was like watching a car wreck. Or a Madonna movie. She couldn't tear her gaze away, no matter how horrible it was to see.

Denise lingered a little too long behind Michael, like a bulldog over a new bone. She took way too much time fussing over the apron and touched his body far too much in the process. *How damned hard is it to tie a bow?*

Well, she hadn't been able to manage it. But he'd distracted her with all that flirting. She watched the two of them talk, their faces animated, friendly. Apparently, she wasn't the only one who'd fallen prey to his charms. Michael laughed at something Denise said and she reached over, her hand lingering on his arm with all the possessiveness of an apostrophe "s".

"Hey! Where'd they get you? Klutzes 'R' Us?"

Candace jerked her attention away from the romantic tableau to her left. An irate man stood in front of her, glaring. Little bits of chicken, celery and noodles dripped down the front of his shirt, across the table, slowly spreading in a puddle on the floor. "Oh! I'm so sorry!" She grabbed a cloth and started to mop up the mess with one hand while dabbing at the man's clothes with a napkin in her other.

"Never mind." He brushed her hand away with a grunt. "It gives me a snack for later, anyway." She refilled his bowl and he stomped off, muttering about the quality of help these days.

From that point on, Candace made a point of conversing with many of the people who came through her line, hoping it would help her concentrate on the soup, not on the tall man whose voice seemed to carry over the hubbub of the busy room.

Even though she didn't turn her head to look, she could

hear Denise and Michael's laughter, spurting out between bursts of conversation. They were working the front of the line, dispensing bowls and spoons and putting out new tureens as needed. Candace's chest tightened and her gut twisted every time she heard them laugh.

Either she was coming down with West Nile or she was . . . Jealous.

Impossible. Michael wasn't hers to begin with. He had a right to flirt with anyone he wanted to. She should be glad. After all, if he became interested in Denise, he'd stop messing with Candace's heart. And she could go back to marrying Barry in peace.

But she wasn't glad. At all.

The line trickled to a couple of people. Jerry came up to her as she started the cleanup, offering a helping hand. "Love is in the air; it's so romantic," he sang. He stirred the soup spoon into the chicken soup like it was doing a ballet, swooped up the bits of chicken and noodle, then dropped them into the waiting bowl of Kenny, who had come for thirds. "Strangers in the night, exchanging glances . . ." He paused, lowered the ladle to the bowl and turned to Candace. "Dance with me, Candace."

"I'm not the best partner."

"Doesn't matter." He turned her around in a humming spin, then went back to his work.

She laughed. "What has you all worked up today?"

"Love, my dear. The most ancient of God's gifts."

"Love? I thought you gave up on all that. Didn't you tell me last month that Jewish people are supposed to suffer?"

"Pshaw," he waved a hand at her. "Not when there's love to be celebrated."

"How do you know if it's love?"

"Ah, she's my soul mate. I feel it in my heart."

Candace moved down the line and started wrapping up the extra sandwiches. "You believe in all that?"

"Of course I do. Meeting her was preordained." He laid a

hand on Candace's. "God always leads you to the right one, if you listen to your heart."

She prodded at the pile of bread, straightening it. "And where does it say that in the Bible?"

"Well, it doesn't, not exactly. You know the word of God. It's about as precise as a buffalo in the Philharmonic orchestra pit. But God made Adam as the perfect man for Eve. One man, one woman."

Candace snorted. "Jerry, if God had put a Bennigan's and a few eligible males in Eden, I bet Eve would have found more than one soul mate over a Coors Light."

"Ah, you are too jaded, my dear. When people believe they will find the right one, they do." He gave her a slight jab with his elbow and cocked his head toward Michael. "Isn't that your intended?"

"Oh, no. I . . . I just work with him."

Jerry gave her a look. "Are you sure about that?"

"Of course."

"I don't know. I feel love in the air."

She rolled her eyes and went back to the sandwiches. "That's the fan blowing the hot air around."

Jerry shook his head. "Tsk, tsk. True love is blocked by negative thoughts."

"Since when did they incorporate feng shui into the Jewish faith?"

His laughter was deep and hearty, the kind that said Jerry lived life from his gut. Then he glanced at the doorway, stopped, and pressed a hand to his heart. "Ah, I see my Lucy has arrived."

"*Lucy* is the one you're in love with?" Candace glanced at the uniformed female officer who often provided security for the shelter on her off-duty hours. She stood on the top step, all boxy and stern. But when her plain face met Jerry's, it lit for a brief, privileged smile.

"She's a strong woman," Jerry said. "And Lord knows I need a strong woman to keep me in line and away from my vices." He gave his beard a thoughtful stroke. "Weakness is what made me descend into this hellhole in the first place."

"I bet you were an interesting rabbi." Candace gave his shoulder a squeeze.

"Ah, I provided a lot for the temple to gossip about, but not much leadership, I'm afraid. Now, though, with love in my life, I'm changing." He let out a sigh. "Taking risks, saving money, having hope for an even better life. It's a brand-new day every time I see my Lucy's face."

Taking risks. Geez, that seemed to be the message of the week. Everywhere Candace went, someone was telling her to take a risk. Maybe if she signed up for a bungee-jumping course, they'd all get off her back. Or heck, she could jump off theirs.

Now *there* was a thought.

She was getting hysterical again. Maybe one of the guys singing "Goodnight Irene" at the corner table would have a paper bag she could use.

As if pulled over by the word "risk," Michael appeared at her side, the pink apron still tied around his blue pin-striped waist. "Need some help?"

"Candace needs some company. I'm off to woo a woman." Jerry tipped an imaginary hat, then made his exit.

One of the other volunteers dropped off a plastic container and Candace started spooning the leftover soup into the bowl. "I've got it under control," she told Michael. "Go back to your little conversation."

He laid a hand over hers, immediately setting off an electrical storm inside her skin. "Are you mad at me?"

The heat coiling between them could have boiled the chicken noodle. No need for a chafing dish at this end of the table. "No, not at all. You and Denise can go finish whatever you were 'working' on." She couldn't keep the sarcasm from her voice no matter how hard she tried.

"Are you jealous?"

"Of what?" She topped off the plastic container, laid it on

the counter behind her and turned to grab the disinfectant spray and a rag from one of the other tables.

"Of me talking to Denise."

"Talk to whomever you want." She sprayed orange cleanser on the table, then wiped it off in furious little circles. "It doesn't bother me."

"Uh-huh." He moved several dishes out of her way, clearing them as fast as she moved down the table sections. Then he stopped, laid the dishes down and stood in front of her.

"You're in my way."

"On purpose."

"You're supposed to be helping." She started in on the table again. "Go find something to do."

"No."

She stopped wiping the table and looked up at him. "No?"

"I have a better idea. Let's go shopping."

"Shopping?"

"While I was talking to Denise—and you thought I was flirting with her," he said, grinning, "I was finding out what the shelter needs, which is pretty much everything. We spent two hours here helping, but I feel like we didn't even make a dent in the problem. I want to do more." His gaze traveled over the room, lighting on the young girl and her mother, who'd remained behind to help with cleanup. For a long moment, he didn't say anything. "Help a few more people."

The room buzzed with activity around them, as people chatted over the remnants of their meals before heading out the door, back to the streets, to jobs, some staying behind at the shelter. "You surprise me," she said.

"Good." He took the cleaning cloth out of her hands and placed it on the table. "Now, let's go shopping."

She smiled. "If more men said those words, there'd be a lot more happy women on earth."

* * *

"That was fun." Michael held the door for her as they exited the shelter for a second time later that afternoon, after dropping off thousands of dollars in supplies and gifts.

She quirked a brow. "Fun? For a guy?"

"Well, yeah. I've never done anything like that before."

"Why not?"

The question threw him. Why hadn't he? All those years of complaining about being in a wealthy family, all the comments criticizing excess and ridiculous purchases. Why hadn't he done something real instead of only talk about charity? "I'm not exactly sure. I guess it's not the first thing you think of."

"It's easier to send a few bucks to the Salvation Army before the tax loophole closes, isn't it?" She bit her lip. "I'm sorry. That was harsh. I was out of line."

"No, you're right. It's easier to write a check than dish up a bowl of soup. Easier to throw money at the problem than see it face to face."

"That's part of why there's such a problem."

"True."

They walked along in silence for a moment, their shoes making soft twin patters against the sidewalk. They had dropped off the blankets, pillows, clothing and other supplies they'd bought and had arranged for delivery of several dozen new mattresses tomorrow. Michael had insisted on buying presents for some of the people he'd met, including a suit for Jerry to wear when he took Lucy out for dinner or went on job interviews. Jerry had proudly modeled his finery, then boxed it with all the care of a new mother handling a preemie.

"It was sweet what you did for Ginny." Candace smiled again, remembering the smile of the child when Michael had presented her with the toy.

He shrugged. "It was nothing."

"To her it meant a lot. Telling her the new bear was a

friend for her old bear and then buying a coat to keep the old bear warm." Candace touched his shoulder. "You knew, didn't you?"

"Knew what?"

"That you couldn't replace the one she had." She let her hand remain on his arm. "You must have had a teddy bear when you were a kid, huh?"

The sky darkened and a soft rain began to fall. Michael cleared his throat, leaving the question unanswered. He'd had bears, and everything a kid could have asked for, but none of his possessions had ever meant as much to him as that one stuffed animal did to that little girl. He'd thought her childhood was lacking. Now he realized his had been. Maybe more than hers. "We should get inside."

"I like the rain. It's not too heavy. Let's walk."

They strode along, one of a handful of people out in the lumbering shower. "I've never done this, either."

"What?"

"Purposely walked in the rain."

She laughed. "What, do you live in an envelope?"

"Seems like it." When Michael grinned at her, she returned the smile. Something warm settled in his gut. He liked this. He liked her. More than just casual like, too. "And here I thought I was so cultured."

"Don't look at me for culture. I have trouble telling Chianti from Lambrusco. That's why I stick with tequila."

"Smart woman. Wine can give you a killer headache."

"So can tequila," she pointed out.

"Ah, but the fun leading up to the headache is worth it."

A faint blush crept into her cheeks. He could only hope she was remembering their tequila-inspired night together. They hadn't rounded any bases together, but seeing her in his bed, so angelic and sweet, he'd felt like he had when he'd hit a home run in high school baseball years earlier. Good. Satisfied. Fulfilled.

He reached out and took her hand in his, a move as easy and natural as if they had been together for years. "I'm not good with wine, either."

Candace tipped her jaw to catch a raindrop in her mouth. "Then we'll never go to Europe together."

"Agreed."

Her joke with the word "we" in it was something he liked. A lot. She hadn't let go of his hand, which he took as a good sign. A very good sign. The air bristled with humidity and electricity. Between them, the same sizzling hummed, growing with the feel of her delicate hand in his.

It was only five fingers and a palm. But together they felt like an erotic tool designed to take his mind down paths he'd never traveled.

They came to a crosswalk and he pulled her against him. She collided against his chest, stumbling a bit. He caught her with his free arm. "Candy, I really had fun today." His palm cupped her chin, thumb tracing her lip.

She gulped. "You already said that."

"I don't want the day to end. Don't go back to the shop. Don't go anywhere but with me."

"I—"

He pressed a finger to her lips. "Don't. Don't say it. Take the day off." He closed the remaining distance between them. "Live dangerously."

"I already am," she breathed.

He ran the back of his hand along her cheek. It was soft as a feather. His fingertips brushed against tender, pale skin. Her eyes widened and she inhaled a sharp whistle of air. "You can't live dangerously if you still keep your seat belt on."

"Michael—"

She was cut off by the storm, which, held in abatement for too long, now started gushing with a sudden rumble from the clouds. Rain let loose around them in a steady stream, slapping against the pavement and streaming down their faces.

"Come on!" He grasped her hand tighter and they dashed forward, running the last couple of blocks to his car, which was still parked in front of Gift Baskets to Die For.

They piled inside and he turned on the engine, putting the Lexus in gear before she could change her mind and head into the shop. "Let's go get dried off," he said.

"Where?"

He turned and looked at her heart-shaped face. Want pounded in his veins, louder than a Rolling Stones concert, more insistently than the early morning nudges of Sam. She was dripping wet, bare of makeup and dressed in nothing more complicated than a pale yellow sundress, and he wanted her like he'd never wanted anything in his life. "My bathtub."

Candace's Taste-of-Sin Chocolate-Caramel Apples

5 small apples
5 wooden sticks
7 ounces of caramels
7 ounces semisweet chocolate
¼ cup heavy cream
1 cup chopped pecans

Yes, these are the same things that got Eve into all that trouble. But when they're dipped in chocolate, they work better than a fig leaf at covering up the worst of your foibles. Insert a stick into the stem end of each apple. Then, in a saucepan, combine the chocolate, caramels and cream, heating over low until they're melted and smooth as the snake's voice. Now dip the apples and coat them well. Double-dip them for extra flavor, if you want. Roll them in the pecans, then place dipped on wax paper. Chill until ready to serve.

Warning: one taste of this sinful treat and you'll definitely be back for seconds. Put the guilt on the backburner until you're done tasting the temptation. I guarantee eating this won't get you into quite the same trouble as Eve did.

CHAPTER 18

Oh, this was a bad idea. A very, very bad idea.

But Candace didn't ask him to stop or turn around or call the dumb mistakes police. Instead, she listened to the heat swirling in her gut, the tightening, twisting need that had roared to life when he'd said the word "bathtub."

She didn't say anything on the ride over to his apartment, afraid of what might come out if she did say something. She wasn't a stupid woman. She knew where this was leading.

And half of her wanted it anyway. They'd been playing this game for days now, with each moment together raising the stakes like a poker game with professionals who were determined to take the whole pot home.

What about Barry?

She looked down at the ring on her finger.

What about me?

What if everyone was right? What if she married Barry and always wondered, "What if?" How horrible was it to be with Michael for one afternoon?

Well, it was probably the kind of horrible that would land her on the *Maury Povich Show* later in life. Best not to think about tomorrow. That philosophy had worked for Scarlett O'Hara and Della.

Of course, their lives were a complete mess.

"We're here." He parked the car, but didn't get out. "If you don't want to come in, I can take you to your house."

"I want to . . . and I don't." She ran a hand through her hair. "I don't know what I want."

He chuckled. "Join the club. All I do know is I don't want today to end." He took her hand in his. "Where it goes from here is completely up to you."

"Well, I know I don't want to sit here in the car in my wet clothes and get all musty."

He chuckled. "That's a first step. And we can take just that one if you want." He opened his door, got out of the car and then came around to open her door.

From her vantage point behind him, she watched Michael walk up his stairs and into the building. Here was a hot, sexy, incredible man who wanted her. No strings attached. Nothing to worry about tomorrow. He didn't want a commitment. He'd made that pretty damn clear. It was the kind of sex men dreamed about every four seconds, according to the survey in *Cosmo*. Why not women, too?

Why couldn't she have one last fling? Get rid of those doubts once and for all—those questions that had been lingering in the back of her mind for so many years, ever since that summer at her father's lake house. There'd been so many "What ifs" that Candace had kept quiet. Too many. And if she married Barry with those still swirling in her mind, could she ever truly be happy with him? Or would she always wonder what the grass looked like on the neighbor's side of the fence?

Michael paused inside the lobby of his apartment building. He turned and looked at her, bending down as if he were about to kiss her, then withdrawing. He held her gaze a moment longer, then turned away, but the heat still held in the air between them. "I, ah, I should probably get the mail." He reached to insert his key into one of the brass boxes that lined the wall. When he did, a little muscle flexed in his arm.

It was a small movement, but enough of one to turn the switch inside Candace's brain from "maybe" to "oh, yeah."

"Screw the damn mail." She stepped forward, grabbed his shirt and turned him around to face her, tugging his face down so she could kiss him. His brows rose in surprise and he took one step back, colliding with the mailbox wall.

Good. Something for traction. She pressed herself against the length of his body and kissed the hell out of him. Their kiss started out soft at first, his hands tangling in her hair, lifting and releasing. Then harder, the need sparking in each of them, fueled by the long day together, the hours spent shopping and laughing, the unspoken possibilities between them.

"What . . . what the hell was that?" he asked when she let him come up for air.

She grinned. "I'm hungry."

"I don't think there's anything in my fridge. I'm not much of a homebody. I can get some take out—"

Her fingers teased along his hairline. "I'm hungry for something else."

"I might have a—" He stopped. "You're not talking about food at all, are you?"

She shook her head.

"What about—"

"I don't want any questions. I don't want to talk about this. I just want to have sex."

"Uh . . . uh . . . okay." He nodded. Very quickly.

Her smile widened. "Good."

Michael, she realized, could move pretty damn fast for a guy in shock.

Michael barely got his door unlocked. He and Candace kissed their way up the stairs, hands roaming, clothing coming untucked. At his door, he fumbled with the keys, nearly dropping them. Twice. Then he got inside, shut the door, and managed to lock it while she fingered his buttons and got his shirt undone and off. She dropped her tote bag to the floor, the contents spilling on the hardwood floor. Neither of them stopped. Or cared.

Sam came over to greet them, saw his master was otherwise engaged and plodded back to his dog bed and Nylabone. Michael had a vague thought of apologizing to poor Sam later with a warehouse-sized box of Milk Bones.

And then the thought was gone. Candace's tongue was doing acrobatics in his mouth and his brain short-circuited.

Here he'd always imagined this big seduction scene. Move slow and easy, tease her until she was begging for him. Because he sure as hell had been wanting her since the moment she'd spilled her chowder on him and then apologized so nicely.

But he'd been wrong about Candace Woodrow. Nice wasn't how he'd describe her right now.

Hot, demanding and consumed with a passion to have him. Yeah, those were better adjectives.

She had his shirt out of his pants, her hands beneath the fabric, nails scratching lightly against his skin, awakening nerve endings, sending little screams of desire into his groin. Never had he been with a woman so aggressive. Who seemed to want him more than she wanted to breathe. The thought of it caused a heady rush of desire in him and he surged forward, sliding the straps of her dress down her shoulders, then the straps of her bra, slipping his hands into the cups and lifting her enchanting, perfect breasts out and into his palms.

She moaned, her head falling back, mouth open, eyes closed. He thumbed her nipples in tiny, tight circles and Candace squirmed her pelvis against his. His erection went stone hard, and he almost lost control right there in his front hall.

Then she jerked her head forward and grabbed at his

head, pulling it down to her breasts. He obliged her demands, tasting the sweetness of her skin, teasing at the tips, hearing her gasps and feeling like he would die inside if he didn't have her right now.

He pulled back, wrestled with the last couple of buttons on her dress, then finally managed to get enough of it undone that it fell to the floor in a puddle at her feet. Beneath it, she wore tiny lace panties, so sheer they were nearly transparent.

Oh, God.

He lowered himself to his knees and trailed kisses along her abdomen. Then he hooked a finger into each side of the string bikini and eased it down, one centimeter at a time, watching her face as he did. She bucked a little, clearly in agony with want and impatience. "If you don't get those goddamn things off me now, I swear—"

"What?" He grinned. "What'll you do?"

"I'll . . ." She took a moment to inhale. "I'll make you wait. And tease you until you can't breathe." She lowered her mouth to his, swept her tongue inside, then nipped at his bottom lip, sucking at it for one long, sweet second before releasing him and holding his gaze very, very steady. "Until you beg to fuck me."

Hearing *that* word out of her mouth was the last straw for him. His brain exploded with desire, every nerve in his body screaming for her.

He tugged at her panties, and she stepped out of them as quickly as he slid them down her legs. He tossed them to the side, then stood, moving to his release his own pants.

"I'll do that, thank you very much." She gave him a teasing grin. "You keep your little hands busy. Right where they were."

He didn't move for a second. "Did I pick up the wrong woman somewhere along the way?"

"Didn't expect this side of me, did you?"

"Hell, no."

She undid the clasp of his belt and yanked it out of the loops with all the drama of David Copperfield. "Guess I've been holding myself back for a long time."

He cupped her face with his hands. "Before we go any farther and while I can still think . . . are you sure?"

"I want you." She dropped his belt to the floor. The buckle hit the wood with a clatter. "You don't want anything else out of me but this, right?"

A tiny flicker of disappointment ran through him. Just sex. Any man in his right mind would give up his left arm and his retirement account to get that. He'd had plenty of no-strings-attached sex. Women who wanted a good time in bed, a partner for a night or two, and not much more.

But for the first time in his life, the thought of that sounded almost . . . empty. How crazy was that? It was the exact thing he'd been telling her he wanted. Against his cheek, he could feel her diamond, which had spun around her finger. Just sex. Nothing more. Because she belonged to someone else. "Yeah, that's all."

"Good. Then stop talking." His zipper went down, his pants fell to the floor and before he knew it, he was naked, carrying her into his bedroom and leaving coherent, sensible thoughts back in the living room.

Maria's Lose-Your-Mind Chocolate and Rum Mousse

6 ounces semisweet chocolate, chopped
1 ½ cups heavy cream, divided
3 tablespoons rum

He's damned good at what he does, isn't he? Well, show your appreciation, girlfriend, by making him a dessert to remember. You don't want to be gone from bed too long, so make it delicious . . . and make it fast.

Melt the chocolate and three tablespoons of the cream in a double boiler, then add the rum and remove it from the heat. Let it cool for, oh, fifteen minutes, long enough to get his motor running again.

Beat the remaining cream in a separate chilled bowl until stiff, but not dry, peaks form. Get that mind out of the gutter. I'm talking about the dessert here. Really, I am.

Fold the whipped cream into the chocolate. Gentle; don't want your peaks to fall. Spoon into four dessert dishes: Two for now. Two for *later*. Top with any extra whipped cream.

Serve in bed so you can get back to your own little dessert-making sooner.

CHAPTER 19

Michael didn't disappoint her. Sex with him was mindless, intense. He used every ounce of his body to please her, tasting, feeling, then sliding along her and slipping into her with an expertise that made it seem as if he'd memorized her body. The first time she came, she nearly wept.

"What?" He paused, catching a single teardrop on her cheek with his fingertip.

"Nothing. It's . . . it's been a long time since . . . Well, since I had one of those."

"Oh, Candy." His smile was so, so tender, it forced the tears into her eyes again. The smile turned to a grin. "Then let me make you do it again."

And he did. Three times more before he finally climaxed with her in a swirling torrent that seemed to blur the room and him and her into something she couldn't recognize. Stars exploded in her mind and she arched her back beneath him, clawing at him, wishing she could hold onto that feeling for the rest of her life.

And then it was over. The stars twinkled for a few long seconds, then her heartbeat slowed. And she came back to earth.

Sex with Barry had *never* been like this. Not even on the good days when his stamina was at its highest.

She stretched along the bed, replete and utterly satisfied. Michael had reached places, touched parts of her, that she hadn't even known existed. Was it because it was forbidden sex? With a man who wasn't her fiancé?

Or did it mean something more?

Candace refused to spoil the afterglow with analysis. Later . . .

Yes, later she'd deal with all of this.

Michael left the bedroom only long enough to order some Chinese food to be delivered, then he climbed back into the four-poster and pulled her into his arms, kissing at her hair. He trailed a hand along her chest, down her abdomen—a light, tender touch that seemed almost reverent. "You surprised me."

She let out a shaky laugh. "Got to keep you on your toes."

"I had no idea you could be so . . ."

"I'm not all planners and spreadsheets."

"You most certainly aren't." He smiled.

Her gaze connected with his cobalt-blue eyes. And Candace realized she hadn't merely had sex. She'd lost control. The one thing she'd vowed *never* to do again.

Oh, shit. What had she done?

"What's the matter?" he asked when she tensed in his arms.

"Nothing. I . . . I should go."

"No. Don't run from me. Not now."

"I shouldn't have done this." *Shouldn't have shared part of myself. Shouldn't have let go like that. Shouldn't have . . .*

"Don't have regrets, Candy. Not for going after what you want."

"Thinking with my vagina just leads to stupid mistakes."

His hand traced her cheek. "Sometimes it does. And sometimes it doesn't."

She turned away, putting her back to him before she could get swept back up in those eyes.

"What stupid mistakes have you made?" He snuggled closer to her. "You're so sensible. I can't imagine you doing anything you haven't planned out."

She arched a brow and glanced at him over her shoulder.

"Oh, yeah. Except this." He grinned.

"See, I'm not who you think I am."

"You're a well-rounded woman. There's nothing wrong with that."

"I'm insane. The last time I did something like this—" She cut herself off.

"What?" He tucked a tendril of hair back behind her ear. "What happened, Candy?"

What would it hurt to tell him? The basket job was finished. She could, conceivably, never see him again after this. After all, hadn't that been her real plan? Get him out of her system, then be Barry's wife for the next fifty years and never, ever think about this night again?

Regret squeezed at her chest, but she ignored it.

"If you talk about it, maybe it won't seem so bad."

"I've never told anyone," she whispered.

"Secrets are heavy weights to carry around."

She sighed. "Yeah. They are." Outside the bedroom, the sun was setting, casting the room in dark gold shadows. Michael pressed a kiss to her shoulder and waited, silent. If she didn't want to tell him anything, he wouldn't push her.

But he was right. All those years and that one mistake still felt like she was carrying around thirty extra pounds. She let out a breath, took another in, then figured today was a day of new beginnings. "My last year in college, I spent the summer at my dad's lake house in New Hampshire. I hadn't seen my dad in a long time. He moved to Florida after the divorce and it was hard to travel and get down there to see him."

"But he kept the lake house?"

"It was his dad's. My grandpa had died that spring and I went up there to help my dad clean it out, get it ready for selling or keeping or whatever he decided to do. It was a chance to kind of reconnect, too, you know?"

"I don't, but I wish I did. My parents aren't the connecting type."

She filed the information away. Later, she'd ask about that. It explained something about him. But now, she'd begun her story and couldn't seem to stop. "In New Hampshire, I met someone. A guy named Danny. He was there for the summer, too."

"A summer romance?"

"You could call it that. But I thought it was . . . something more."

"You fell in love."

"Yeah. I jumped in headfirst, didn't bother to check the depth of the water. And Danny was everything a girl could want. Gorgeous, good with words."

"But not good with commitment?"

She snorted. "Not at all. I got really wrapped up and . . ."

"What?" he prodded gently when she didn't finish.

"Nothing." No, she wasn't going to finish the story. She rolled to face him, slipping her body into the concave of his. "I thought you promised me a bath."

"You're changing the subject."

"Yes, I am." Her hand slipped between them and began stroking him back into an erection. "On purpose."

"Why not talk about Danny and everything that happened?"

"Because that would be a string. And we agreed not to have any." She tugged lightly on his penis and his mind went blank for a moment. "Sex only. Nothing more."

"Hmmm . . . seems a pity, though."

"You going soft on me?"

He chuckled. "Quite the opposite."

She bit her lip, her smile devilish. "Good. Then get the water running. I have plans for you."

Candace had been wrong. It wasn't she who had any plans at all. Michael was in control from the minute he touched the tap and then turned to lower her into the deep, inviting whirlpool tub. "This time, I'm calling the shots," he said, kissing her neck, trailing down to her breasts.

"I'm used to being the one in control."

"Letting go is very liberating." His voice was almost a growl. His tongue circled her nipple and that was all the convincing Candace needed to quit trying to be the leader.

And let Michael hold the reins.

The second time was slow and easy. He took his time, lathering her with the soap in his deep whirlpool tub, treating her like a precious gem. Then washing her with the nubby washcloth, awakening every nerve ending, sending her spiraling down the same desire track as before. A thousand times she wanted to beg him to end the teasing and the wait, but he'd catch her with that grin of his, reminding her that he was the one calling all the shots. Oh, and he did it so well. By the time he took her in his arms and kissed her, Candace was nearly panting with want.

"Not so fast," Michael said. "Take your time and you'll enjoy it even more than you did the first time."

Damned if he wasn't right. Between the steady thrum of the jets, the slickness of the water and the easy rhythm of Michael on top of her, it felt like one long, sweet orgasm.

She slid her hands along his body when they were done, stroking and holding. Knowing this would be the last time and wishing it wasn't.

He pulled her into his lap and placed an easy, slow kiss on her lips.

Precious. Tender.

Almost like he loved her.

She pulled back suddenly. Water sloshed over the side of the tub, puddling with suds on the ceramic tile. "What was that?"

"A kiss. Unless I've flunked Sex Ed 101."

"That wasn't just a kiss. It was much more than that."

"Yes, it was."

"This isn't going any further. It can't."

"Why not?"

"I'm getting married in two weeks to someone else." She climbed out of the tub, grabbed a towel and wrapped it around herself. "Why are you messing with that?"

"Because I'm not happy."

"Well, go get some Prozac and quit messing with my life." She dipped her head. "Sorry, that was a little mean."

Towel in hand, he stepped out of the whirlpool tub and stood before her. His hair was wet and curling a little on the ends, looking both boyish and sexy all at once. She wanted so badly to touch it, to tease at the curls with her fingers, but knew that would only lead her back to the bed.

She couldn't go there again.

Ever.

"What I meant is I'm not happy with just sex," Michael said.

"I said, no strings. I meant it."

"Well, I want more."

"Why? So you can get scared in two weeks or a month and run for the hills? Barry is the kind of guy who stays around. For good. You, on the other hand, don't." She took a step forward, peering into his eyes. "Why is that?"

"Because fairy tales aren't real. Happy marriages with two-point-five kids and a dog don't exist."

"Bullshit. That's just something you've told yourself so you don't have to get close to a woman." A chuff of disgust escaped her. "It's like the secret code for entry into the men's club." She exited the bathroom, heading into the front room.

With one hand, she collected her clothes into her arm and dumped them into a pile on the couch.

He followed, pulling on a pair of sweatpants. His naked torso only looked more bare and enticing over the loose gray pants hanging low on his hips. Damn. She needed to leave. Or all those reasons she'd come up with for going would get sucked up by her libido.

Michael dropped into a chair to the left of her, turning his head enough so she could get dressed out of his sight. Ever the gentleman. Damn him.

"When I was growing up, my parents were always gone. Parties, openings, trips to Europe. They were always together, but never really together, if that makes sense. It was like they were escorts for each other. I never saw them kiss and never heard anything more than civil 'pass-the-butter-please-darling' conversation around the house."

Her hands stilled on the buttons of her dress. She crossed to the sofa and perched on the edge, listening.

"My sister and I were raised by a succession of nannies, none of whom had a whole lot of warmth." He shook his head. "It's not always like *The Sound of Music.*"

"Didn't you have anyone?"

"I did when I got older. At boarding school, I made friends with a guy who didn't come from much. He'd gotten a scholarship to come to the school. His mother was always sending him goodies in the mail or knitting him something. His parents were always there on the family days. And he always had a place to go during school breaks."

"And you didn't?"

"I had the nanny. And my sister. But one Christmas, when my parents were in Italy or Greece or wherever, and Rachel had gone to stay with a friend, I went home with Robert to spend the break at his house." He got up and crossed to the window, stopping to stare at the skyline for a moment. "It was all I'd ever imagined. Simmering wassail. Singing carols. Hugs and fudge and presents all around."

"It must have been wonderful."

"It was at first." He toyed with the windowsill. "And then I was introduced to their daughter. They seated me beside her at the dinner table. It took me a while before I noticed the conversation turning from the new restaurant down the street to my family's net worth."

"They wanted you to marry their daughter?"

"Yes. And the sooner the better. They were facing bankruptcy and," Michael pivoted away from the window, "the whole family thing had been a bit of an act. For me. It's a tactic my businessman father would have been proud of. Bait and switch."

"But you didn't get hooked?"

His Adam's apple bobbed up and down. "I did, in a way. But no, I didn't marry her."

"And that's what has made you so jaded?"

He shook his head. "Not just that, but it's one of those moments that I can point to and see my path going another way. I've never really seen myself as cut out for the white-picket fence life."

"Why? Because you haven't met anyone who did it successfully? Michael, there are people out there who do live happily ever after."

"Oh, yeah? Show me one. You said your mother is a serial marrier. Your parents are divorced."

"I'm getting married, though."

He took a step toward her. "And how long do you give it?"

She jerked to her feet. "I'm not going to stand at the altar like a gambler placing odds before the seventh race."

When he rose, his height gave him a several-inch advantage over her. "You think you can love Barry forever?"

"That's the plan."

"You think you can forget me and what happened here today that easily?" He was closer now, inches from her.

"I will. I have to."

"And what are you going to do? Lock the other Candace, the one I saw today, away in the closet? Only pull her out for party tricks?"

Before she could think about what she was doing, Candace had raised her hand and slapped Michael across the face. "How *dare* you?"

He didn't flinch. "I can't bear to see you do this, Candy. You won't be happy with a life of predictability."

"And what are *you* going to do? Ride in on your white horse and take me away from it all? Then when we get too close to the castle, start feeling penned in and go off for another princess?"

"That's not what I meant."

"You read Eliot, but you missed the point in the poem. He's saying it takes courage to make a commitment. Barry has that. You don't." She spun on her heel, grabbed her tote bag and slipped it on her shoulder. "You want to know why I'm marrying him? Because he isn't like you."

And then she was gone.

Rebecca's Can't-Make-a-Decision Chocolate Banana Split Pie

1 cup sugar
⅓ cup cocoa
¼ cup cornstarch
2 ½ tablespoons all-purpose flour
¼ teaspoon salt
2 ½ cups milk
1 egg
2 tablespoons butter
1 teaspoon vanilla extract
2 bananas, peeled and sliced
1 ready-made graham cracker crust
frozen whipped topping, nuts and cherries for decoration

For those fence sitters, this is as easy as it gets to cook. Put the first seven ingredients into a bowl and mix well. Microwave on high, covered, for six to eight minutes, stopping every couple of minutes to whisk it. When the mixture begins to boil, microwave for another minute to thicken like the muddled mess your brain is right now. Add the butter and vanilla, then put plastic wrap over the surface and put it in the fridge to cool.

Slice the bananas and arrange them over the bottom of the crust. Pack 'em in tight like the tense muscles in the back of your neck. No need to get fancy, since you can barely make a decision right now. Pour the filling over the bananas, top with plastic wrap and then refrigerate until it's time for dessert.

Top with the whipped topping, nuts or cherries. If you can't make a decision, throw all of them on there. It's dessert, not a life-altering choice. Eat enough pie to clear your mind so you can make a good decision.

Not enough pie for that? Then make more.

CHAPTER 20

"Michael, you have to save me." Rachel stood in his apartment an hour after Candace had left, hands on hips, a demanding glare in her eyes. "If you don't, I'll kill you."

"No need for death threats," he said. "I'll talk to Mother and Father. Tell them an all-girls school will turn you into a lesbian."

She tapped a silver polished fingertip against her lips. "Oh, that's a good one. I wish I'd thought of that." Then her gaze narrowed and she took a step closer, zeroing in on him. "Speaking of loving women, have you done anything about *your* little problem yet?"

"What problem?"

"Oh, don't 'what problem' me, big brother. You're not that good at lying and I'm not that stupid." She brushed past him, made herself at home in his kitchen and started rooting around in the refrigerator. "Jesus. Don't you eat?"

"Not at home."

"What's the point in having your own place if you never spend any time here?" She shoved aside some Heinekens and a moldy block of cheese, then slammed the fridge door shut. She pivoted, spied the paper bag of takeout Chinese on the counter and peeked inside. "So you do eat at home." She withdrew a couple of boxes and read the labels on the sides. "Moo Shu Pork. Chicken Chow Mein. Pu Pu platter for *Two*. Hungry . . . or otherwise engaged?"

"You are underage." He took the moo shu away. "I'm not telling you a damn thing."

"She was here?" Rachel looked at his face, then at his rumpled clothes and beyond him, to the sheets and pillows on the bedroom floor. "Oh my God, you slept with her? And you didn't tell me?" Rachel smacked his arm. Hard. "I'm cutting you out of my will."

"What will? And what do you own?"

"A hell of a good personality. And you're not getting any of it." She grinned, then flipped up the lid of the Pu Pu Platter container, grabbed a fork out of the drawer and speared up a boneless rib. "So tell me what I missed."

While Rachel was munching, he put the rest of the take-out into the fridge. After Candace left, the Chinese food had arrived, but Michael's appetite had deserted him. So the food had sat here, waiting for him either to eat it, pitch it . . . or for Rachel to come along and put two and two together. "You didn't miss anything."

His little sister let out a gust of disgust. "Did she break it off with her floppy fiancé?"

"Floppy?"

"I figure he must be if she slept with you."

"Hey, I take offense to that."

She shrugged and popped a piece of shrimp toast into her mouth. "You should."

"You really need some feminizing." He crumpled up the empty paper bag and tossed it into the trash compactor. "I've changed my mind. I'm giving Mother and Father my hearty recommendation for finishing school."

She gaped at him. "You wouldn't."

"Only if you find a major and a college and do something

with your life after graduation," he said, emphasizing the point with his index finger.

"Oh, all right." She sighed. "I was planning on it anyway. After I took a year to see Europe."

His head was shaking before she even finished the sentence. "Not at your age. Why, you could—"

She cut him off with an exasperated sigh and a roll of her eyes. "And they say you start turning into your parents when you hit your thirties."

"That was low."

"I'm better at this game than you." Rachel smirked, dove into the container again and came up with a second piece of shrimp toast. "So, are you in love with her?"

Michael crossed to the kitchen window and hovered there, staring at the bustling city streets below him. "Yeah. I think I'm starting to feel that way."

"Are you going to run this time, jackrabbit?"

He let out a breath. "I want to."

"What the hell is wrong with you? Did you get dropped on your head as a kid?"

He spun around. "What do you mean?"

"I may not be the legal age to drink yet, but that doesn't mean I don't know a thing or two about love. True love doesn't come along twenty-five times in a lifetime, you know." She jabbed her fork at his chest. "And I see something in your face. You get all goofy when you talk about her. It's sickening." She withdrew her eating implement from his torso and stirred at the Chinese food. "But it's kind of sweet, too," she added in a mumble. "You should do something about it."

He should. But was he prepared to deal with the consequences if he did?

By the time Candace got home, Saturday afternoon was over and evening had begun. She'd taken a cab back to Gift

Baskets, picked up her car without going into the shop, then drove around Dorchester for the better part of an hour, searching for answers.

Unfortunately, there weren't any to be found in the narrow side streets, white-painted colonials or weather-worn Cape Cods. She did find one shopping cart without its wheels, a street preacher screaming about the evils of something or other, and one old woman watering her lawn in her underwear.

She pulled into the driveway of the duplex and parked her Civic. All she wanted was a hot shower, a stiff drink and enough trash TV to shut her brain off. For the past hour, she'd thought way too much. About Michael. About Barry. About Michael and Barry—that last thought, in particular, had told her she needed to get out of the sun.

Then about how stupid she was. And about how damn good those few hours in his bed—and his bathtub—had been.

Stupid, stupid, stupid. To throw away a marriage—a lifelong commitment—for a bit of afternoon delight. Choosing Michael over Barry was like eating marshmallow fluff instead of kielbasa.

She needed substance. Not sex.

No. She needed chocolate and alcohol. And a lot of time alone to beat herself up.

She opened the Civic's door and started up the walkway. Before she could reach her door, Della came bounding out. "Oh, you're home! Finally!"

And then Candace remembered. Her bridal shower. Oh, damn. She was not in the mood to put on a happy face among a bunch of blenders and distant cousins.

But Della was already prancing ahead, leading the way into Grandma's house with more glee than she'd ever expressed about being near her former mother-in-law. "Let's stop in for a quick hello to your grandmother."

"Mother, give it up. I told you. I already know this is my shower."

"Oh, stop. You'll spoil everything." Della flung open the door. Four dozen female voices shouted "Surprise!" with Della providing backup harmony. Maria came over, took Candace's tote bag from her shoulder and hung it on one of the coat hooks.

Candace opened her mouth into an appropriate little "O" of shock. "I had no idea."

"Bullshit," Maria whispered in her ear. "But thanks for playing along."

Candace was dragged over to a chair decorated with pink and blue streamers and balloons, an upside-down paper umbrella suspended over it. As soon as she was seated, Della pulled the rip cord, dumping two pounds of pastel-colored confetti on Candace's head and lap. "It's shower time!" Della cried.

Clearly, her mother was in her element.

Bernadine sat in the large orange La-Z-Boy on the other side of the living room, arms crossed over her chest, looking about as merry as an underpaid mall Santa in a roomful of kids on a sugar high. She eyed Candace with a look that bordered on suspicion.

Did she know? Did it show on her face? A little sign that blared: I JUST HAD SEX WITH A MAN WHO ISN'T YOUR SON?

Another thought occurred to her. If Bernadine was back, that meant Barry had returned earlier than she expected. Was he here? Oh God, she hoped not. She wasn't ready to face him yet.

"Hi Bernadine," Candace said, leaning forward. "How's Aunt Miriam?"

"Not going to die today." Her future mother-in-law pursed her lips. "But she's sure making it sound like she could go at anytime. The woman has complaining down to an art."

Gee, wonder who inherited that trait? "Where's Barry?" Candace forced a polite smile to her face.

"Since you haven't called him back after he left two messages, you probably don't know."

Her face started to hurt from keeping that goofy grin pasted on it. "That's why I'm asking you." *Mommy dearest.*

Bernadine gave her a return smile of smug satisfaction. "Tonight was his bachelor party. His friend Jim has taken him and a few other friends to the movies."

"The movies?" Candace chuckled. "Barry at *that* kind of movie would be something I'd pay to see."

Bernadine cast her a look of horror and disgust. "My son would never go to one of *those* films. He's not Pee Wee Herman, you know. He has standards."

"Oh yes, you're absolutely right." Candace caught herself before she choked on the words.

"Maybe you would have remembered tonight was his special night out with his friends if you weren't so busy lollygagging in cars with your cust—" Bernadine's mutterings were cut off by a series of hacking coughs.

"Gee, nasty cough you have there," Candace said, innocent as a lamb in a lion's den.

Bernadine scowled. "Touch of bronchitis. That's all."

"Be careful Barry doesn't catch that. It would be awful if he got sick right before the wedding." Candace exchanged a glare battle with her future mother-in-law. When Bernadine looked away, she knew she'd won the war. "So what movie did they see?"

"The newest Clint Eastwood film. My Barry, he loves the Wild West. If we lived in another day and age, he would have made a great cowboy."

Candace nodded. "If only he wasn't allergic to leather."

"Ah, yes." Bernadine sighed. "Poor Barry."

Grandma Woodrow came up and, thank God, interrupted the conversation with her Dustbuster. She vacuumed up most of the confetti, inserting her spandex-clad self between Candace and Bernadine's view.

Boy, did Candace love her grandmother.

Della got to her feet and started tossing out lacy things in neon colors, trying to launch a rousing game of "guess the lingerie." Undoubtedly her new boyfriend had helped her find some of the more unique items in the store because it wasn't long before the crowd, made up mainly of great aunts and maiden cousins, was stumped.

"We tried to stop your mother," Grandma said, "but you know how she is when it comes to these things."

"That's okay. It makes her happy."

Grandma winked. "Think of all the free garter belts you're going to get."

"I'd get more use out of a Crock-Pot." Candace sighed and sagged back into the chair. The movement tipped the umbrella, showering her anew with a few stowaway pieces of confetti, like a party that wouldn't quit.

Grandma shook her head, brushing the pieces to the floor. "Honey, are you sure—"

Candace put a hand over her grandmother's. "Don't ask me that. Not today."

"You're right." She smiled. "Probably not the best timing."

"No, not at all."

Grandma's soft palm felt like a balm against her cheek. "You okay, sweetie? You look a little green."

"Nothing . . . really. Just prewedding jitters."

"I'll get you some chocolate cake. That'll help."

"Bring me a big slice." Candace grabbed Grandma's arm before she walked away. "On second thought, bring the whole damn thing. Leave the guests the crumbs."

Grandma laughed. Like she thought Candace was kidding.

Three pieces of cake, two toasters, three negligees, five china place settings and untold towels later, Candace sat back and thanked her friends, relatives and mother for the shower. Della beamed with pride, gathered up the note cards she'd distributed for her homemade "Tips to Candace for Avoiding

Housework" booklet, then handed out parting gifts to every-one—thigh-high fishnet stockings and little hot-pink garters that played "Here Comes the Bride."

Note to self: Never ever let Della plan my baby shower.

"You okay?" Rebecca came up and picked up Candace's empty plate.

Candace had to resist the urge to dab up the crumbs with a finger. Surely there were leftovers in the kitchen she could sneak in and grab. As soon as no one was looking. "Why does everyone keep asking me that?"

"Because you look like you're about to hyperventilate again. And because I remember how panicked I felt when it started getting close to my wedding date. Like the world was about to close in."

She sighed. "Yeah, it's like that."

Rebecca patted her arm. "Don't worry. It'll work out. In a couple weeks, everything will all be over and you'll wonder why you worried so much."

"It's not that, it's . . ." She suddenly realized she needed to talk to someone, to tell someone who would understand. "Come on in the kitchen. I have to talk to you. And I need more cake."

They found a quiet corner in Grandma's bright yellow kitchen. Candace poured herself a glass of milk, then took a seat on the counter and dove into another piece of cake. "I did it," she said with a sigh.

"Did what?" Rebecca scooped up some veggie dip and celery. "I wish I could have that cake, but I swear, once you have a kid, you gain weight by just *looking* at a Twinkie. It's not the kids that drive you crazy—it's the years of being forced to eat salad and—"

"I slept with him," Candace interrupted.

"And carrots and . . ." Rebecca blinked. "Wait a minute. Did you just say what I thought you said?"

"Uh-huh."

Rebecca lowered her voice and leaned closer. "You *slept* with Michael?"

"Twice. In one day. So technically, maybe, that's once."

"When?"

"After lunch."

"Today?! Before you came to—"

Candace nodded.

"Oh. Oh . . . oh my God." The celery in her hand tumbled onto the counter. "Screw the veggies. I'm having cake with you. Does Grandma have anything to drink?"

"There's some Kahlúa in the cabinet over the stove."

"Good. I think I need a shot or two." Rebecca paused, then looked at Candace. "Oh, yeah, and you, too." She pivoted, reached above the Kenmore and got the brown bottle out of the cabinet, giving each of them a liberal amount mixed in with their milk. She took a big gulp, then exhaled. "Okay, start at the beginning."

Candace did, relating the details of the trip to the shelter, the shopping, and the crazy couple of hours she'd spent in his apartment.

Just after she finished, Della popped her head into the kitchen. "What are you doing in here? You should be out there, saying good-bye to everyone."

"I will. Just give me a minute."

"Did you enjoy your shower, sweetie?"

"It was perfect. You did a great job."

Della beamed. "Thanks." She wagged a finger of admonishment at her. "Now, don't be a hermit!"

When the kitchen door had swung shut again, Rebecca turned to Candace and topped off her Kahlúa. "What are you going to do?"

"Nothing. It was a mistake."

"Are you sure about that?"

"Yeah." She nodded, telling herself that as much as Rebecca. "Yeah, I'm sure."

Rebecca bit her lip, swirling the drink in her hand. "Did it clear up your doubts?"

"Oh. Absolutely." Candace threw all the conviction she had into her voice. "It was like putting chlorine into a cloudy pool."

Rebecca slipped off the counter and drew Candace into a hug. "Okay, but watch out you don't drown in the deep end."

Candace's Nerves-of-Paper Chocolate Soufflé

8 ounces semisweet chocolate
⅔ cup corn syrup
4 eggs
¼ cup milk
3 ounces cream cheese, softened

First thing—breathe. When you're feeling calm enough to cook, melt the chocolate and corn syrup in a saucepan. Cool slightly, pacing while you wait to expend that nervous energy.

Whip up the eggs and milk in a blender until smooth, then add the cream cheese a little at a time. Keep breathing (make sure you have a paper bag handy in case your nerves get out of hand). Add the chocolate, blend until well mixed. Pour into an ungreased one-and-a-half-quart soufflé or baking dish. Bake at 400 degrees for fifty-five minutes. Don't make any sudden moves or loud noises, or your soufflé will fall apart, just like you.

Eat with a large spoon. The faster you can get that chocolate into your system, the sooner it can start its calming effect. Don't forget—breathe between bites. It'll all work out.

And if it doesn't, there's always another chocolate recipe to be tried.

CHAPTER 21

By Sunday morning, the paper bag and the remains of the chocolate cake had become Candace's new best friends. She'd lugged all the gifts back to her apartment, then left them in the corner of the living room, too tired to do anything with the piles of dishes and small kitchen appliances.

Barry showed up at her apartment that morning, as early as a robin looking for a worm. The minute she saw him, she felt an odd mixture of relief and remorse.

She wanted to undo yesterday, but couldn't. If she didn't think about it—ever—maybe she could move on, get back to where she'd been with Barry before Michael Vogler had come into her life.

And thrown it into a wood chipper.

"Hey," Barry said. "I brought you something." He pulled his hand out from behind his back and handed her a Starbucks Vanilla Breve Latte.

"You read my mind." She sighed, slumped into a kitchen chair and inhaled the fragrance of the drink, then took a sip. From the living room, she could hear the snores of Della on her couch. Percy was running circles around the kitchen table, playing tag with Bob. And losing, considering Bob didn't have a tail to catch. "You did that thing again, didn't you?"

"What?"

"Took the top off for exactly seven minutes so it gets just cool enough to drink."

He shrugged. "I know that's how you like it."

She took a long gulp, then gave him a big smile. "You know me so well." *This* was why she was marrying Barry. Because he could read her mind like Sylvia Browne predicted Montel's future. "So, how was your movie?"

"Okay. Sure made me want to buy a horse, though." He knelt down beside her chair and caught her gaze with his own. "Listen, I'm sorry about the dress. I could see you weren't pleased. It's your wedding, too, and it's your dress. I should have thought of you. I told Mother it was wrong for us to buy it for you. We'll take it back." He took her hand in his. "Your happiness is the most important thing to me."

Guilt ricocheted through her faster than Keanu Reeves in *The Matrix Reloaded*. How could she have ever done what she did with Michael? Barry was the one who was here, coffee and apology in hand.

She thought of returning the dress, then realized the only other one she could imagine wearing was that one at Reverie Bridal. And that was not only out of her price range; it was out of the question. Especially when she'd modeled it for another man. "No, it's okay. The dress is fine. I was just . . . surprised."

"I shouldn't have done it. I thought it was a good idea. Save you some time. Money. You know."

Candace got to her feet and gave him a one-arm hug, careful not to spill the Starbucks on his neatly pressed golf shirt and khakis. He had been thinking of her, and that meant a lot. He'd seen the stress on her face, and in his own Barry-esque way, thought he was doing the right thing. "It was a wonderful thought. The dress may not have been exactly what I would have picked out on my own, but it's okay. Really."

"If you don't like it, we'll take it back. I mean it." Barry grasped her hand in his. "We can shop for something *you* like. Together."

Taking the dress back and starting the whole nightmare shopping process all over again seemed too big of a job. Too stressful. Barry's choice wasn't *that* bad. "It's only a dress, right? What's important is the wedding. And what happens afterward."

He smiled. "See? That's why I love you. You're always so sensible. You don't care about the stupid details like what you're wearing. You think about the practical stuff." He grinned and chucked her under the chin. "That's my girl."

"Yeah, that's me." Candace tipped the coffee into her mouth and wondered if there were any cookies left in the jar on her counter.

"Hey, I stopped by for another reason, too. I have some bad news about the honeymoon."

"What bad news?" What more could possibly go wrong with this wedding?

"A tornado hit the island down in the Keys where we had reservations. The hotel's pretty badly damaged. "But I was able to exchange our tickets for a trip to"—he did a little drum roll on the edge of the kitchen table with his fingers—"Phoenix."

"Arizona? In June?"

Barry scoffed. "It's sunny. Just like the Keys. And the hotel has a pool. What more do you need?"

"You should have asked me first. We might have thought of other options besides Phoenix."

"There weren't a lot of choices this close to the wedding, not on our budget and not during the biggest wedding and graduation month of the season. Most places are already booked up. Besides, Mother said it would be the perfect environment for my allergies."

Candace forced a smile to her face. Leave it to her future mother-in-law to recommend the top retirement community as a hot honeymoon location. Either way, it was only a week. An escape from all of *this* with Barry. "Then Phoenix it is."

What was important was the marriage, not the honeymoon. Or the dress. Just marrying Barry and beginning their life.

"Great. I need to call the caterer, too, and confirm a few things. Do you have her number in your planner?"

"Sure. Let me grab it." Candace crossed the kitchen, picked up her tote bag and reached inside. And came up empty. There was plenty of other stuff in there—a tube of lipstick, a bunch of pens, a pad of paper, a calculator—but no planner.

Oh, shit. Oh, shit. Oh, shit.

"I, ah, don't have it with me."

Barry laughed. "That's impossible. You never go anywhere without your planner."

"I must have left it someplace." Her mind raced, trying to retrace her steps.

"Where?"

And then she knew. The image came back, clear as a block of ice. Michael and her at the front door of his apartment, so hungry for each other, they were tossing off clothes and shoes . . . and tote bags. The planner had to have slipped out then, lost in the rushing tumble to get into bed and devour each other. *Oh, double shit.* "I probably left it at"—she scrambled for an answer—"Maria's."

"Oh." He frowned. "I didn't know you went over there."

"You know us girls." She let out a little laugh. "Friends are always dropping by each other's houses."

"Well, I'm sure you'll be going right over there to pick it up." He grinned. "I don't think you can go five minutes without that thing."

Get it back? That would mean returning to Michael's apartment. She'd had a hell of a good exit—the kind of line

Rob Reiner would be proud of. She didn't want to rewrite that ending. Wasn't sure she could.

And seeing him again? There wasn't enough chocolate on the planet to help her get through that.

"Candace, are you okay?" Barry asked. "You got really silent there for a minute."

"I'm fine." She ran a hand through her hair. "Just have a lot on my mind."

"Hopefully your fiancé." His arms stole around her waist, and when he spoke again, his voice dropped into the deeper octaves. "I've missed you so much this weekend. I dropped my mother off at the Cut 'N Go just now." He flipped out his wrist and glanced at his Timex. "I've got, ah, thirty-nine minutes until she's all done with her set and dry. Want to go back to my place and get reacquainted?" He gave her a grin and wriggled his pelvis against hers.

Hint, hint.

"That's, uh, not very much time," Candace hedged.

"Oh honey, you know us. In and out before the last scene of *Frasier* is over. Plenty of time to catch *Law and Order*."

This was what her life was going to be like, she realized. It was what she'd always been seeking, she reminded herself.

Dependable nights. Dependable sex. A dependable man.

"Come on," he said, bending down to nuzzle at her neck. "I've missed you, honey."

"I can't. I-I-I still haven't made all my calls."

He broke away from her. "What? How could you let that slide? This is our *wedding*, Candace. It's important."

"I know. I've been busy."

His gaze zeroed in on hers. "Busy or . . . unsure?"

"Unsure?" Her laughter was a little nervous. "About what?"

"About marrying me." He took her hand in his, flipped her palm over as if studying it for a lie line. "Lately, you've been a little distant."

He'd noticed. Oh God, how could she have done this? What

kind of woman threw her fiancé to the side mere weeks before the wedding? How insane was it to be doubting him this close to their marriage? This was the kind of thing a teenager did, not a twenty-seven-year-old woman. She forced another bright smile to her face and gave Barry a kiss on the cheek. "I'm sorry. Just a lot on my mind. I'll be fine as soon as we say 'I do.' "

"That's my girl," he said again, then kissed her back, gentle as a pillow over her face. "I can hardly wait to be calling you Mrs. Barry Borkenstein."

"Hey Michael," the voice on the other end of his phone purred. "Where've you been?"

Michael cleared his throat, pushing the disappointment out of his voice. He'd been hoping it would be another woman calling. But no, she'd made it pretty clear she wanted nothing to do with him. "Just get back into town, Monica?"

"Landed an hour ago. Did you miss me?"

"Don't I always?"

"Did you save a place in your bed for me?" she asked, her voice now dropping into a kittenish range. "It's been a lonely few days at that boring IT conference in Phoenix. I swear I was about ready to do it with a pocket protector by the time I got on the plane."

He chuckled. "You've always been an inventive lady, that's for sure."

"Oh, I've come up with a few new tricks. All that time to myself to think and all." Over the phone line, he heard the clink of ice in a glass as she took a sip of a drink. "You want to try them out tonight? Say, my place. In an hour?"

A week ago, Monica's voice would have charged his libido like a truck full of Energizers. She was the kind of woman he usually dated—no strings, no commitments, no expectations. A quick time in bed and a phone call when she was in town.

But that was last week. Yesterday he'd had a full-course dinner. Going back to the McDonald's drive-through suddenly seemed distasteful.

"Michael? You there?"

"Yeah. Listen, I'm not going to make it tonight. I have a little touch of indigestion."

Her laughter was throaty. "Hopefully you're not sick of me."

"Actually, Monica, I've met someone."

"In a week? Come on, Michael, I know you. It's a temporary thing. You'll screw her, then come back to me for dessert."

He toyed with the cord on the phone. "I don't think so. Not this time." He said good-bye and hung up.

It felt better than he'd expected. Less terrifying. Maybe there was hope he could grow up after all.

His doorbell rang and he crossed to answer it. Standing on the other side was Candace, looking simple and pure in a pair of denim shorts and a simple white V-neck T.

She'd come back.

Joy flooded him, washing through his heart like a dam that had suddenly burst. He hadn't realized just how much he'd missed her until she returned. Now he knew. And the want for her was ten times stronger than he'd thought it would be. It all originated on the left side of his chest, right in his heart.

"Hi," he said, opening the door wide.

She didn't move forward. "I left my planner here. I only stopped by to get it."

A concrete block of disappointment sunk to the bottom of his stomach. "Oh. Yeah, sure. Come on in."

Her head was already shaking no. "I think it's best if I don't."

He leaned against the doorjamb. "You were right about me, you know. And you put it pretty well, too."

"I'm sorry, I probably shouldn't have said what I did. I didn't mean to hurt you."

"Hey, I can take it." He smiled at her. "And I needed to hear it."

"Well, I'm glad." She glanced at the carpeted floor, then back up at him. "Anyway, do you have my planner?"

"So, this is how it's going to be?"

"This is how it has to be. I'm getting married soon."

"For a woman who cares about other people so much, you're pretty damn cold when it comes to yourself."

"What?"

"I mean it. I've seen you with your friends. With the people at the shelter. You care. You give. You don't see status or age. You see just the people." He stepped forward, knowing he was invading her space. "That's a very rare quality."

She swallowed, a faint blush in her cheeks. "I don't know what to say to that."

"But when it comes to yourself, you hold back. As if you don't think you deserve the best. Why is that? Why do you give and give and hold nothing in reserve for Candace?"

"I do. I take care of myself."

"No, you don't." He shook his head. She was the kind of woman he'd never thought existed. One who lived life with an honest kind of goodness—something he thought had disappeared long ago. Being with her filled something in him, like adding color to a black-and-white picture. But she couldn't see that for herself. "What did you do? Use up your credits on yourself years ago? Decide to live a life of deprivation in penance for something?" He let out a gust. "I don't get it. You're a beautiful, vibrant, passionate woman, but you're keeping it locked inside as if you have to keep a rope around yourself so you won't fall off the cliff."

Tears shimmered in her eyes and she looked away for a long, long moment. "You don't know anything about me."

"I know everything. We're more alike than you think, Candy. Only difference is, I'm not afraid to fall off the cliff anymore."

Her gaze swiveled back to his. "Why?"

"Because I know you're there to break the fall." He grinned. "Because I'm falling in love with you."

"No. No. *No.* You can't do this to me, Michael." She backed up several steps, hands up, warding him off. "I don't want to hear this. You only *think* you're in love. It's some kind of postcoital bliss or after-sex high or something. Go have a cigarette and you'll feel totally different."

"No, I won't." He sucked in a breath and tried to keep his frustration at bay. "This is permanent. And it has nothing to do with spreadsheets or pro-con lists. For the first time, Candy, I believe that white picket fence life is possible. I can imagine myself sitting across from you fifty years from now. Teasing you. Happy as hell to see you still there." He moved forward, grabbed up her hand and pressed it to his chest. "It's all in here, Candy. Listen to your heart, not your head."

"Stop it!" she cried. "Don't do this. I know men like you. You think you feel love for five minutes and then the feeling passes like a bad cold." She shook her head, tears shimmering in her eyes. "Don't say things to me that you aren't going to mean tomorrow. I have my whole life figured out. I can't write a new plan."

"Can't? Or won't?"

Instead of answering, she jerked her hand away, brushed past him and dashed into the apartment, grabbing up her planner from where it still lay in the corner by his door.

"Please, just leave me alone," she said as she exited his apartment. "I'm marrying Barry. For better or worse."

Then she ran for the stairs like a woman on the lam. She *had* stolen something, he realized.

His heart.

Grandma's Layers-of-Truth Chocolate Baklava

½ cup butter, melted
1 cup each of pecans and peanuts, lightly toasted and
    chopped
1 ¼ cups semisweet chocolate chips
2 tablespoons sugar
1 teaspoon ground cinnamon
1 box frozen Fillo dough, thawed
Grandma's Taste of Love Chocolate Syrup

If the truth ain't coming out, then you gotta peel back the layers and find it, honey. Getting down to bare naked honesty isn't easy, but it sure makes you feel free once you've done it. Start by mixing the nuts, chips, sugar and cinnamon in a bowl. Lay one sheet of Fillo on a breadboard, then brush it with butter, starting on the outside and working your way in (kind of like searching for the truth about yourself).

Do the same with three more sheets, stacking them on top of each other at a forty-five-degree angle so the truth comes out pretty, too. Lay the stack inside a buttered nine-by-thirteen-inch springform pan, then put one-third of the nut mixture inside. Trim any excess, just as you should in your own life. Repeat three more times, topping with another stack of Fillo and any extra pieces. Drizzle remaining butter on top.

Bake at 400 degrees for thirty-five minutes. When it's cooking, do some soul searching. Later, while the baklava's cooling in a pan on a wire rack, think about coming clean.

Serve with chocolate syrup and a strong dose of honesty. You'll feel as good as a goose who's finally laid a stubborn egg.

CHAPTER 22

Candace threw herself into the wedding plans like a drowning woman going after a life preserver. There was enough to do to keep her busy for a year and yet, no matter how long of a day she put in or how many hours she spent running from here to there, she still had time to think of Michael.

And then Barry.

And the incredibly stupid complicated mess she'd created.

She'd lied to Rebecca. Sleeping with Michael hadn't made the waters any clearer. They'd muddied them like a herd of water buffaloes. Three weeks ago, she'd been so sure. She'd known what she wanted. Where she was going. And now . . .

Now she'd be lucky if she could find her way out of the Callahan Tunnel.

The front door opened and closed. Percy came skidding into the kitchen.

"The poet doesn't rhyme with me anymore," Della said with a sigh, coming in and taking a seat across from Candace.

"Too bad. I really liked the discount he gave me at Lingerie for Lovers."

"Well, maybe you should look for someone who works at Bloomingdale's." Candace waved her cereal spoon at Della. "Get some shoes out of the deal."

"I don't think so." Her mother dropped her head into her hand.

How many times had they sat here like this, in one kitchen or another? Della with a broken heart, Candace offering whatever solace she could. Ever since she'd been nine, she'd been her mother's sounding board after dates went sour. She shoved the bowl of Cocoa Puffs to the side and reached for her mother's hand. "Maybe you should try someone closer to your own age," she said gently.

"Those men are old. Boring."

"Dependable. Home when you want them to be."

"Gray. Paunchy."

"Loyal." Candace smiled. "Grateful for the sex."

Della laughed. "There is that." She toyed with the napkin holder. "I've never been much of a grownup for you, have I?"

Candace shrugged. "I turned out okay."

"Yeah, you did."

"Listen, why don't I introduce you to some people I know? Take you out on the town. Fix you up with—"

Della shook her head. "I don't need you to take care of me."

She cast an askance eye at her mother.

"Really, honey. I may not make the best choices, but that doesn't mean I need a keeper." She got to her feet. "What I do need is a trip to the mall. That's the way to solve a broken heart. You up for some shopping?"

"Nah, I think I'll stay here. I have some things to figure out."

"Well, don't wallow too long." Della laid a soft hand on Candace's shoulder. "And don't forget to worry about yourself once in a while instead of everyone else."

Then her mother toodled a wave, called for Percy and had him hop in her purse. Within a few minutes, she was over garter-belt guy and on her way to greener pastures, armed with a Visa and good walking shoes.

Candace went to the sink, rinsed and dried her dishes, and thought about her mother's advice. All these years she'd thought Della had been the one needing to be taken care of. Maybe she didn't.

Maybe her mother wasn't cut from the same cloth as she was. Could it be possible Della was happy with her topsy-turvy life? Maybe she didn't need fixing at all.

How ironic. Maybe the one who needed fixing was Candace.

You know where the answers are, the little voice in the back of her head told her. *You've known all along.*

Traffic was light on the way down to Providence. It hadn't taken much to track him down, thanks to the Internet and its amazing ability to completely erase anyone's efforts to remain private. Within half an hour of searching, she'd known his address and come up with a newspaper article that profiled him at work.

Candace stood outside Ray's Fish Market on the day before she was supposed to marry Barry, took a deep breath, then confronted her past. "Danny?"

He was taller now, broader in the shoulders and not as blond as he'd been at twenty-one. When she entered the shop and spoke his name, he looked up from his fish. It took a while for him to recognize her, but then the light in his eyes dawned. "Candace! What a surprise. Are you here for a cod?"

"No, I wanted to talk to you. Do you have a minute?"

"Yeah, give me a sec." He hoisted the massive fish into his hands, balancing it in beefy palms. "Jerry! Heads up!" Danny tossed the bulky silver fish across the shop. Jerry caught it on his forearms, taking a step back as he did, then laid it on a fresh bed of ice. "All right, let me wash up and I'll be right out."

A few minutes later, Candace met him on the sidewalk. They started walking toward a café at the end of the block.

"So, how you been?" he asked.

"Okay. Busy. I own a gift basket shop in Boston now."

"Really? That's great. I knew you'd do something like that. You were always so . . . determined. Ambitious."

She snorted. "Boring, you mean."

"Nah, not at all. Being determined is good." He ran a hand over his receding hair line. "I wish I had been. Gotten my ass in gear and had a better career going for myself than flinging fish guts around."

"Are you happy, though?"

He shrugged. "I smell like cod all day. How happy do you think I am?"

"You looked like you were having fun in there."

"I am." He snatched a leaf off a maple as they passed underneath it, then began tearing it into shreds and scattering the pieces on the ground. "But I have different priorities now that I've grown up."

She laughed. *"You* grew up?"

"Hey, it happens to the worst of us eventually. Took me until last year." He grinned. "I'm a slow learner. I was having way too much fun sleeping late, kicking it on the beach and slugging beers." He laughed. "The ideal bachelor life."

"So what made you change?"

"A kid. Nothing can make you grow up like having a kid of your own."

Surprise, mixed with hurt, burst inside her. He'd never even asked about her that summer, never even known about what had happened the night the two of them had forgotten to take precautions. He'd been gone and off in another woman's arms, leaving Candace to pick up the pieces of her heart . . . and everything else. *"You* have a child?"

"Yeah. One now, another one in the works." He ran a hand through his hair and squinted against the sun. "I used to be quite a shit when I was young. I'm sorry about how I treated you back then. If a guy like me ever came near my daughter, I'd probably kill him."

The apology surprised her. She hadn't come here seeking one, but hearing it felt good all the same. "It's okay. It was a long time ago."

"Yeah, it was." He turned and grinned at her. "But hey, just so you know, there's hope, even for guys like me. Even I fell in love eventually. Made me give up my evil ways. When she got pregnant, all of a sudden getting married made a hell of a lot of sense."

"You're *married,* too?"

He nodded, smiling like a happy loon. Held out his left hand as proof. "Legally bound and hog-tied."

"Didn't you plan it out? Think about it first? Make sure she was the right one?"

"Hell, no. I mean, I thought about it and all, but geez, how am I supposed to know what kind of woman I'm going to want when I'm forty? I can barely figure out what I want for breakfast in the morning."

"Then why this woman?"

He stopped, and in his gaze, she saw a brightness she'd never seen before in Danny's eyes. "It's the strangest thing, Candace. I just *knew.* I know that sounds nuts, but that's how it was. I felt it here." He punched at his chest. "Like someone hit me with a hammer and told me to wise up before I let this fish get away. So I hooked her on my line." He grinned. "And I'm damned glad I did."

She'd come here for answers, to fill in the blanks from six

years ago. But after seeing the love in his eyes for his wife and the happiness on Danny's face, it no longer seemed so important. What had happened between them was in the past. He had his own life. He'd moved on.

And so could she. Finally.

Candace pulled into the driveway, just in time to avoid a cherry-red Porsche convertible screaming to a stop outside the duplex. Grandma flung open the driver's side door, followed by pounding rock music. "Showed them who's boss," she crowed, pumping a fist into the air.

"Are you drag-racing again?"

Grandma toed at the driveway. "Uh . . . no?"

"You are, aren't you? Grandma, that's illegal."

Her grandmother waved at her friend Ted, who'd switched seats and was pulling away at the wheel of his car. "It's only illegal if they catch you."

"Most people your age are having their licenses taken away for being a menace on the road."

"I'm only a menace on the racetrack." She winked. "But I taught that Martha Winton a thing or two. She thought that Dodge Dart of hers actually stood a chance." Grandma snorted.

Candace laughed and bent to retrieve her tote bag out of her car. "I'd worry about you, but I don't think it's going to do any good."

Together they walked up the paved walkway and climbed the steps. "It's you I worry about," Grandma said. "Are you okay?"

They'd reached the front door of Grandma's duplex. Candace waited to answer until her grandmother had finished unlocking the door and opened it. "No, I guess I'm not."

"I didn't think so. You want to talk about it?" Grandma gestured toward her leopard-print loveseat.

When she sagged into the velvet surface, it felt as if she'd taken half the weight on her shoulders and laid it on the animal print. "I went to Providence today," Candace began, "to see Danny."

Grandma had sat in the zebra-patterned armchair opposite the sofa. "Danny?"

"I dated him. A long time ago." She shrugged off her light cardigan and laid it beside her. "The summer before my senior year of college. Remember, I went to New Hampshire and stayed with my dad at his lake house?"

Grandma nodded. "I do."

"It was one of those typical summer flings. Stupid me thought it meant more than it did. Apparently I was the only one." Candace rose, crossed to the mantel. It was odd, really, how she could be in this jungle-themed living room and feel more at home than she did in her own Pier 1 Imports environment. Here, zebras coexisted with leopards in comfortable zaniness. "It was one of the only times in my life I didn't act before thinking it all out first."

In the reflection of the mirror, she saw Grandma nod. "You thought he was Mr. Right."

"Or something like that. I guess I was more of a romantic back then."

"Nothing wrong with that."

Candace spun around. "There's plenty wrong with it. All it does is lead to trouble."

"One bad relationship—"

"This wasn't just a bad relationship, Grandma," she cried. "I didn't think with my head. I didn't think at all. I . . . I got pregnant."

Her grandmother stood and crossed to her, laying a soft palm against Candace's cheek. "I know."

"You know? Everything?"

Grandma nodded. "Why do you think I asked you to move in here?"

"To keep an eye on you."

Grandma laughed. "I may need that, but at the time, you needed someone much more."

Candace had never told anyone how Danny had broken her heart by cheating on her with someone else. How she'd realized three weeks later that her stupidity and her lack of common sense had gotten her pregnant. She'd been so wrapped up in Danny, in the wild, swirling emotions of that summer, that she'd forgotten about precautions. About what could happen. About the mistakes she could make so easily in a moment of passion.

He'd never called her, not even sent so much as a smoke signal; just moved on to other girlfriends, unaware she was going through the most agonizing summer of her life. When she'd miscarried at eight weeks, she'd told herself it was a blessing. But it hadn't been. It had been the most painful experience of her life, one she relived every September twenty-third. She'd vowed never to make the same mistake twice, and dedicated her life to helping other people who had stepped off life's path.

For six years, those choices had served her well. But now . . .

Now she wasn't so sure she'd made the right decision.

"How did you know?" she asked her grandmother.

Soft blue eyes crinkled with love. "I've known you all your life. You're part of me, which gives us a connection that can't be explained away. When you finally came back home that summer, I saw it all over your face. And I knew you needed me."

For once, Grandma's beliefs in the cosmic alignment of life and spirits made perfect sense. "I'm glad you were here."

"I'm glad I was, too." She smiled. "Some things are meant to be."

The clock in the hall chimed. "I better get home. There's a lot to do before the wedding tomorrow."

Grandma withdrew her hand and pursed her lips, as if she

wanted to say something, then didn't. "Get some rest, then. It's a big day."

"The biggest." And then Candace had to leave because her throat had closed up and her eyes had filled with tears.

She was turning into a human spigot. At this rate, she'd be using her veil for a tissue.

Della's Pipe-Dreams-in-Chocolate-Clouds Cookies

3 egg whites
⅛ teaspoon cream of tartar
¾ cup sugar
1 teaspoon vanilla extract
2 tablespoons cocoa, sifted
1 ¾ cups really good semisweet chocolate chunks

Get your best boa on, then preheat the oven to 300 degrees. Cover a cookie sheet with parchment paper. Keep an extra piece to the side to doodle pictures of your dreams. Post it on the refrigerator as a reminder that pipe dreams can come true. Look at Cinderella—it worked for her.

Beat the egg whites and cream of tartar at high speed until soft peaks form that look like cloud nine. Add in the sugar and vanilla a little at a time (don't want to do it too fast and deflate your dreams), until the mixture is as glossy as a silver lining. Fold in the cocoa, then the chocolate chunks. Do this gently   and watch that you don't get any feathers in the mix.

Drop by tablespoons onto the parchment paper. Bake thirty-five to forty-five minutes, or until dry. Cool slightly, then peel paper backing from cookies, pop them in your mouth and dream of a good-looking, rich and luscious future. If it helps you to indulge more, wear a nice pair of feathered mules and stretch out on the divan à la Elizabeth Taylor.

CHAPTER 23

"You know you're insane, don't you?" Rachel said. She'd arrived bright and early, albeit with a few grumbles about being roused from bed before noon on a Saturday morning.

Michael grinned. He folded the top layer of tissue paper over the gift, then carefully fitted the lid onto the giant box. "Yeah, probably."

"She's never going to accept this from you."

"That's why *you're* going to deliver it." He withdrew a sheet of stationery from the top drawer of his desk, wrote a note, sealed it in an envelope, wrote "Candy" on the outside, then attached it to the top of the box. "Just make sure you give it to her personally."

"How will I know which one she is?"

"She's the bride. Pretty hard to miss."

Rachel put a hand on his shoulder and gave it a little squeeze, then released him quickly, as if she didn't want to be caught by the affection police. "You know, you're not so bad for a brother. If I weren't your sister, I might actually think you were boyfriend material." She bent to pick up the box, but not before he saw a faint sheen of red in her cheeks.

"Hey, thanks . . . I think."

She grinned, toting the big box in both arms. "So what are you going to do after I drop this off?"

"Wait. Hope. Pray." He took in a breath. "But first, I have one more stop to make."

"We're here!" Rebecca came into Candace's apartment the morning of the wedding, dispensing a hug and a bright smile. "Best friends to the rescue."

"And we come with lots of supplies." Maria held up a bag of sweets from the shop. "All the chocolates you can eat and more."

"Thank God." Candace grabbed the bag out of her hand and peeked inside. "All my chips went ahoy in my stomach sea an hour ago."

"That bad, huh?"

"My nerves are shot. I'd kill anyone who got between me and a Hershey bar."

"Hey, you're a woman. Craving chocolate is in your DNA." Maria patted her on the shoulder.

"So, where's your dress?" Rebecca asked. "I'm surprised you're not wearing it yet. The limo's supposed to be here to take you to the church in fifteen minutes."

"I haven't put it on. I guess I've been a bit distracted this morning." Della had left two hours before, to ensure perfection with everything. Grandma had already headed over early to get a good seat before big Aunt Bertha from Somerville arrived and blocked the view. That had left Candace alone, to stew—and chew—in nervous anticipation.

She led the way toward her bedroom. Trifecta tagged along, hobbling into the room and leaping up onto the corner of the bed. Bob stationed himself in front of the fish tank, hoping in vain for a tetra to make a leap for freedom.

Candace lugged the big white bag out of the closet, pulled down the zipper and released the enormous white cloud from its plastic coffin. "Ta-da!" Her voice held all the enthusiasm of Eeyore's.

"Oh," Maria said.

"Oh my," Rebecca said.

Candace sighed. "I kept the one Bernadine picked out."

"I can see that." Maria picked up and released a piece of the faux suede edging. "The question is, why?"

Candace dropped down onto her bed, the dress landing like a smooshed cream puff beside her. "I don't know. It seemed easier. I thought about shopping for another one, and Barry even offered to buy me a new dress, but . . ." There was that tightening feeling starting in her chest again, clawing at her throat, blocking her breath, squeezing at her heart.

Air. She needed air. No, not air. She needed . . .

Candace lunged for the bag of treats Maria had brought, tore it open and grabbed a double chocolate macadamia cookie, stuffing it into her mouth before her throat closed up and left her unable to sugar up.

Rebecca took a seat beside her on the light blue plaid comforter. "I thought you picked out a dress you loved the other day when you went shopping with . . ." She didn't finish the sentence, as if saying his name would invoke the temptation to think about Michael.

Too late. He'd been on her mind for days.

"I did." Candace sniffled and dug in the bag for another cookie. "It was perfect. I loved it. The saleslady even said it looked delightful." And then she was crying, the tears streaming down her face faster than Porsches on the autobahn. She shoved another cookie into her mouth.

"Then why didn't you buy it?" Maria placed a third cookie in Candace's palm.

"Because . . . because I couldn't imagine marrying Barry in it." Now she had a full-fledged avalanche of waterworks running down her face.

"Who else would you wear—" Maria started to say. "Oh. *Oh.*"

Rebecca cast Maria a look that said, *Don't say it.*

"I'm marrying Barry," Candace said, and started to sob again.

But after all that had happened . . . could she still go through with this today? Wearing that *thing* that was sitting on her bed?

Rebecca's emerald satin gown rustled as she moved closer and turned Candace's chin up to meet her gaze. "Are you really, really sure?"

"Everybody's already there. The priest is waiting. I have a dress. Sort of." This time she grabbed a fudge brownie from the bag and downed it in two gulps.

"If you aren't sure, don't do it. A marriage isn't a temporary thing."

"I know. But . . . but Barry is just like me. That makes him perfect, doesn't it?"

It was the logic she'd built *everything* on. Barry was perfect because he was her identical match. If he was all wrong for her, then all her carefully laid plans were wrong, too. That would mean all the planning and objective thinking in the world wouldn't save her from making another mistake.

That was exactly the kind of chaos Candace couldn't handle. There wasn't enough chocolate in Hershey, Pennsylvania, to help her face that truth.

Maria pulled up the ottoman, took a seat, and then fished out a second brownie and handed it to her. "Do you remember the conversation we had in the shop about your planner?"

Candace thought for a minute, chewing. "Yeah, I think so."

Maria bit her lip, as if weighing her words carefully. "Well, I told you there's more of your grandma in you than you think. And . . . I think you should take her approach to this."

"What? Get married naked?"

"No. Look at what's going to make you happiest. What's going to make you excited about beginning every day? If

Barry isn't the man to get your motor running, as Grandma would say, then"—she glanced at Rebecca, who nodded support, then returned her gaze to Candace—"you shouldn't go through with this."

Candace jerked to her feet, shaking her head. "I can't let sex rule my decisions."

"Hey, it works for me," Maria said with a grin.

"We're not talking about sex. Well, *I'm* not, anyway," Rebecca said. "Who knows what goes through Maria's mind. I think we should get her spayed." She winked, to show she meant no harm.

"Hey, I think about things other than sex." Maria smoothed out her skirt. "Like shopping. And donuts. And donut boys. I can't help it if Krispy Kreme hires cuter help than Dunkin' Donuts. I go there solely for the donuts."

Rebecca rolled her eyes. "I can smell the bullshit from here."

Candace toyed with the tulle edging of her dress. "I just can't see myself running out and getting a new husband every time I get an urge for a devils food instead of a honey dipped."

"You look terrified today." Rebecca draped an arm over her shoulders. "What is it, Candace? It's more than being afraid of repeating your mom's marriage record, isn't it?"

"Yeah."

"Then what?"

She shook her head. "How do you ever know you're making the right decision? I mean, I thought planning it all out, analyzing my choice, was the way to go. It made sense, at least to me."

"That works when you're picking out a minivan. Not a husband."

She flipped the brownie over and over in her left palm. It crumbled, breaking into several pieces, each as delicious alone as they had been together. Grandma would have found some kind of sign in the broken brownie, but all Candace saw was a need for the Hoover. "I just don't know if I can trust my heart."

Rebecca and Maria both drew Candace into a huge, supportive hug. "Hey, if there's anyone who has a good heart, it's you," Maria said softly. "Trust it. You deserve to be happy."

"You're going to be okay," Rebecca told her. "It's all going to work out."

This was what friends were for. To put the brownie bride back together when she crumbled.

"Aw, I love you guys." Candace nodded, sniffling. "Even more than chocolate."

Bernadine's When-the-Truth-Falls-Apart Chocolate Cherry Crumble

1 ½ cups chocolate cookie crumbs
¼ cup pureed prunes
¼ cup semisweet chocolate chips
2 cans (20 ounces each) of cherry pie filling

You've made your bed, now it's time to pay the piper with a little prunes—bound to bring out the truth in anyone. Mix the crumbs and prunes with a pastry blender until it looks as crumby as your lies have been. Add the chocolate chips, one for every untruth spoken in the last three weeks.

Spread the pie filling evenly in a pie plate; cover it up with the chocolate crumbs, just like you've been covering your own tracks. Bake at 375 degrees for twenty minutes and think about how the truth can set you free.

Or ruin your life.

CHAPTER 24

By the time she had her dress on and had consumed every treat in the bag, Candace had decided she couldn't marry Barry with this secret between them. Screw Dear Abby's advice about keeping an affair to yourself. That wasn't fair to Barry, or to their marriage.

The limo pulled up to the church and Candace got out before the driver could even open the door, leaving Rebecca and Maria behind. "I have to talk to Barry," she told them.

Candace hurried into Our Lady of Faith, through the doors, down the white-pathed aisle and toward the door at the back of the church where the groomsmen waited. The white tulle bell of a dress swirled around her legs like an upside-down melting soft serve.

She yanked open the door. "Barry. We need to talk."

He jerked up in surprise. His face reddened and he shoved the Sears catalog he was holding to the side, exposing pages of ads for high-heeled women's sandals on perfectly pedicured feet.

"Uh, okay. Sure." He gestured toward the two tuxedoed groomsmen, who left the room with a look of "uh-oh" on their faces.

"I have something to tell you." She moved to plop into a chair, missed, grabbed at the wooden armrests and felt around under the massive skirt for the cushion. On the second try, she managed a seat.

"Is something wrong, dear?"

Father Pete's dish of Hershey's Kisses sat on the table to her right. Bless the man. She'd finished off the treats from Gift Baskets in the limo, leaving a little trail of chocolate shavings on the leather seat.

Surely one chocolate kiss wouldn't hurt. It would . . . coat her tongue. Make the truth come out easier. She unwrapped a kiss and popped it into her mouth.

"You've been eating a lot of chocolate lately."

"Yeah?" she said around a mouthful of Hershey.

"You know, chocolate is filled with nothing but empty calories."

"It's food for my endorphins." Candace popped another into her mouth.

"Honey, you're aware we're supposed to get married in five minutes, right?" He gave her an appraising glance, then a soft smile. "The dress looks very nice on you. Better than it did in the store."

"Thanks." Candace sighed and dropped the unwrapped kiss back into the bowl. "I'm here because I need to tell you something."

He nodded, his lips thin and tight. "I already know."

"You do?"

"I could see it in your face. You didn't think you could hide it, did you?"

"Well, it's not like I'm wearing a sign or anything," Candace said. "That went out about the same time they stopped hanging dancing women for being witches."

"Well, I can't say I'm proud of what you've done, but I know you can make it right." He patted her fluffy knee. "Mother and I were talking about it and we thought after the honeymoon would be the best time for you to start working on changing."

"You told your *mother?*" No wonder she'd been giving her the evil eye at the shower.

"I had to. She guessed before I did."

Maybe Bernadine was psychic. Or maybe she hadn't been visiting Aunt Miriam. Maybe she'd been following Candace's every move. Either way, Barry knew. She wished again she could undo what had happened. Guilt hovered over her, heavy and thick.

She dropped her head into her hands. "I'm really sorry, Barry. I never meant to hurt you."

"You didn't hurt me. You only hurt yourself, dear."

"You know . . . and you still want to marry me?"

He tipped her chin up and smiled into her eyes. "Of course I do, honey." His grin widened, full of support and understanding. "You've gained a few pounds from all that chocolate you've been eating, but if you're willing to work on the problem, I'm willing to overlook it until after we get back from our honeymoon in Phoenix."

She blinked. "You . . . you think I came in here to confess I'd put on a little weight?"

"Of course. What else could you have done? You're as perfect as a pin."

She shook her head. Oh, this was going all wrong. "Barry. There's more I haven't told you. I—"

Father Pete stuck his head in the door. "Candace! Here's where you are. Everyone's looking for you. It's time to get marching down the aisle. The organist has already started. Barry, get into place." Father Pete gave them an excited thumbs up. "Next time you see each other, it will be as husband and wife."

Barry scrambled to his feet and gave Candace a quick kiss on the forehead. "See you soon, darling."

"No, Barry! I have to tell you something. Don't—"

But he was already gone.

Candace took the bowl of kisses with her back to the bride's room. She doubted she'd burn in hell for stealing Father Pete's chocolates.

This was, after all, an emergency.

"This came for you," Della said, pointing to a big white box that lay on the crushed red velvet love seat in the bride's room. "Some teenage girl dropped it off. She was wearing combat boots. I do hope she's not part of the wedding party. My flowers don't go with camo."

"Teenage girl?" Candace started to undo the pale pink bow that held the box shut. "I don't know anyone who's a—"

She stopped talking when she saw the handwriting on the cream-colored envelope. Only one person called her "Candy." Her hands shaking, she opened the envelope and unfolded the single piece of linen stationery. "In this box is the wedding dress of your dreams. But there's a catch. You can only wear it to marry me. I love you. Michael."

"Oh honey, you look so pretty in your dress," Della said. "Like an angel tree topper. I think these flowers are going to—" Her mother stopped when Candace didn't respond. "What is it?"

Tears sprang anew in Candace's eyes. "A marriage proposal."

"Oh, that Barry. How silly. You're already getting married today."

She shook her head. "It's not from Barry."

The air in the room seemed to weigh more than all the water in Boston Harbor. After a long moment, her mother let out a breath. "Oh."

Candace folded the paper and stuffed it back into the envelope, then pushed the box from Reverie Bridal aside. Percy, a little wrist corsage dangling from his diamond-studded collar, leaped up onto the love seat and nosed at the top of the cardboard box.

"You aren't going to look inside?"

"No. What's in there is for a dream, not a reality."

"Dreams are good, honey. A life of all reality is about as much fun as sitting through a twelve-day seminar on tax law."

Candace shook her head and dove into Father Pete's candy stash again. Half the Kisses were now in her stomach instead of in the bowl. "You don't understand. I can't undo what I've done. It's all planned out. Everyone's waiting."

"You haven't said your vows yet. It *can* be undone."

She had three more Hershey's Kisses unwrapped and in her mouth before she spoke again. "I don't live my life like that. Not anymore."

Della took a step closer, her face soft. For a moment, she didn't look like the zillion-times married divorcée who bought fishnet body stockings and pink boas on a whim, but more like . . . a mom. "Not since the summer you went to your dad's?"

"How do you know about that?"

"Just because your father and I got divorced doesn't mean we never have a conversation about you." Her mother brushed a tendril of hair off Candace's forehead. "You're about the only thing we *can* talk about anymore. I kind of miss the days when we used to talk, just your dad and I."

"But . . . I never told anyone what happened, not even Dad."

"I know. But your father knew you'd been hurt pretty badly, so he called me." Della cocked her head, her hazel eyes studying Candace's face. "And after that, you became the complete opposite of me, didn't you?"

"It's not that I didn't love you or anything." Candace sighed. "I felt like if I planned things better, made better choices, didn't go off all hari-kari again, I wouldn't end up hurt like that."

"What'd you think, honey?" Della said. "If you controlled everything, you'd never make a mistake?"

"That was the plan."

Her mother shook her head, then stepped forward and drew Candace into a hug. Tears welled up in Candace's eyes and a new kind of tight feeling sprung to life in her chest. "Baby, life is not about control. The more you try to keep a thumb on it, the less you really have in your grasp."

She let out a shaky laugh. "You might be right about that, Mom."

Della stepped back and swiped a tear off her own face. "I've made a lot of mistakes in my life. But the only one I've never regretted is having you." She smiled. "I wish I *had* found a man I could love and settle down with for years and years. I didn't value the one good man I had when I had him—your dad. I should have trusted my heart more back then." She pointed toward the box on the couch. "If you find someone who loves you that much, who'd send you a marriage proposal on your wedding day to try and get you to change your mind, then you need to listen to your heart." Her mother cupped her face. "Don't marry a man you don't love. And don't walk away from a man you do just because you're afraid of being hurt."

Candace glanced at the box again. "He's crazy if he thinks—"

"He's crazy about *you.*" Della smiled, straightened Candace's veil. "But, if Barry's the man who makes you happy, then marry him. Don't try to control your feelings, honey. Just *listen* to them."

Before Candace could listen to anything besides the nervous, rapid thuds of her heart, the music started and her father was at the door, ready to escort her to her groom.

Candace's The-Decision-Is-as Clear-as-Mud Cake

1 ½ cups margarine, divided
4 eggs
1 cup cocoa, divided
1 ½ cups all-purpose flour
2 cups sugar
¼ teaspoon salt
1 ¼ cups peanuts, chopped
3 cups mini marshmallows
35 vanilla wafers
1 tub chocolate frosting

Beat one cup of the margarine, the eggs and half of the cocoa until well mixed, all the while talking out loud and discussing your options with yourself. Add the flour, sugar, salt and nuts. Try not to think about how you'd be nuts for choosing bachelor number one or . . . choosing bachelor number two.

Spread the cake batter in a greased nine-by-thirteen-inch pan and bake at 350 degrees for thirty-five minutes. Plenty of time to write a pro-con list, maybe a few of them. Sprinkle the marshmallows on the hot cake when it's done baking, then pop it back in the oven for a couple of minutes until they puff up like Grandma's s'mores. Top with wafers, then frost.

If you still haven't made up your mind, serve cake with milk and keep eating until a sign as big as a billboard comes along and guides you in the right direction.

CHAPTER 25

The sounds of "Trumpet Voluntary" swelled through the air. One of the groomsmen escorted Della down the front of the church to her seat. The entire church seemed to reverberate with each note, the organist pounding out the music with a fervor unmatched by the Boston Pops.

"You ready, honey?" her father asked as they waited in the vestry for the bridal march cue. He'd arrived the night before, in time to walk his daughter down the aisle. She hadn't seen him in several months and he looked at her now, happily unaware of the turmoil churning in her stomach like an undercooked burrito.

"Of course." Candace bit back the scream that tried to escape from her throat.

"Oh no, you're not." He pulled a handkerchief from his tuxedo pocket. "You have some chocolate on your face." He dabbed at her cheek. "There. All better. You almost walked down the aisle looking like dessert instead of like the bride." He tucked the handkerchief away, then wrapped her arm around his own and gave her hand a pat. "Your mother looks beautiful in that blue dress. Very beautiful."

"She said you didn't look so bad yourself."

"Really?" He turned to glance at his daughter. "She talked about me?"

"Yeah. And she said nice things."

"Huh." Jacob Woodrow paused a second, peering over the crowd ahead of them. "Where's her husband?"

Ahead of them, Rebecca's daughter, dainty in her flower girl dress, began to strew rose petals along the white path. Barry's four-year-old nephew reluctantly tagged along with her, dragging a ring pillow at his heels and making his displeasure at being seen in public with a girl obvious by sticking out his tongue at the back of her head.

"Mom is currently unattached."

"Oh. *Oh.*" Her father cleared his throat. "Well, maybe I'll ask her to dance later."

"I think she'd like that."

He thought a minute, then cast her a worried glance. "Barry does have a retirement account, doesn't he?"

"Yes, Dad, he does. And stock options. And life insurance."

Rebecca and Maria made their march, sedately stepping along the flower-strewn path. Too quickly, they reached the end of the aisle and stepped into place on the left side of the church.

"Disability?"

"Long- and short-term."

Her father patted her arm again. "Then you have my blessings."

The bridal march began and the people in the church turned and stood, an expectant wave of guests waiting for the main act. With her arm linked in her father's, there was nowhere else to go but forward.

Toward Barry.

Keeping pace with her father, she began the slow journey

down the aisle, clutching the bouquet of lilies and orchids like a lifeline. Her ankles trembled, her hands started to shake.

Ten pews to go.

At the end of the aisle, Barry was watching her, a nervous grin on his face. She looked around at the other dozens of faces awaiting her arrival. Friends. Family. Acquaintances.

Five pews.

And then, at the end, Maria and Rebecca. Grandma and George. Della. Bernadine. Dressed in a rhinestone-studded purple muumuu, she was the only one in the crowd wearing a scowl as an accessory.

Father Pete, his hands on a Bible, stood in the middle of the group at the altar. Her friends were all beaming proudly, encouraging her with their smiles. Her mother nodded at her. *They're waiting for you. It's time.*

Three pews.

The tightening swelled in her chest. She swallowed, sure one of Trifecta's tennis balls was wedged in her throat. Her step faltered.

"Are you all right?" her father whispered in her ear.

She nodded and took another step. Five more feet and she would be standing beside Barry, pledging to love him for the rest of her life.

To become Mrs. Barry Borkenstein. Forever.

She swallowed again and wiped a bead of sweat from her brow. The chocolate in her stomach churned in disagreement.

She glanced again at the altar. Something was missing. The candles? The flowers? But no, all was in its place. Everything except—

And then, the realization came to her, clear and true. There was only one face she wanted to see, only one man who should be there at the end of the aisle, only one man she wanted to marry.

And he wasn't there.

She halted in midstep. Her father teetered forward, then jerked back. He glanced over at her, surprise in his face. Father Pete's eyes widened, the organist missed a key, and the entire crowd fell silent.

"I can't do it," Candace said, giving her bouquet to her father. Her voice sounded twenty decibels louder than usual, as if the voluminous skirt created a megaphone effect. "I've made a terrible mistake. I'm sorry."

Then she turned and ran like hell, abandoning her own carefully made plans.

Barry was the first one out of the door of the church. He charged down the steps, then slowed when he saw Candace sitting on the bottom step in the June sunshine. "You okay?"

"No. Yes." She sighed. "I don't know."

"Is it something I did? Were you overcome by the heat? I can have Father Pete turn on a fan." He took a seat beside her on the step and ran a hand over his face. "Maybe it was all the chocolate you've been eating. You might be having a sugar reaction."

She turned to him, taking in his big, brown eyes. So trusting. So ready to believe the best of her. And all she'd done was let him down. "No, Barry, it's nothing like that." She sighed. "I can't marry you."

"Can't?" He blinked. "What *exactly* does that mean?"

"I changed my mind." She bit her lip and felt a heaviness descend into her chest. "I'm so sorry."

"You decided this *now?* As you were walking down the aisle?"

"More or less."

"But . . ."

The silence was the hardest part. She knew she should offer some kind of explanation, something concrete. But for the first time, she'd acted on a gut reaction, not on anything she'd planned or thought about ahead of time.

Barry, however, deserved a reason.

"I was walking toward you and I felt . . . I felt like if I went through with it, I'd be making a huge mistake. It's not that I don't care about you. Or that I don't think you're a great guy. Or that I don't think you'd make a wonderful husband."

"Just not for you."

"No, not for me." She sighed. "I should have figured this out earlier. We've dated for two years. I know you pretty well. And I thought I knew myself, what I wanted. *Who* I wanted."

"What was I, an old pair of shoes you didn't want to get rid of? Is that why you stayed with me all this time?"

"No. It's not that." She laid a hand on his arm, but he jerked it away. She'd hurt him, which was exactly what she'd been trying to avoid.

And the Screwup of the Year Award Goes to . . .

Candace took a breath and searched for a way to explain. "I've lived my whole life—well, a lot of my life—trying not to be like my mother."

"I understand that."

"I was so afraid of acting without thinking that I thought *too* much. Do you know what I mean?"

He looked at her, blinked several times. "No, I guess I don't."

Her smile was watery. "And maybe that's the problem. There's a whole other side to me I've kept tucked behind the planners and the lists and the spreadsheets. Hoping that if I did everything by the book, I'd never make a wrong turn."

Barry draped his arms over his knees. The black tuxedo sleeves rode up on his wrists. "And today you thought marrying me was one of those wrong turns?"

"Yeah. And I'm really, really sorry." This time, when she laid a hand on his, he didn't move away. "You deserve someone who appreciates you for who you are. Not someone who's marrying you because she's afraid to really be who *she* is."

He thought for a minute, looking out over the grassy knoll across the street from the church. A bird fluttered by them, and a faint breeze whispered through the trees. Traffic came and went, humming along as if nothing monumental had occurred on the steps of Our Lady of Faith.

"You're really sure about this? You don't want to take a few minutes and think about it?"

She shook her head.

"Then I guess that's it. I wouldn't want to be married to someone who wasn't a hundred percent sure." He grinned—albeit a small grin—but when he did, Candace knew why she'd spent two years with him. He was a nice guy. A safe guy. One she'd never, ever regret meeting and dating. "I'm an accountant. I like it when all the numbers in the column add up to a hundred."

She returned the smile. "There's a girl out there who will be the right balance for your credits and debits."

"Yeah." He dusted invisible dirt off the knees of his tuxedo, then got to his feet. "Do you need a ride or anything?"

"No. I'll be okay."

"All right." Barry took a step, then pivoted back. "If you ever need a coffee that's exactly the right temperature, you know where I am."

She smiled. "Thanks."

He gestured toward the church. "I'll go in and tell them all. I think I should be the one to break the news to Mother."

"Somehow, I think she's going to take it just fine."

Just as Barry was heading in, Marcy, the photographer, was coming out of the church, camera in one hand, open planner balanced in the other. "Did you want me to get a shot of you two out here? It wasn't on the list. And we're running six and three-quarter minutes behind schedule. The caterers—"

"There's not going to be a wedding," Barry interrupted.

The brunette paled. "No wedding? But I have this schedule and—" She bit her lip, clutched the leather book to her chest. "I've never had this kind of glitch happen before. Wh-what do you want me to do?"

"Come on back inside with me," Barry said, waving the slim photographer ahead of him as he pulled open the door of the church. "I have a feeling there'll be a few photo ops inside in a few minutes."

Marcy scooted inside, her open-toed sandals making little clacking sounds against the marble threshold.

"Nice shoes," Barry said.

"Oh, thanks. I'm a shoe addict, I swear." She let out a laugh.

"Oh, *really?*" Barry said. The door began to swing shut behind them, but not before Candace heard him asking, "By the way, where *did* you get that planner?"

A few seconds later, Candace snuck back inside to retrieve Michael's box and her tote bag from the bride's room. She ducked around the corner, avoiding the doors to the sanctuary, and the murmuring, gossiping crowd inside. She could hear Bernadine crying about her "poor Barry" and moaning she'd never be a grandmother before she died.

Grandma Woodrow came running up to Candace the instant she entered the tiny bride's room. "What happened out there?"

"The signs became a billboard." Candace sagged onto the love seat. "I decided not to marry Barry."

"Good for you. You deserve a man with a backbone bigger than yours."

"Grandma!"

"Did he take it okay? Do you need a getaway car? I can get up to a hundred and ten in the Chevy, you know."

Candace laughed. "I'm fine, Barry's fine. It's all going to work out okay."

"Good." Grandma sat down beside her and gave her shoulders a squeeze. "All's well that begins well. And you're getting a new beginning today, angel pie."

There was a knock at the door and then Maria and Rebecca poked their heads in. "Hey, there you are," Rebecca said. "You okay?"

"Yeah." Candace nodded. "Definitely."

"If we come in and tell you something, do you promise not to kill us?" Maria asked. "I have a date on Saturday and I don't think James is interested in kissing a corpse."

Candace laughed. "Your life is safe with me. You guys are my best friends."

"Best meddling friends, actually." Rebecca swished into the room and sat in one of the armchairs. "Michael called the store yesterday."

"He did?"

"He begged us to tell him where the wedding was. He was clearly desperate and hurting, so we had to put him out of his misery," Maria said. "We figured he had something up his sleeve, but we didn't know what it was. When he didn't show up this morning—"

"Oh, he showed up. In a way." Candace held up the box. "He sent me a wedding dress. And a marriage proposal." She took off the lid and showed them the exquisite gown from Reverie Bridal.

"That's the biggest damn billboard I ever saw," Grandma said. "That kind of sign hits you like a Mack truck."

"You're one smart grandma," Candace said, giving her grandmother a one-armed hug. She recovered the box, then slid it onto her lap. "Why didn't you guys tell me he called?"

"Because you had to make up your own mind. If anyone else made it up for you, you'd always have doubts." Rebecca gave her shoulder a squeeze.

"You're right."

"Hey, that's why we're women," Maria said. "Because we're always right."

"So what are you going to do now?" Rebecca asked.

"I don't know." She picked up the box, slung her tote bag over her shoulder and headed toward the door. "And for once, that thought doesn't terrify me."

On her way out the door, she spied Father Pete's bowl of Hershey's Kisses on the table.

Candace kept on walking, right past the chocolate.

Grandma's The-Treasure-is-Hidden-in-the-Center Dinner Rolls

3 cups all-purpose flour
3 tablespoons sugar
1 package (¼ ounce) active dry yeast
1 teaspoon salt
1 cup milk
3 tablespoons butter, softened
1 egg
8 ounces milk chocolate

Sometimes, you gotta peek inside to find the real gift. These cookies will help you keep that little bit of wisdom in mind. Combine the milk and butter in a saucepan and heat until the mixture reaches 130 degrees. Add the egg, then stir in the flour, sugar, yeast and salt. Ooh, it's magic. You've made dough, and pretty damn easily, too.

Knead on a floured surface, making sure you get a good workout in to prevent those chicken wing arms. Shape the dough into a ball, put it in a greased bowl, then smear a little grease on the dough ball, cover it and let it rise until it's twice as big as it was before. Yeast is baker's Viagra, don't you know?

Punch it down, then knead again for a minute and break off into eight pieces. Put an ounce of chocolate in the center of each hunk, being sure to close it up good and tight. Put the chocolate-stuffed delights on a greased cookie sheet, then set it aside to rise again for a few minutes. When they're good and puffy, brush them with a bit of milk, then bake at 400 degrees for about fifteen minutes.

These may look like ordinary dinner rolls, but inside is a treasure to be enjoyed. Remember that bit of advice—sometimes the best things are right there under your nose.

Take a big bite out of life and you'll find the sweetness under the surface.

CHAPTER 26

Michael screeched to a halt in front of the church. He didn't bother parking, just slid the Lexus haphazardly into the first space he found. He tossed off a quick apology to his passengers for the whiplash, then hopped out and ran up the walkway toward the double doors of the church.

Candy hadn't responded to his note. He thought she'd call. Tell him the wedding with Barry was off. Or at least tell him to go to hell. Either way, his misery would be over and he'd have an answer.

But he didn't have squat. After an hour of pacing a hole in his apartment floor and barking at Sam, he'd finally jumped into the car and headed over to the church.

Out of the corner of his eye, he spied a marshmallow, striding down the sidewalk with determination. No, not a marshmallow. Another kind of candy.

His Candy. Carrying the box he'd sent and looking like the most delicious thing he'd ever seen, even though the puffy dress was all wrong for her.

So was Barry. And if Michael couldn't make her see that, he was going to make a damn good fool out of himself trying.

"Don't do it," he shouted, running to catch up with her.

She spun around like an angel on a Christmas tree. The sun bounced off the curls in her hair with glints of gold. God, he'd missed her smile. Her eyes. Her touch. It was all he could do to hold himself back from pulling her into his arms and kissing her until she promised to be his.

Forever. And the day after that, in case forever wasn't long enough.

"You already missed the part where you put in your objections."

His heart plummeted into his gut. "You aren't . . . ? You didn't . . ."

She smiled. "I didn't marry Barry."

The relief that flooded through him could have swamped California. And now he did move forward, taking her into his arms. Well, taking her as best he could, with an enormous dress box between them. "I see you got my gift."

"Every girl needs two wedding dresses. And a backup plan." She winked at him.

"*I* am not a backup plan." He studied her hazel eyes, hoping for a clue, finding only a tease. "Did you read the note?"

"Uh-huh."

"And . . . ?" He held his breath, his pulse beating faster than a Michael Jackson record played at seventy-eight revolutions per minute. "What was your answer?"

She cocked her head to the right. "Isn't this the time when you get scared?"

"Oh, I'm terrified. Feel my heart." He took the box, laid it on the ground beside them, then placed her hand against the left side of his chest.

Beneath her fingers, Candace could feel the steady rhythm of his heart, thudding quick and strong and causing an answering call in her own veins. "Do you still mean what you said in the note?"

"Every word. I'm not so afraid of commitment anymore, not since I met you." He lowered his mouth within kissing distance. Heat curled between them, tensing the thread of want. "What I *am* afraid of is you running off on me."

"I'm not going anywhere." She grinned. "Especially not in this dress."

"Good. But just in case, I brought along some insurance."

She quirked a brow. "Insurance?"

"Yeah." He grinned, then grabbed the box and led her down the sidewalk toward the Lexus. When he opened the door, two heads leaned out to greet her.

"Shalom, Candace!"

"Jerry? Lucy? What are you two doing here?" Jerry was wearing his new suit, his hair slicked back and his beard neatly trimmed. Lucy had on, of all things, a blue calico-print dress and sensible navy pumps. Candace hadn't even known the tomboyish Lucy owned a dress, never mind knew how to wear one.

"We're here to convince you to follow your destiny," Jerry said, giving her a stern but friendly look. He got out of the car, then cupped a hand around his mouth and tilted his head toward Candace's ear. "And we figured if you weren't using that priest, we'd get your dollar's worth for you."

"But you're *Jewish.*"

"My Lucy's not. A minor detail." He shrugged. "I figure we might as well cover all the bases. We might run over and pay a visit to the Trappist monks later, too, just in case."

Candace laughed. "I don't think they perform marriages."

Lucy had gotten out of the car and come around to Jerry's side, clasping his hand in hers and looking like a woman in love, even though she towered a good foot and sixty pounds over her intended. "He's just anxious for a wedding night," she said. "He'd get married by the swan boat operator in Boston Common if he thought it would be legal and binding. My Jerry is a gentleman. Wants to do it up right."

Jerry laughed. "For love, I'll make any sacrifice." He raised a skinny arm and flexed. "Climb any mountain."

"The only mountain you'll be climbing tonight is me, mister," Lucy said. Then her face reddened and she stepped away. "Well, we better get going. Uh, good luck, Candace." And with that, the two of them were gone, holding hands and giggling like two seventh graders dashing off to their first dance together.

"I like Jerry's philosophy," Michael said. "Spontaneity and creativity."

"Gets the girl every time."

"And did it?"

She opened the back door of the Lexus, laid the dress box carefully on the back seat, then shut the door again. "Well . . ."

He spun her around to face him. "You're not having second thoughts on me, are you?"

Oh, she was going to love teasing him over the next fifty years. Who knew it could be this much fun? That a few words and a smile could make her heart sing like the ending of a Disney movie?

For now, though, she decided to go easy on him. Later, there'd be more teasing. And much, much more fun.

"Nope, no second thoughts at all. Not anymore." She took a breath, then met his gaze. "When I was younger, I made one really stupid mistake because I got more wrapped up in feelings than common sense. I thought if I planned everything out, I'd never make a mistake again. But it was a pretty stupid plan because I almost married the wrong guy."

"Damn good thing you came to your senses."

She smiled. "I had a little help. From my friends. My family. And you." She stepped forward and kissed him. There were no doubts, no hesitations, no regrets in her kiss. Just everything she was feeling in her heart.

And a few things she was feeling elsewhere, too.

"Whew," he said after a few moments. "I'd say that's a nice way to begin."

She captured his cobalt gaze with her own. "I suddenly don't crave chocolate anymore at all. I want something else much more."

His smirk sent a little thrill through her. "Something you can't get enough of?"

"I don't think my appetite will *ever* be satisfied."

"Good." He cupped her face in his hands, his thumbs tracing the outline of her jaw. "Because I love you, Candy."

Never had anyone said those words to her the way Michael had. Deep and solid. The kind of love she'd been searching for, even if she hadn't known she'd been looking.

"I love you, too." The answering smile on his face soared through her heart. She leaned forward, sealing the words with a kiss.

Behind them, the doors of the church opened and the guests began spilling out, talking amongst themselves. The volume of the gossip raised several decibels when people spied the bride kissing a man who wasn't the groom.

"Quit gawking, you bunch of rubberneckers," Grandma Woodrow said. "There's better stuff to watch on *Celebrities Uncensored*. Leave my granddaughter to her life."

"Let's get out of here." Candace tugged at his hand.

"Good idea." Michael opened the door for her, then ran around to the other side and slid into the driver's seat, putting the car into gear and pulling out onto the street. Within seconds, they were heading toward the on-ramp for the expressway. "Where to?"

"Anywhere. See where the road takes us."

He laughed. "That isn't much of a plan."

She dug into her tote bag and pulled out the black-and-purple wedding planner. Then she lowered the electric window and chucked it onto I-93. "I'm done with plans. For now."

He grinned at her. "And how long is that going to last?"

From the side mirror, Candace watched the pages fluttering sadly against the concrete. "Probably just until I get myself to an office supply store."

He laughed. "I love you, Candy. Planner and all."

Candace and Michael's Recipe for a Happy Ending

1 lonely bachelor
1 slightly committed bride-to-be
1 meddling grandma
3 well-meaning friends
1 flighty mother
1 brassy sister
large vials of sexual attraction
equal parts honesty and commitment

Take all of the above, mix well and bring to a boil. When the flavors are completely melded, sprinkle in a proposal from the bachelor to the bride. Let sit in a church crowded with loved ones. Bring in extras as needed, including one ex-rabbi and his policewoman wife.

Wait until all the vows are exchanged, then toss cookie crumbs and good wishes at the new Mr. and Mrs. Michael Vogler.

Please turn the page for an exciting preview of
Shirley Jump's next book in this series,
THE DEVIL SERVED TORTELLINI.
Available in March 2005 from Zebra

Maria let go of Dante's hand abruptly, as if she'd just realized she'd been holding it. She wrapped her arms around herself. "It's cold out."

"That's March in Boston for you." He shrugged out of his leather jacket and draped it over her shoulders.

"Thanks. But won't you be cold?" Even as she said the words, she snuggled a bit into his coat. The action thrust her breasts forward, and before he could think better of it, he was drawing the jacket shut across her front, the backs of his knuckles grazing her chest.

"I'm not cold right now. At all." He released his grip on the coat, before he gave in to the urge to rip it and everything else she was wearing right off that delicious body and then, against the brick wall, show her a warmth of a very different kind.

"Thank you for the flowers."

"My pleasure. You probably saved my business Tuesday night, you know. The review came out Thursday morning and we've been hopping ever since. Every day, before I get into work, our answering machine is already full of reservation requests."

"That's wonderful. Good for you." She stepped back, as if she were about to say good-bye and to go into the house.

Dante moved forward, no longer maintaining his respectable distance. The scent of jasmine teased at his nostrils, drawing him in like a siren song. "Why are you avoiding me?"

"I'm not."

"Yes, you are." He reached up and captured one of those stray ringlets in his finger, twirling the velvet tendril in a leisurely, sensual movement. "Is it my antipasto?"

She blinked. "Your . . . your what?"

He smiled. She wasn't as immune to him as she thought. "The salad, remember? Was it so terrible that you decided never to see me again?"

"No, not at all. It was . . . delicious." She gulped. "I've just been thinking since I met you Tuesday night and . . . I don't think getting involved with you is a good idea."

He took a half step closer, the cloud of his breath mingling with hers. He trailed his finger down her jaw line, along soft, smooth skin that glided beneath his touch like silk. Her eyes widened; her lips parted. He'd never wanted to kiss anyone so damn bad in his life. "Who said anything about getting involved? Why can't we just have mind-blowing sex? A few hundred times or so?"

She laughed, a rich sound that flowed from her like wine from a bottle. "Only a guy would say something like that."

He cupped her chin, tracing her lower lip with his thumb, slowly. Tenderly. The way he'd do it if it were his tongue instead of his finger. "You aren't interested in mind-blowing sex?"

"I . . . I wouldn't say that," she breathed.

"Good." And then, he decided to hell with waiting and

with arguing about whether or not she was interested in him. He lowered his head, taking her cranberry lips with his, teasing at first, then not teasing at all when she moaned and opened them for him, her arms spreading wide and reaching for his back.

She fit against him like butter on bread, her body molding to his in perfect harmony. He roamed his hands down her back, feeling the slight bump of her bra strap through the fabric of her shirt. His mind skipped forward, imagining his fingers undoing the hooks, her breasts spilling forward, his mouth tasting them as thoroughly as he was tasting her right now.

Her hands tangled in his hair, pulling him closer, demanding more. She pressed her pelvis against his, then away, the tease sending his brain into other stratospheres. "Mmmm," she murmured, pressing, withdrawing again.

She was as much of an aggressor as he. Lord, what fun that would be in bed.

"Maria. Oh God," he whispered against her mouth, wanting to say much more. But he'd left his vocabulary somewhere between his fly and his brain.

With a start, she broke away from him, stepping back several paces and swinging his jacket off her shoulders. "I—I—I can't do this."

"What?" He wished like hell his body had an on/off switch. He definitely still felt *on* and it was damned hard to concentrate on anything but the memory of her body touching his.

"I can't get involved with you." She handed him the coat and took another step back.

"Why not?"

"You wouldn't understand," she said. "It's complicated. I'm not even sure I can explain it to myself."

"Tell me." Hot desire still pulsed within him. He hoped

she'd get to the explanation soon so he could show her the error of her argument and get her right back into his arms.

"Well," she paused, then let the rest out in a rush. "Mary Louise Zipparetto, for one."

He raced through his mental little black book. "I don't know anyone named Mary Louis Zipparetto."

Say Yes! To Sizzling Romance by
Lori Foster

__Too Much Temptation

0-7582-0431-0 $6.99US/$9.99CAN

Grace Jenkins feels too awkward and insecure to free the passionate woman inside her. But that hasn't stopped her from dreaming about Noah Harper. Gorgeous, strong and sexy, his rough edge beneath the polish promises no mercy in the bedroom. When Grace learns Noah's engagement has ended in scandal, she shyly offers him her support and her friendship. But Noah's looking for something extra . . .

__Never Too Much

0-7582-0087-0 $6.99US/$9.99CAN

A confirmed bachelor, Ben Badwin has had his share of women, and he likes them as wild and uninhibited as his desires. Nothing at all like the brash, wholesomely cute woman who just strutted into his diner. But something about Sierra Murphy's independent attitude makes Ben's fantasies run wild. He'd love to dazzle her with his sensual skills . . . to make her want him as badly as he suddenly wants her . . .

__Say No to Joe?

0-8217-7512-X $6.99US/$9.99CAN

Joe Winston can have any woman—except the one he really wants. Secretly, Luna Clark may lust after Joe, but she's made it clear that she's too smart to fall for him. He can just keep holding his breath, thank you very much. But now, Luna's inherited two kids who need more than she alone can give in a small town that seems hell-bent on driving them away. She needs someone to help out . . . someone who can't be intimidated . . . someone just like Joe.

__When Bruce Met Cyn

0-8217-7513-8 $6.99US/$9.99CAN

Compassionate and kind, Bruce Kelly understands that everyone makes mistakes, even if he's never actually done anything but color inside the lines. Nobody's perfect, but Bruce is about to meet a woman who's perfect for him. He's determined to show her that he can be trusted. And if that means proving it by being the absolute gentleman at all times, then so be it. No matter how many cold showers it takes . . .

Available Wherever Books Are Sold!

Visit our website at **www.kensingtonbooks.com**.

Contemporary Romance By
Kasey Michaels